The Other Black Widow

Widow

The Black Widow – Book Three

ERNEST WALWYN

DEDICATION

To my brothers Rudy and Louis and my sister Pauline.

The male black Widow spider is normally considered an inconsequential non-entity whose sole purpose seems to be a sex object for the female. If he is lucky, he can have sex with her and live to see another day. If he is unlucky, the female forgets what his purpose was and uses him for food, if she is hungry and he is near.

But, what if . . . What if the male Black Widow spider becomes more than just a sex object? What if the male Black Widow spider becomes more than food for the female? What if the male Black Widow spider becomes a force of nature in his own right? What If ?

ACKNOWLEDGMENTS

I want to thank Inge-Lise Goss for her insightful corrections and additions, Debbie Prince for her shaping of the tone of my story and Nancy Buford for helping me keep one foot grounded in reality.

PROLOGUE

When Blaire Winslow, (daughter of Myra James, the Black Widow) was nineteen and growing up in Prescott, Arizona, Jake Stettler was five, growing up in Milton, Nevada. None had knowledge of the other.

***

Jake and his father shared a 3-bedroom, 2-bath ranch house in a quiet neighborhood. The neighbors were friendly, but not nosy. They spoke when they met on the street yet only on rare occasions did they visit each other's houses.

After the death of Mrs. Stettler, a nanny, Mrs. Burns, was hired to take care of the house and Jake when Mr. Stettler was at work.

One day, Jake and his father were playing catch in their back yard. Jake missed a throw and the ball rolled under the hedges.

When he went to retrieve the ball, he thought a thorn had pricked him. He yanked his hand back then sucked on the wound for a few seconds. He tried to retrieve the ball again and got pricked again. After a few seconds, he used his gloved hand to get the ball.

He threw the ball to his dad and prepared to catch his father's throw. Before the ball was tossed back to him, he collapsed.

His father ran to him, yelling his name. Mr. Stettler picked Jake up and ran to his car. He put his son on the back seat and drove to the hospital Emergency Room. He explained to the ER doctor what had happened.

The doctor looked at the wounds. "I've seen this before," he said. "He's been bitten by a Black Widow spider. They are prevalent in this area so we have the antidote on hand."

He turned to the nurse who stood by and instructed her on where to find the serum.

Jake was moved to a room from the ER. The doctor administered the antidote. "It will take a while for the serum to take effect. He'll probably be in a coma for 24-36 hours. You don't have anything to worry about. We'll take good care of him. Why don't you go home? There's nothing you can do here."

Mr. Stettler looked at his son, then at the doctor. "Are you sure he'll be okay?"

The doctor put a hand on Stettler's shoulder. "Leave him with us. He'll be all right. Call tomorrow to see how he's doing." He paused. "Why don't you have his mother come stay with him in the meantime?"

"His mother's dead. She died from breast cancer when Jake was two."

"Oh. I'm sorry to hear that. How difficult has it been bringing up a son by yourself?"

"Yes, but I have a nanny who is fabulous. She stays with him while I'm at work. She also takes care of the house."

"I see. I guess the only thing you need to do then, is go home, try to relax and call us in the morning."

Stettler fidgeted for a few seconds, indecision creasing his face. He was silent as if looking for words. Finally, he nodded. "Right. I'll call in the morning." He bent over the bed and kissed his son on the forehead. With one last look at the doctor, he turned and left the hospital.

***

It was a few moments short of 36 hours after the injection that

Jake woke up. In less than a minute, a nurse was by his side.

She checked the readings on the monitor. Frown lines creased her forehead. The monitor showed a low heart rate of only 58. His blood pressure measured 90 over 42. She asked, "How do you feel?" *The doctor will be concerned about those.*

"I feel funny, like I'm not really all here."

She tilted her head to one side. "Can you explain that a little more?"

Jake thought for a moment. "I feel like I'm not solid, like I could walk through the wall if I tried."

Just then, the doctor walked in. "Hi, Jake. I see you're awake. How do you feel?"

The nurse told him what Jake had said and what the monitors read.

He nodded and turned to Jake. "Your blood pressure and heartbeat are rather low. I think you'll be all right in a little bit but, we'll have to monitor your vitals to make sure. Part of what you feel is from the venom and part from the antidote. Take it easy for a day or two. You'll be back to normal before you know it."

"What happened to me, doctor?" Jake asked.

"You were bitten by a Black Widow spider. Her venom is very powerful but, is only dangerous to young children and older people." He looked at his watch. "I called your dad. He should be here in a few minutes. I'll stay with you until he arrives." Less than a minute later, Mr. Stettler arrived.

"Hello, doctor. Hi Jake. How do you feel?"

"I still feel a little funny, but the doctor said I should be okay in a day or two."

Stettler turned to the doctor.

Before he could speak, the doctor said, "I told him to take it easy for a little bit. He should be back to normal soon."

Stettler nodded. "Okay, doctor. I'll make sure he follows your advice." He took Jake's hand and led him out of the room. At the door he stopped and turned. "Thanks again, doctor. Will there be any side effects or aftereffects I should look for?"

"Not really. He might get dizzy spells if he exerts himself too much too soon. Just make sure he takes it easy for a while."

Mr. Stettler and Jake waved and left the hospital. They headed home.

CHAPTER ONE

My early life wasn't too unusual. I first got interested in soccer when I was in the eighth grade. My dad and I were given tickets to see the Las Vegas Lights play the Colorado Rapids. It was different from all the sports I was used to watching.

There was only one team: no offense or defense, like in football. Once a player was substituted, the replaced person was out for the rest of the game. The part that intrigued me most was that although the game was played in two forty-five-minute periods, the clock never stopped during the game. It didn't matter if the ball went out of bonds or a player got injured. Extra time would be added at the end of the period to make up for the time lost due to an injury.

It was thrilling to watch twenty-two men chase a ball back and forth across the field, or pitch, as it's called.

The other interesting fact was that a game could, and often did, end in a tie. This was previously unheard of in American sports.

I tried most other sports in junior high school. I ran track and played volleyball and basketball. I was only good at track. I wanted to try other sports like baseball and hockey. but I had to wait until high school. Dad put a nix on football.

***

I'd been taking part in sports mostly because it was required. I could hardly wait until I got into high school and could try out for soccer. The Europeans call it football, but we already have a game by that name.

***

I found that as I got older, I became stronger and faster. There wasn't anyone in the school that can beat me running. I took first place in everything from the 100-meter sprint to the 5000-meter run. This caused problems. It seemed every other week I was being tested for steroids and other drugs. They never found anything. I didn't do drugs or alcohol, not then, not now.

***

I improved at volleyball, helping the team win almost every game. Couldn't show off too much or they would have thought I was a robot or alien. I should be so lucky. I was just a kid.

***

The rest of junior high school was uninteresting so, I'll skip to high school.

DID IT! I made the soccer team! My position was midfielder. At least I made it. I could run with the best of them, and I mastered ball handling, quickly improving with each game.

***

On my second year on the soccer team. I was good enough to be moved up to be a forward.

It was frustrating to score goals and still lose games. I wouldn't have minded a tie every so often, but no. No matter how many goals we scored the other teams almost always scored at least one more than us. Don't get me wrong, we won a few games, but we were very near the bottom of the league. I decided to talk to coach about being the goalie. That's our weakest position. I think I could do better than the two guys we had.

***

The coach let me try out for goalkeeper.

I had been watching the other guys and had a good idea on how to keep the ball out of the net.

"You have to move," the coach told me.

"Got it, coach." I stood before the goal, waiting for the ball to come to me. Even though this was a practice session, I still missed the first two.

On the sidelines, I could see the coach shaking his head. *Better not let any more get by.*

The next time the ball was coming my way, I concentrated all my attention on it. I found I could track the ball, no matter who had it. Even on the first tryout, I could not only sense, but also predict where the ball was going.

The ball was brought forward on the left side. It was passed across the front of the goal toward the foot of another player but, I stopped it before it reached it' destination.

Holding the ball, I looked over at the coach. He was standing with his hands on his hips and his mouth open.

In the meantime, I was being congratulated by my teammates.

The guy who was supposed to score came up to me. "How did you manage to stop the ball?" he asked.

I shrugged. "I concentrated on where it was and where I thought it was going. I guess I was right."

He shook his head and walked away.

During the rest of the scrimmage, my side scored three goals. No ball got past me. I was pretty proud of myself.

Later, in the locker room, the coach made an announcement. "Guys, it looks like we have a new goalie." He motioned to me. When I stood beside him, he put his hand on my shoulder. "This is Jake Stettler. He'll be wearing number one from now on."

The other two goalies were not happy. Especially the one who had to give up his number. His name was Aaron Kosch.

***

After school, Aaron and Craig Turner, the other goalie, stopped me.

"Think you're hot shit, huh?" Aaron asked.

Craig said, "If you're not careful, you could get hurt out there, or maybe hurt yourself."

I smiled. "I can take care of myself."

They closed in on me. "Maybe we should take care of you." Spittle from Aaron's mouth hit my face.

I wiped it off. "You're drooling. I thought only babies and old men drooled. Since you're not that old . . ."

He grabbed my shirt. "You calling me a baby?" he yelled. His face almost touched mine.

Not smiling, I said, "Back off. Your breath stinks."

He growled and raised his other fist.

I caught it and held it for a second.

A bewildered look crossed his face.

I started to squeeze, slowly.

He tried to pull away but couldn't.

I kept squeezing.

"Bastard! Let go before you break my hand. Let go!"

I stared into his eyes. I had never seen pain and fear in another person's eyes before. It was fascinating. His pupils expanded then contracted several times at an uneven rate.

Then the tears started to flow.

I didn't realize he had let go of my shirt until his other hand tried to pull mine loose.

I stopped squeezing and just held him. I looked at Craig. Confusion changed the contours of his face.

I could see he wanted to help his friend but wasn't sure what to do.

I let go of Aaron's hand and relaxed. "You were saying?"

"My hand. It's ruined," he cried. He held it with his other hand trying to rub life back into it.

"You should be able to use it tomorrow. Keep flexing it so it won't get stiff." I smiled. "Gotta go, fellas. I got homework to do before school tomorrow." I turned, got on my bike and headed home.

***

Several days later, I headed for my bike to go the practice field. The crowd around the bike stands confused me.

As I approached, the crowd parted. Some of the students looked me in the eye; others turned their faces away.

Then I saw it, or rather; I saw what was left of my bike. I stood open mouthed. *Who did this? Why? When?* My bike was a mangled mass. Every part of the frame had been broken. The wheels were bent beyond repair; the tires were cut in pieces.

I could only stare at it open mouthed and dumbfounded. Again, the questions: why, who, how, when?

As I stared at the mangled mess that had once been my bike, tears started flowing down my face. They were tears of anger. I was angry because of what had been done and angry because I didn't know who did it. I had my suspicions, of course, but no proof.

With my head hanging, I turned to walk to the field. We had a game on Saturday and we all needed to practice.

I hadn't taken three steps when a voice called, "What's going on here?"

It was Dr. Temple, the principal.

"My God!" He looked at the mess, his eyes wide and mouth open. "Whose bike was this?"

Several students said, "Jake Stettler's"

He turned and saw me. "Mr. Stettler."

I turned toward him.

"My office, now!" He strode towards the building.

I followed trying to match his pace.

He didn't stop until he reached his office. There, he held the door and closed it when I was inside. "Sit."

I plopped down in the nearest chair.

He leaned against his desk; his arms crossed over his chest. He stood and stared for what seemed like an eternity.

When I started to fidget, he asked, "Who hates you that much?"

I shook my head. "I'm sure I don't know, sir."

He stared at me some more. "In other words, you know but won't say."

I remained silent. My eyes focused on his shoes.

He pushed himself from the desk and stood with his hands in his hips. "I'll notify your father. If you decide to talk to me, let your teacher know or stop by my office." He walked to the door and opened it. "You're excused."

I stood and walked out the door. I didn't meet his eyes.

***

On the way to practice, I thought about my bike, or rather, what was left of it. *Could Aaron and Craig have done this? When would they have had the time? Where would they have found the tools?*

I put it all out of my head when I got to the locker room. I forced myself to focus on being a goalie.

After practice, I wondered how I would get home. It was six miles, which was easy with the bike. I sighed and let my shoulders droop. It would be a long walk.

I had taken just a few steps when a car horn sounded and someone called my name.

It was Mrs. Burns, our housekeeper. I was surprised, but glad to see her.

"Your principal called your dad and he called me to pick you up."

"Thank you," I mumbled.

We rode in silence for a little bit.

"I saw the bike. You must have made someone really angry."

"I guess," was all I would say.

***

Mrs. Burns drove me to school the next day and was there to pick me up after practice.

On Wednesday, after first period, I was summoned to the Principal's Office. When I got there, Aaron, Craig and another student I didn't know, were there. The Security Guard and the shop teacher were there also.

When I entered, Aaron and Craig shot daggers at me. The other student, Dan Crews, sat staring straight ahead.

"What's this all about, sir?" Aaron asked.

"You'll see," Dr. Temple told him.

The principal pressed a key on the computer on the table next to his, and the video began. It showed Aaron, Craig and, Don Crews, enter the shop. Each selected a large sledgehammer and large shears from the array of tools. While there was no audio, the video was damning enough. The date and time was recorded.

Another segment showed them returning the tools, laughing and giving each other high fives.

The three criminals sat dumbfounded.

"Motion activated video cameras," the shop teacher said.

The principal said, "Mr. Crews, you are suspended for two weeks for breaking and entering and abetting in a crime. Mr. Kosch and Mr. Turner, you are expelled for the rest of the school year. The parents of all three of you will be notified of the crimes committed and the punishment meted out. There will be no appeal. If your parents decide to fight this, you might end up in jail." He took a few seconds to compose himself. "Return to class Mr. Stettler. You three will be escorted off the school premises." He nodded to the Security Guard.

I headed for my next class. *My suspicion was right. I didn't think they'd go that far. I guess I'd better watch myself when I'm off campus.*

The rest of the day was uneventful. I continued to keep the ball out of the net during practice. The following Saturday, my dad told me we were going to get me a new bike.

"That's great. I'm sure Mrs. Burns can find better things to do than be my chauffer."

"I was thinking the same thing," dad said. "We'll go to the bike shop in the city. The bikes are expensive, but they're worth the money."

"Dad, I don't need a real expensive bike to get back and forth. Why don't we go to Wal-Mart and get a cheap one? If it breaks or gets stolen, it won't be a big loss. I'm sure a cheap one will ride just as good as an expensive one. I only need it to get back and forth to school."

Dad crossed his arms over his chest and looked at his me. He nodded. "So be it. Wal-Mart it is."

When we were in the car, I said, "Thanks Dad. It's the thought that counts."

He laughed.

***

At Wal-Mart we found a bike for little more than $100.00. It even had gears. It was also the only one in blue, my favorite color.

CHAPTER TWO

The rest of the school year went smoothly. Our soccer team was undefeated thanks to my goal keeping.

There was a summer tournament that our school signed up for. What I couldn't understand, no one else could either, was that I didn't get bigheaded about my skills. I just accepted them.

Of course, members of some of the other teams were suspicious of my abilities.

I was tested for drugs every week.

***

For our first game we travelled to Jonesville to play against their school.

Before the game started, several of the members of the other team somehow caught me alone in the locker room. I had returned to get an extra set of gloves.

Their leader, Chris, a heavy-set boy about a year older than I, said, "We've heard about you. We don't care what you can do or how you keep the ball out of the net. We've won this tournament every year. We're going to win it this year too. Do I make myself clear?"

I shrugged. "Clear enough."

"Good." He turned to walk away.

"Just one thing," I said.

When he turned back, the look on his face should have frightened me.

He put his hands on his hips and pushed his face towards me. The move caused a lock of hair to fall across his face.

I almost laughed. He looked like one of the comics in the black-and-white movies. I cleared my throat. "My job is to keep the ball out of the net. I'd be letting my teammates down if I didn't do my job."

"You plan on keeping us from scoring?"

I nodded. "Yes."

His face turned red. He blew the loose lock of hair away. He reached out and grabbed my shirt. Very slowly, he said, "Didn't you understand what I told you?"

"Yes."

"Do you want to get hurt, or maybe die?"

"No."

"Then you will let us score."

"No, I won't. Please let go of my shirt and back off. Your breath stinks."

His face turned even redder.

"Let go of my shirt before you tear it."

He started to twist his hand as if he meant to ruin my shirt.

"Don't," I said as I grabbed his fist. "Promise to let go and I won't break your hand."

His expression changed from anger to surprise to pain. He tried to pull away.

"Let go," he said. "You're gonna break my hand. Let go!"

"Promise not to rip my shirt?"

He was almost on his knees; tears were flowing down his face. "Yes, yes, I promise, I promise."

I looked at his companions. "Touch me and his hand will definitely be broken."

They backed sway.

I slowly released his hand and removed it from my shirt.

Holding his hand to his chest, he turned his head and yelled at the three other boys he had brought with him. "Why didn't you do something? He almost crushed my hand."

They looked at him bewildered. One of the said, "What were we supposed to do?"

"Stop him from hurting me, that's what."

One of the others said, "But if we would have tried to help, he probably would have broken your hand."

Chris climbed slowly to his feet, still cradling his hand. "This is not over." There was hate in his eyes.

The four of them walked out of the locker room.

I sighed. *Why can't people accept me for what I am and what I can do?*

I left the locker room to join the rest of the team on the field. Game time. Neither of our teams scored during the first half.

In the locker room, coach Spears gave us a pep talk.

"Okay, guys. We all know that they won't score as long as Jake is goalie. They can't beat our goalie, but we can beat theirs. At least I thought so when we started. I have only this to say before we go back on the field. Execute the plays we've been practicing. Get the ball in their net. Do it at least once before the final whistle blows. Now, get out there and do it."

***

We did it! The final score was 1-0. Of course, we scored the one.

After the game, Chris and his three buddies approached me on the field. I didn't think they were going to congratulate me on helping my team win the game. I was right.

"Hi, Jake," Chris said. "You didn't let us score."

"No, I didn't. My job is to keep the ball out of the net. I was only doing what I'm supposed to do."

"Well, asshole. Your job is going to cost you. I'll let you decide. Would you like to lose a leg, an arm, or both?"

I shook my head. "I wouldn't make promises I couldn't keep."

He laughed. "I have to admit, you've got balls. What do you think you can do against the four of us?"

I shrugged. "Defend myself as best I can."

He crossed his arms over his chest. "You better bring some of your teammates. That's the only way to keep from getting hurt."

"Okay," I said. "I'll think about it." I turned my back on him. I'd know if he made a move toward me. He didn't disappoint me.

He reached out and grabbed my arm.

I wrapped my fingers around his hand and pulled it loose. Pulling him forward, I jammed my other hand in his armpit. I dipped and spun to get momentum. Using his body weight, I threw him into his three buddies. He went crashing into them sending the group to the ground.

While they were untangling themselves, he looked at me, his expression bewildered.

"What are you, some kind of Kung Fu expert?"

"No. I'm just a goalie that can move fast." I turned and walked to the locker room smiling so hard my face hurt.

I didn't see or hear from Chris for the rest of the tournament.

***

Our coach, Mr. Spears, was happy. The team was ecstatic. We had been on the road home for about thirty minutes when Mr. Spears used the mike to quiet us down.

"Guys, we have a lot to celebrate. We won the school championship and now the end-of-season tournament. This is the first loss for Jonesville in three years. They get rough and like to intimidate the other teams. This year, we intimidated them. It wasn't enough that we scored against them but, thanks to Jake, they didn't score against us. This is also the first time they've been shut out. Their coach congratulated me. Of course I told him congratulations should go to my team. I only coach. They played and won the game."

The bus resounded with a tremendous roar. I think we startled the driver because the bus swerved across the road a few times.

The guys had called ahead with the news. The whole town was waiting for us when we arrived.

It was a good thing school was out. We partied for three days. Even our small police force made sure we had transportation so we wouldn't have to drive. They overlooked our under-age drinking but drew the line on our driving drunk.

***

As had been said many times, all good things must come to an end. Our celebration was no different.

More than half the graduating class headed off to college. Most of the rest started jobs either in town or in nearby cities. A few stayed home to help run the homesteads or family businesses.

My dad expected me to go to college. I told my him I was going to become a professional soccer player.

He looked at me with one eyebrow raised. "Think you're good enough?" he asked.

"No, Dad," I said. "I know I'm good enough. I even know which team I'm going to play for the Franklin Thunder."

He looked shocked when I named the team. "The Frequent Blunders? Why do you want to play for the last place team? They've had the worst record for the last four years. If the Kindergarten had a girls' team, they couldn't beat them and would have been relegated two years ago."

"Dad," I said. "With my goal-keeping skills, I'm going to take that team to first place. With me as goalie, we'll win the championship at the end of the year."

"You sound very cocky."

I didn't like the look on his face.

"I'm not cocky, Dad. Winning a game is more than scoring goals. It's also keeping the other team from scoring. It doesn't matter how many times we score. If the other team doesn't score, we win. I've perfected my skills to the point I can guarantee no one will get the ball past me into the net."

He crossed his arms over his chest and leaned back in his chair. "You think you're that good." It wasn't a question; it was an accusation.

"Dad, I KNOW I'm that good. During the last season in school, only one ball got past me, and that was when one of my team members sent the ball into our goal. In the summer tournament, no one scored against me."

He uncrossed his arms and rested them on the arms of his chair. "You're just barely seventeen. Isn't that kind of young?"

"No. Some guys start as young as fourteen. I can make it, Dad. I know I can."

He sat quietly for what seemed like forever. Then he stood up and said, "Go to bed. We'll talk more in the morning."

I nodded. "Goodnight, Dad."

"Goodnight, Jake."

We both headed off to bed.

It took me forever to get to sleep. *Would he support me or find a way to shoot down my goal?* I couldn't tell from his expression and he made no comment to help me know which way he would decide. Since I was only seventeen, he still had control over my life.

***

In the morning, at breakfast, he asked, "How are you going to get on the team?"

I smiled. "I already have a plan. I'm going to challenge the other goalies on the team. If I beat them, and I'm pretty sure I will, then I'll be the primary goalie."

He sighed, then took a forkful of scramble eggs and followed it with a bite of bacon. He washed them down with a sip of orange juice. When his mouth was empty, he asked, "When do you plan to start your new career?"

I couldn't help smiling. He approved. "The team has a home game a week from Saturday. I thought I'd make my bid the Sunday after that game."

He picked up a slice of toast, put some egg on it, then bit into it. He looked at me while he chewed.

I wanted him to hurry up and swallow so he could talk.

He finally did. "Okay. What do you need me to do?"

Trying not to jump out of my chair, I said. "I just need your moral support. Oh, and maybe book a hotel room for me for a week."

He laughed. "If that's all you need, consider it done. You'll want a room close to where the team is. No problem."

He picked up his coffee cup, drank some of it, then pushed his chair back and stood up. "Gotta go. You'll still need my support until you get hired." He came around to my chair, hugged me, then got his stuff together for work.

***

My dad works for the District Attorney in Las Vegas. This means working late nights at least two or three times a week. It just happened that he had to work late on Thursday night, Mrs. Burns' night off. I can usually find things to do on nights like this. Tonight would be a little harder. No schoolwork, nothing interesting on TV.

While I was wondering what to do with myself, the doorbell rang. I answered it and, much to my surprise, there stood Chris and his three buddies.

"I guess you didn't get enough at the game. I can break your wrist for real thus time," I said.

His smile was more of a sneer. "Can you come out to play? We don't want to mess up the house."

"How thoughtful of you. I'm sure my dad will appreciate your concern." I stepped out and closed the door behind me. With my back against the door, I asked, "What kind of fun and games did you have in mind?"

"Oh, I thought we'd break a few bones. Some in your arms so you can't catch a ball and maybe some in your legs so you can't run."

"You can forget about the legs. I would never run from you."

He took two steps back and hooked his thumbs in his belt. "You might want to lock the door. Can't leave the house unsecured."

"Are we going someplace?"

"Yeah. For a ride."

I was about to protest when I saw the gun in his hand. "Oh," I said.

"Thought you'd like a nice surprise."

The four split up leaving a path for me.

"To the car, if you please," Chris said, waving the gun. "By the way, just in case you try to use your speed and strength, we are all armed."

The other three brandished their guns.

I did a quick calculation. They each had a pistol that could hold up to fourteen rounds. I didn't fancy my chance running from fifty-six 9mm bullets.

I nodded and headed for the car parked by the curb. Since it was late at night and there was no moon, I could only tell that it was a dark sedan.

Of course, I sat in the back, flanked by two of his buddies.

"What's your name?" I asked the one on my left. No answer. He just stared straight ahead. I asked the one on the other side the same question. No response from him either.

***

After about thirty minutes, we pulled off the road. All four doors opened and we piled out.

"Nice quiet place, don't you think?" Chris asked.

I looked around. It was more than quiet. It was desolate.

"There's nothing here," I said.

"Walk," Chris said.

I headed into the desert, away from the car.

I asked, "How far are we going?"

"Walk until I say stop."

"You guys didn't bring shovels, " I observed.

"Won't need them. The animals and buzzards will take care of you."

I continued, "Would I be correct in assuming you plan to kill me and leave me out here?"

"You got it, smart ass. Keep walking."

While we walked for only ten minutes. The desert march seemed to go on forever.

Finally, Chris said, "This is far enough."

I stopped and turned to face the group.

Each had a gun pointed at me.

For some reason, I wasn't afraid. I felt calm. *Don't I know I am about to die? Why am I so calm? I guess I'll find out what Heaven or Hell is like.*

I took a deep breath and relaxed. I looked each guy in the eye, one by one.

They returned my stares with hard, cold, steely glances.

Are they robots or on drugs?

Chris was another story. There was so much hate in his eyes that they had turned red.

I closed my eyes and forced myself to relax. I knew it would be loud and there would be a lot of pain, at first, at least. Then, I imagined the darkness would overcome me and the pain would go away.

I waited. I didn't hear the sounds of the guns firing. I waited some more.

I sensed movement. I opened my eyes and found myself moving back through the desert toward the car. After a few steps, I stopped, turned and looked back. The darkness of the landscape hid everything from me.

I shrugged and continued walking. When I reached the car, all the doors were still open, and the keys were in the ignition. I closed the doors and climbed into the driver's seat. I sat quietly behind the wheel for what seemed like forever. I had no idea what had happened, except that I was still alive and the other four were missing.

CHAPTER THREE

I started the car and drove, not stopping until I was four blocks from my house. I went home and got a wet washcloth. Back at the car, I wiped down every surface, inside and out.

When I was done, I wiped the keys and dropped them on the driver's side floor. I left the doors unlocked. I knew the car would be considered abandoned in a day or two. I thought I'd make it easy for our small police force.

Back home, I checked the time. It was almost midnight.

When I walked through the front door my dad yelled, "Jake! Where the Hell have you been?"

He caught me by surprise. I forgot he'd be home. "I couldn't sleep so I went for a walk. I didn't realize I'd been gone so long."

He snorted. "Next time leave me a note."

"I will, Dad."

"Goodnight."

"Goodnight, Dad."

***

I didn't get much sleep that night. I couldn't figure out what had happened. I should have been dead, riddled by bullets from four guns. Yet, here I was, alive, and my executioners were missing. *What the Hell happened out there?*

***

I slept late the next morning. Why not? I'd graduated from high school and didn't have a job. Yet.

Mrs. Burns smiled at me when I entered the kitchen. "Do you want breakfast or lunch?" she asked.

I checked the wall clock. It was quarter to eleven. "I guess I'll have brunch."

She laughed.

"What are you going to make?" I asked.

"Something you'll have to eat. Don't worry," she added. "You'll enjoy it."

She was right. She made a green salad with scrambled eggs on toast. When I was done, I went to my room to play video games. I was just getting comfortable when my cell phone rang. It listed an unknown caller. At first, I was going to ignore it, but something told me to answer it. "Hello."

"Where the hell is my car, asshole?"

"Chris. How nice it is to hear from you. How are you and where are you?"

"Never mind how I am. Where is my car?"

"You don't have to yell. It's four blocks from my house on Maple Street. The keys are on the driver's side floor. By the way . . . Hello . . . Hello?" He had already hung up.

Damn. I wanted to ask him what had happened last night. All I could remember was waiting to get shot, then walking toward the car.

Frustrated, I typed his name in my computer, thinking I could get his number and address. I forgot that info would be listed under his parents' name. *I guess I'll have to do things the hard way.*

I went to my dad's study and located a phone book. I was surprised he still had one. There were four families in Jonesboro under the name Kelly. I found him on the third try. The woman said he wasn't home. He was visiting some friends in Milton.

I thanked her and hung up. The only person I could think of him visiting would be me. *Maybe I can catch him at the car.*

"Mrs. Burns, I'm going out for a walk. I shouldn't be long."

"Okay," she called. "Be careful."

"I will." I walked at a quick pace to where I had left the car. When I reached the street, it was gone. *He must have been close by to have gotten it so soon.*

After a few seconds, I turned and headed home. I put my hands in my pockets as I strolled leisurely back to the house. I didn't want to get home too soon. Mrs. Burns might ask questions.

***

When I got home, I took my bike out of the garage and went for a ride. I rode to the school, knowing no one would be there, then rode home using a different route just to kill time.

On the way, I thought I saw Chris' car. I didn't know his license number and dark blue Honda Civics were very popular.

Still, I took my time getting home. I didn't think he and his buddies, for want of a better term, would bother with Mrs. Burns if I weren't home.

***

I was right. I'd been gone a little over an hour. As soon as I walked in the door, Mrs. Burns said, "There was a young man looking for you. He didn't give me his name and never said if he'd be back."

I thanked her and checked my phone for messages. His number hadn't registered before when he called. *Oh well, I guess he'll call back.*

He did, but not until the next day. "Meet me at the school practice field. Immediately! We'll be waiting."

Again, he hung up before I could respond. I told Mrs. Burns I was going for a bike ride.

On the way, I thought, *I hope I don't have any problems. I have to make my pitch to the soccer team manager in two days.*

***

When I got to the field, the four of them were waiting for me. At first glance, they didn't appear any different from the last time I'd seen them. They still wore the same T-shirts, jeans with holes in the knees and cowboy boots that looked like they'd been polished with cow dung. I wondered if they all shopped together in the same shop.

I got off my bike, put the kickstand down and walked over to them. "I wanted to ask you . . .? I started.

"Another time," he interrupted. "How did you do it?"

I blinked. "Do what?"

"We were about to blow you away and suddenly, you weren't there. Where did you go? How did you get away so fast?"

I shrugged. "I went back to the car. That's all I can remember. What happened to you guys?"

He put his hands on his hips and snorted. "Like I said. One second you were there, then you were gone. How did you manage to disappear like that?"

I rubbed the back of my neck. "I'm just as confused as you are. I thought you could tell me what happened."

"I wish. I knew you could move fast," he conceded. "But that was more like disappearing." From his tone I couldn't tell if he was angry, confused, or what.

I put my hands in my pockets. "I don't know what to tell you. I'm confused too."

He crossed his arms over his chest. "I never want to see you again. Get out of my sight and out of my life. When I leave here, I will wipe you out of my mind. Go. Now!" The look on his face was not a pleasant one.

I think I really pissed him off. I turned and walked to my bike. When I looked back, they were already gone.

"Huh. And he talked about me disappearing." I still had no answer as I rode home.

***

Saturday, my dad drove me to the bus station.

"Be careful, take care. Call if you need anything."

"I will, Dad." I hugged him, then boarded the bus.

I spent my time trying to decide what I was going to say to Coach Spears to convince him I should be his primary goalie.

I was lucky. The bus depot wasn't very far from the hotel, just a few blocks. Since I didn't have a lot of luggage, I walked.

After I checked in, I called my dad to let him know I arrived safely.

Dad had arranged for all my dinners to be included. Breakfast came with the room.

I had dinner, then wandered through the town getting familiar with the stadium and its surroundings.

***

Sunday morning, after breakfast, I gathered my gear and headed to the stadium.

The team was arriving, so I joined them.

I got a few weird looks. More than one guy asked who I was.

"I'm the new goalie," was all I said.

This raised a few eyebrows, but the questions remained unasked.

Inside the locker room, I started changing into my gear.

The coach came over and, with his hands on his hips, demanded, "Who the hell are you?"

I smiled. "I'm your new goalie."

"Since when?"

"Since today," I said matter of factly.

"By whose authority?" He was starting to get red in the face.

"Yours," I said with my best smile.

He sputtered a few times. "When the hell did I hire you as goalie?"

My smile got broader. "Just now."

There were quite a few snickers around the room.

He took a few deep breaths. "Why did I hire you?" he asked calmly.

"Because I'm the best goalie you've ever seen. Also, because of my skills, I'm going to take the team to first place. Then, we'll win the championship."

For what seemed line forever, the locker room was deathly quiet.

Then, one by one, everybody started laughing.

I waited.

When they were finished, I said, "I'll prove to all of you how good I am." I waited for that to sink in. Then I hit them with it. "I challenge the whole team, all twenty-three of you, to a penalty shoot-out."

I was almost deafened by the roaring laugher. I was the only one not laughing.

When they had quieted, I crossed my arms over my chest. "Here's the deal. If three or more balls get past me, I will disappear, and you will never hear from me again. Otherwise, I will be your new primary goalie and I'll wear number one."

The other members were on their feet and crowding around the coach and me. Their bodies leaned forward, eyes on their coach.

He stared at me for a few moments. "How old are you, kid?"

"I'm seventeen, but why does my age matter?"

"It doesn't, but because of your age, you can't sign a contract."

"Not a problem. My Dad can be here in less than a day. He works for the DA's office in Las Vegas."

"Does he even know you're here?"

"He bought my bus ticket, drove me to the bus and booked my hotel room."

The coach was quiet. I could sense he wasn't sure about what to do. "Let me talk it over with the team."

I nodded. "I'll be in the bathroom."

I walked out, crossing my fingers on both hands once I was out of sight.

***

I waited in the bathroom, trying to wear a groove in the tile floor. When one of the team members came in to get me, I was so relieved I almost wet myself. Then, I thought, maybe they voted against me.

Before I had a chance to explore that possibility, we were back in the locker room.

"What's your name, kid?" the coach asked.

"Jake. Jake Stettler."

"Well, Jake Stettler, you offer sounds intriguing. The team thinks this would be s good way to practice their penalty kick skills."

I smiled. "When do you want to start?" I asked.

He raised his eyebrows. "Glad you want to get this over with quickly." He motioned to the team and they exited the locker room, yelling and whooping.

On the field, (in soccer, it's called a pitch). I picked the nearest goal. "Ready when you are," I called.

***

One by one, they lined up. One by one, they tried to get the ball past me into the net. One by one, I frustrated their efforts.

I found out later that twenty-nine men had tried to get the ball past me. Six decided my skills were a fluke and tried a second time. They didn't make it.

"Want to try your luck, Coach?" I called.

I could see he was amazed and angry. Breathing hard, he put the ball in the spot and turned his back to it.

His shoulders rose and fell as he took a few deep breaths.

Suddenly, he turned, ran and kicked the ball.

I took two steps left and caught it.

He stood staring at me.

"How the Hell do you do that? I've never seen anybody move so fast."

I walked toward him, pulling my gloves off. "It's a natural ability," I said. "I grew up with it."

He held out his hand. "I'm Coach Spears. Welcome to the team."

Except for the other three goalies, everybody cheered and either shook my hand or patted me on the back. I was elated. I was on the team. Now would come the work.

CHAPTER FOUR

Well, we didn't quite make it to first place at the end of the season. The team had already played twelve of the thirty-four games scheduled. They had won four and lost eight by the time I joined the team, but we finished the season winning every game.

At the closeout speech, I asked Coach Spears if I could say a few words.

He stepped aside.

"Guys," I started. "I said I'd take the team to first place. As you are all well aware, we didn't make it. But, now that you've seen what I can do, there's no doubt we'll be in first place next year and every year I'm your goalie. I'll keep the ball out of our net if you guys will put the ball in our opponent's net. Are we agreed?"

There was a thunderous roar, and in groups they punched and slapped my back and shoulders. We had a deal.

I don't remember what the coach's speech was about. I was wrapped up in my own thoughts. There was something going on in my body that I didn't understand. Whatever it was, it had been bothering me for several days.

***

A week after the end of the season, I was back home in Milton. Training would begin in February with the first game in March. I figured we'd have to practice hard just to stay warm.

***

Dad and I were invited for dinner at his boss' for Thanksgiving. We had several invitations for Christmas parties. It made the time go fast.

***

Dad had rented me a small apartment in Franklin and bought me a car. It took a few hours of driving, but I started to really enjoy my VW Beetle. It was easy to handle and could run with just about the best of them. Had to watch my speed, though.

"Don't get caught driving by yourself at night until you turn eighteen. It's only a couple of months away. Think you can manage that?"

"I'm sure I can, Dad. I don't want you to get in trouble and I don't want to lose my driving privileges before I'm even eligible."

We hugged and he headed back to Milton.

***

Just to be on the safe side, I'd take the bus or walk to the stadium. It was good exercise and helped me keep fit.

But there was still the feeling that something was wrong with me. Like my body needed something. However, once in the locker room, I put it out of my mind and concentrated on my skills.

***

We won the first six games with no problem. I did my part and the team did theirs. Our biggest win was 4-0 over Kansas City. They were not very happy about the loss. No one had ever beaten them that bad.

***

During our next game, we had some trouble. I went to catch a ball and someone grabbed my wrist and elbow. It caught me by surprise, but I still managed to tip the ball over the net with my other hand. I then dropped to my knee, pulling my free arm down and twisting my body with all my might.

One of their team members was thrown into three other players, two of his and one of mine.

"You son of a bitch!" he screamed.

I could see death in his eyes.

He untangled himself and got up just in time to face the ref. He stood snorting and glaring. "Get out of the way, Ref. He's gonna pay for what he just did."

Calmly, the referee said, "Let me do this first." He held up a yellow card, then held it up again. He followed this by holding up a red card.

The player looked stunned. "You're red carding me?" He screamed.

"Very observant. You're out of the game."

"But . . . but he grabbed me and threw me into those other guys."

"Yes, I saw him grab you with his wrist and elbow. Quite a nice trick. Now, get off the field so we can continue the game."

The stare down lasted for almost a minute.

The other player pointed at me and said, "This ain't over." He turned and stomped off the pitch.

We won that game 3-0. The usual interaction between the teams after the game wasn't there. The game was over and that was that. Our coach did go to theirs and offer his hand. It was grudgingly accepted.

In the locker room, Coach Spears told me, "It looks like you've made a real enemy. Be careful, he may be lying in wait for you."

I nodded. "I'll watch my step."

As I was exiting the stadium, Coach Spears stopped me.

"Are you driving?"

"No, Sir. I'm walking."

"You're riding with me."

I didn't argue, just followed him to his car. I gave him my address and we drove off.

After a few blocks he said, "We're being followed."

I pulled down the visor and used the mirror to look behind us. Sure enough, a gray Camaro followed our every turn.

After about five minutes, coach pulled into the parking lot of a motel.

"Go up to the stairs to the second floor. On the left, there's a hallway. Go through it and you'll see steps. Take them. I'll be waiting for you."

I put the visor up, got out and called, "Thanks for the ride, Coach." I closed the door and headed up the stairs. As I walked along the pathway, I saw Coach Spears drive away. A few seconds later, the gray Camaro entered the parking lot.

From the corner of my eye, I saw three guys exit the car.

I turned into the hallway and bounded down the stairs. Coach Spears was there with the engine running and the door open. He was moving before I had my seatbelt on, but I didn't mind.

Later, when he had dropped me off at my apartment, he finally relaxed.

"Since this was a home game for us, they should be leaving tonight or early tomorrow. Unless he quits the team to come after you, there shouldn't be any more problems."

"I hope you're right. I don't need that kind of trouble."

"Get some rest. Practice tomorrow at ten a.m. sharp. Don't be late."

"I'll be there on time, Coach. Thanks again for the ride."

I went into the apartment, dropped my bag on the floor and plopped down on the couch. I had the feeling my goal keeping would upset the other teams as well. I didn't think it would get this bad.

***

It didn't get bad, it got worse. I started getting death threats. They would be mailed to Coach Spears and other team members. They all said basically the same thing: either allow other teams to score or major physical bodily hard would come to me or my teammates.

It got so bad the team owners hired full time bodyguards to protect me. I didn't think I needed that kind of protection, but I didn't have a say in the matter.

***

We were halfway through the season when I was attacked. Actually, the car the guards used to transport me was attacked.

I was with the two guards after a practice. We went to the car and got in. As usual, I was in the back seat.

The driver went to start the car and didn't like the way things sounded. "Out of the car! Now!" he yelled.

I scrambled out the fastest I had moved in my entire life. My other guard grabbed me and started running away from the vehicle. A few seconds later, flames burst out of the hood. The driver managed to get out before the flames had totally engulfed the car.

This was getting serious. The FBI was called in. All games were canceled for the next month. There wasn't much they could get from the car. The fire had destroyed any evidence the FBI might have been able to find. The investigation only revealed what was done, nothing else.

The lead investigator said, "This was too professional to be a prank. Pranks don't kill people. This was meant to kill you, not scare you. Be careful. Whoever did this will probably try again."

***

I told Coach Spears we could do one of two things. I could take a break or, start letting the other teams score.

He asked the team their opinion. The consensus was to leave it up to me.

Since we had a couple of weeks before our next game, I went home to Milton to get my dad's opinion.

He wasn't very helpful. "You have to think about other people. One person was almost killed while others could be hurt. No, others *will* be hurt. Think about that. I can't decide for you."

I nodded. I went to my room to think about what to do. I lay on my bed for hours, thinking.

Dad called me to dinner. At the table, he didn't ask me about my decision. He just looked at me. When I looked down at my food, he nodded and continued eating. Our meal was finished in silence.

***

The next morning at breakfast, Dad said, "Tomorrow's your birthday. Any plans?"

I blinked and my mouth hung open. "Oh, my gosh! With all this other stuff going on, I forgot."

He chuckled. "What would you like for your birthday?"

I blushed. I'd never felt so red in my face. I whispered, "I'd like to lose my virginity."

Dad laughed so hard he almost fell out of his chair.

I sat there thinking, *Dad! This is serious.*

It took a few moments for him to regain control. When he did, he wiped his eyes, took a sip of coffee and waited a few seconds, shaking his head.

He cleared his throat. "First, with what's been going on, this should not have been a laughing matter. I apologize for that. It's just that I never expected THAT! It was the last thing I thought I'd hear."

I smiled. "It's okay, Dad. I guess I caught you off guard."

"To say the least. Where do you plan to hold this event?" He leaned forward and put both arms on the table.

"I guess Las Vegas would be the most logical place."

"How much do you think you'll need?"

"Gosh, Dad. I don't have a clue. I don't even know what the going rate is." I sat back in my chair, frustration creeping into my thoughts.

He nodded, poured a little more syrup on his waffle, then said, "How about I give you $200.00 and you can negotiate a price with whomever you choose, or, whoever chooses you."

"That sounds only fair. I'll try not to spend it all in one place."

We both laughed.

The rest of the meal was done in silence.

***

After Dad had left for work, Mrs. Burns peeked around the corner, then watched my dad's car back out of the driveway. "Sit down." She pointed me to a seat in the living room.

I sat on the couch and she sat in the chair facing me.

I waited.

She smoothed her skirt down, took a deep breath, and spoke.

"Try to make sure whoever you pick is clean. I'm sure you can't ask for credentials or a health card. Just use your good judgment." She seemed to lose her patience. "Don't pick the first floozy who approaches you. You pick the one you want." Finished, she stood up abruptly, ending our meeting.

I sat there nodding. I guess she heard more than I thought she did. Sometimes, she's invisible. "I'll remember all that you said and I will be careful. I'll try to make it a memorable experience."

She stood up, patted me on the cheek and disappeared into the kitchen.

I sat for a few minutes thinking about her advice. *I wonder if she had a son.*

***

The next day, after dinner, I said goodbye to my dad and Mrs. Burns. I was nervous as I drove toward Las Vegas.

Dad had booked a night for me in the Starlight Motel on the upper part of the Strip. It was clean and upscale, but not as pricey as the hotels and casinos.

I wandered the streets for a bit until I got hungry. I decided on Mexican and found a place that looked clean. The menu outside showed reasonable prices.

After eating, I went back to the motel to wait for the night. It seemed to take forever to get dark.

Finally, about ten p.m., I left the motel and started walking. I didn't do the Strip. I decided what I was looking for wouldn't be found there. I took a side street between two casinos. It was another world. No flashing lights, no loud music. Except for the sounds of passing cars, it was quiet.

I walked another block and stopped. *Which way?* I looked both ways and decided to go left. That would take me toward the center of town. As I walked, the women appeared out of thin air.

"Hi, Honey. Lookin' for some action?"

"Hey, Babe, I got what you want. Come and get it."

Most of the women had a pitch, some extremely lewd. I actually blushed.

Then I saw her. I don't know what attracted me to her, but I knew she would be the one.

I walked up to her. "What's your name?"

"June. I'll bring the pleasure of summer into your life."

"How much?" I asked.

"How much you got?" She moved forward and caressed me with her body.

"That depends on your price." I stammered.

"What are you looking for?" She put her hands on my arms.

"A good time."

"How much do you expect to pay for this 'good time?'"

"How about fifty?"

She moved back and laughed. "I'm a hooker, not a charity. How about a hundred?"

"Let's split the difference," I suggested.

She pursed her lips, rubbed her chin, then said, "Okay." She turned and started to walk away. Over her shoulder she crooked a finger. "Follow me."

I followed her.

We went into an apartment building and climbed the stairs to the third floor. There was a long hall with closed doors on both sides. She stopped at the third on the right.

Inside was a rumpled bed, small chest of drawers with chips in the edges, a sink covered with a myriad of cosmetics, a chair filled with sexy, lacy underwear and a portable closet jammed with silky, lacy dresses. A lamp with an orange bulb cast an eerie glow to the small room.

She closed the door, put her arms around my neck and kissed both my cheeks. The way her body moved I thought I was with a snake.

At first, she was all over me, then she was standing a foot away. "Strip," she commanded.

I undressed, laying my clothes on the floor, the only place I could find to put them. When I was naked, she nodded. "How old are you?"

"Eighteen today."

She clapped her hands. "I get to make you a man. How cool." She stripped and stood by the bed. "It'll be a hundred."

I sighed. "Okay. But it better be worth it."

"Oh, it will be, Honey. It will be. Get on the bed, on your back."

I did as I was told and she mounted me. "Goodbye virginity,

Hello manhood."

I lay there thinking, *this is worth $200.00.* I gave myself up to the feelings. Everything was going fine until she stopped and lay down on my chest. "What happened?" I asked, confused.

"An unexpected event, I had an orgasm."

"Oh." I thought about that. "What about mine?"

"Roll me over."

I wrapped my arms around her and we rolled over. Everything changed. My whole body was in ecstasy. When I tried to kiss her, she bit my tongue. It didn't matter I kissed her anyway. Then the whole world exploded. I could see stars in a kaleidoscope of colors and shapes. I was spinning in space and dancing among the stars. It seemed to last forever but didn't. I slowly came back to earth and June. I relaxed with my head on the bed next to hers. I was panting. I took a few moments to regain control.

June didn't move and didn't make a sound. At first, I thought she was asleep. I pulled my arms from under her, lifted my body and was about to say how wonderful everything was. I was dumbfounded. Her jaw was broken and her body was scrunched up like she was cold. I found out later that I had crushed her ribs and they punctured her heart and lungs.

I slowly removed myself from her and sat on the floor by the bed. *I killed her. I crushed her to death and broke her jaw. How in Hell did I do that? What the Hell am I?* I sat there trembling, trying to figure out what happened and what to do.

After what seemed like forever, I got up, used one of her washcloths to clean myself up. I got dressed then thought about what to do with her. Part of me said it was time to get out. Part of me said I couldn't leave her like that.

I used the washcloth to wipe down everything in the room. I even wiped her body, front and back, then covered her with a blanket. When I was done, I double-checked everything. Satisfied, I left the room taking the washcloth with me. As I exited the building, I hoped none of the other women would remember me.

CHAPTER FIVE

I wandered the street for what seemed like hours. Too many questions my head with no answers. *Should I tell Dad what I did? If I do, what would he think of me? Since he works for the DA, would he make me turn myself in, or would he have me arrested?* No matter what I thought or did, June was dead, and I killed her.

Two guys who bumped into me and brought me up short. One had a beard the other was clean-shaven.

"Are you blind or just an idiot?"

I shook my head. "Sorry. I had something on my mind." *Why are most bearded men bald?*

"Well, we have something on our minds, your money," he said.

I blinked. "My money? Why are you thinking about my money?"

The one without the beard said, "Because we want it, idiot."

Still confused, I said, "I can't give you my money, I need it."

They looked at each other, then back at me. "Are you stupid or on drugs?"

"Neither. I had something on my mind."

They looked at each other and laughed.

The clean-shaven one said, "Are you awake enough to know what this is?" He had a hunting knife with an eight-inch blade pointed at me.

"Yes. It's a knife."

"Good," Mr. Beard said. "Then you know what this is too." He also had a long knife pointed at me.

I sighed. "I guess you really want my money."

They both laughed again.

They had been standing in front of me. I watched them separate to attack me from each side.

When they stopped moving, I looked straight ahead and waited.

The swift attack would have caught someone else off guard, but I knew what they were going to do.

When they lunged forward, I stepped back and grabbed their wrists. I used their momentum to keep them moving forward.

The surprise on their faces turned to pain as their knives sunk into each other's belly.

One said, "Oh."

The other gurgled.

Letting go of their weapons, they fell, moaning.

I stood watching as their blood started to pool on the ground between them.

Suddenly, I sensed movement behind me. I turned just in time to see another knife on its way down toward me.

I reached up and grabbed the wrist that held the knife, then grabbed the elbow of the same arm. I pushed up on the elbow and pulled down on the wrist. There was a loud crack followed by a blood-curdling scream.

When I let go, my would-be attacker fell to the ground unconscious.

Looking up, I saw another man running away.

I stood still for a moment, still unable to make sense of what had just happened. The death of June was still bouncing around in my head.

***

In the distance I could hear sirens. After a few seconds, I could see the flashing red and blue lights of a police car. Time to disappear.

I ran in the opposite direction from where the sirens were

coming from. A side street took me back to the Strip. *Didn't think I was that close.*

Shortly before I reached the street, I slowed down, put my hands in my pockets and sauntered into the world of glaring, blinking lights.

I made it back to my motel without any more incidents. Inside, I threw myself across the bed and just lay there, trying to wrap my head around the incidents of the evening. *Too many questions: no answers. Not even a hint.*

***

I awoke the next morning still lying across the bed, fully dressed. I sat up. *I should take a shower, have breakfast, then head home. Will Dad detect something?*

***

At home later that day, Mrs. Burns asked me how everything went. She sat on the sofa across from me, her hands folded in her lap.

I tied to smile.

She laughed, taking my nervousness for embarrassment. "Now I have two men in the house. Congratulations."

"Thanks."

"Do you feel any different?" she asked.

I thought for a few seconds. "I do and yet, I don't. Physically, there is no difference. Mentally, I feel like I've entered a different world."

"Well," she said, as she stood up. "At least you've got that behind you."

I nodded. "Yep. I sure do."

***

I knew when Dad got home it would be a repeat of what Mrs. Burns asked.

I was almost right.

He waited until just before dinner to ask. "How much did it cost?"

"At first she said, one hundred and I said fifty. We settled on seventy-five. Then she found out I was a virgin and it went back up to a hundred."

"Do you think it was worth it?"

Mrs. Burns called us into dinner.

As we walked to the dining room, I said, "Oh, yes, Dad. It was worth every cent. After we've eaten, I'll tell you what I experienced."

"I can hardly wait," he said as he sat at the table.

As we ate, we talked about everything except my adventure.

***

While Mrs. Burns worked in the kitchen and dining room, Dad and I settled on the couch.

He put one arm over the back of the couch, turned to me and said, "I'm listening."

I took a few seconds to get my thoughts in order. "I never realized how vast our universe is. I visited planets far beyond our solar system. It was the most beautiful occurrence of my life. It's a shame it only happens once."

He laughed. "Don't get ahead of yourself. When you meet the right person, it will happen time and time and again. Just pray it happens to both of you at the same time."

"Yeah," I said. "That would be great."

He reached over to the coffee table and picked up the remote for the TV. We were just in time to catch some of the evening news.

"Police are saying the woman had her jaw broken. Captain Stroberg and Commissioner Henderson from the Las Vegas Metropolitan Police confirm this is not the first killing of this kind. The Commissioner said they would be working with the FBI on this case."

I looked at my father. His eyes were glued to the set.

"On another note, three men were found not far from the deceased woman's apartment. Two of them died from knife wounds that seemed to have been inflicted on each other. The third man died from shock from having his arm bent backward almost ninety degrees from the elbow. The police said the Medics don't think they could have saved him, no matter how soon they would have been able to reach him.

"A fourth man said the three were attacked by a single man. He couldn't give a description because he was running away when the killings were happening. He also stated he could only see the back of the perpetrator in the dark. The police don't think those three men and the woman are connected in any way.

"In other news . . ."

Dad turned to another channel. "Enough bad news for today. We don't want to sully your experience." He paused, thinking. "By the way, were you in the vicinity of those killings?"

"Not hardly. I wouldn't know what to do if someone came at me with a knife."

He looked at me for some time as if trying to analyze my statement. He then nodded and said, "Okay."

We watched a rerun of *The Hobbit*.

When it was over, I stood and said, "It's back to training. We have a game on Saturday against the Vancouver Rockies. They're pretty good, but we'll beat them anyway."

"Don't get too cocky. Nothing lasts forever."

"You're right, Dad. I'll try to keep my head on straight. Good night."

"Good night."

***

It was on a Saturday a month later that we played the Portland Lumberjacks. It was a good game. Neither team scored during the first half.

When the game resumed, both teams were scoreless until the 10 minutes before the final whistle. Our forwards got lucky and managed to get the ball into their net. Of course, we were ecstatic.

While we were celebrating, two of their members came over and said, "Our turn."

I didn't say anything, just nodded.

***

With only five minutes left, I watched the ball being brought down the field to my right. I expected it to go across the face of the goal and get redirected into the net on my left. I was ready. What I wasn't ready for was the ball going to my right. I had to make a leaping dive to stop the score.

As I lay there with the ball in my hands, I felt it get kicked, then kicked again. I looked up to see an angry Lumberjack trying to kick the ball out of my hands and into the net.

I pulled the ball to my chest and had only enough time to extend my hand before my face. I grabbed the front of his shoe and pushed. I let go when I heard him scream.

I dropped the ball and stood up holding my hand. I could already feel it swelling.

The members of both teams, separated by the ref and linesman, were on the verge of a major battle. Somehow, a stretcher was already on the way for the other guy. I didn't know what his name was and didn't care.

Holding my hand, I walked over to our bench and our trainers. My hand was so swollen they had to cut the glove off. As soon as that was done, it was wrapped in an ice pack. The marks from his cleats were clearly visible on my palm. The trainers gave me a shot for the pain.

Coach Spears came over and said, "Everybody in the stadium saw what happened, several times, from different angles. Whatever you did to him, he deserved it."

"I don't know what I did except try to protect my face."

I found out later I had broken his foot and he would be a cripple for life. I was sorry. I didn't mean to hurt him.

After what seemed like forever, the officials made an announcement. "Because of the unsportsmanlike conduct of the Portland Lumberjacks, the rest of the game will be suspended. The Franklin Thunder is declared the winner."

There were a few more cheers than boos, but essentially, the stadium was quiet as it started to empty out.

The mood of the team was quiet during and after the showers. They got a plastic bag for my hand to keep it dry.

"Good thing it was your left hand," Coach Spears said.

I nodded.

When all had showered and changed, we exited the stadium only to find the parking lot empty, except for our bus. Every window was broken, and every tire was flat.

We looked at the bus in dismay. Our hotel was on the other side of town, more than 15 miles away. From the stadium, it was two miles to the nearest bus stop.

With a sigh, Coach Spears said, "Okay guys, let's see if the local busses are still running."

We found out they were. They left the terminal on the hour every hour after 10 p.m. It was already 10:43, which meant the bus had come and gone.

We dropped our bags and settled down to wait. It was quiet since half of us were barely awake.

***

Sure enough, at 11:27 the bus showed up. The driver opened the door. The sign inside said "Exact Change Only." The fare was four dollars.

Of twenty-six of us, only sixteen were able to make it.

A 12:27, the next bus came and went. We ran and yelled for it to stop. It didn't.

"What do we do now, Coach?"

He sighed. "I guess we wait. If we try to walk, it'll be well after morning by the time we get there."

We decided to wait.

***

About twenty minutes later, a pickup truck pulled up across the street. The driver got out and walked over to us. "What are you guys doing here?" he asked.

"Waiting for the next bus," Coach Spear said.

The guy looked at his watch. "There won't be any more busses tonight. The next one to leave the terminal will be at 4 a.m."

There was a collective sigh of dismay.

"Where are you guys going, anyway?"

"The Holiday Inn Express," Coach answered.

The man smiled. "If you start walking now, you can get there in time to check out." He turned and started toward his truck.

In the middle of the street, he stopped, turned and asked, "Can I give you a ride?"

"Hell, yes," Coach shouted.

Even though it was dark, we could see the smile on the truck driver's face.

"Coach, you ride up front with me. The rest of you pile in the back." He shook Coach's hand and said, "I'm Gary."

Coach said, "No, you're not. You're an angel in disguise. I'm Coach Spears and this is my team from Franklin, Nevada."

"Glad to meet you, Coach Spears. Which is the guy who was involved in the 'Incident'?"

"He's my goalie. Name's Jake Stettler. Never seen anybody like him."

I smiled.

"I guess he's really good."

"No, he's better than good. Challenged the whole team to a penalty shoot-out. Not one ball got into the net."

"Oh, come on now. That's impossible. No goalie is that good."

"Jake is. Check our record. No goals scored against us since he joined the team."

At this point my face was red from embarrassment.

Gary nodded. "Yeah. I'll have to look him up. The Franklin Thunder." He nodded. "I will check it out."

CHAPTER SIX

We arrived at the hotel a few minutes later. Some of the guys had to be woken up.

When coach collected the keys, the desk clerk had bad news. "You'll have to be out of your rooms tomorrow. The hotel is hosting a weeklong conference starting tomorrow. We'll need to have your rooms empty and cleaned by check-in time."

I would have sworn he was looking down his nose at coach. His tone was very nasal.

"We can't get transportation until Monday. Our bus was demolished. We have no way of getting home." Coach looked angry and dismayed at the same time.

"I'm sorry, sir. It is what it is." His tone was very unapologetic.

"Don't you have anything else available?"

At first, he stared at Coach as though he wondered how Coach could have the audacity to ask that question. He looked at his computer screen. "Um, let me see. Ah, yes. There is the Penthouse. It has 6 bedrooms, 5 baths, 2 living rooms and 2 dining rooms. It is, however, only available for one night."

"I think that's all we would need. How much is it?"

With a disdainful look, the clerk said, "It's $3500 per night." The

Cheshire cat would have blanched at his smile.

Coach Spears' mouth dropped open. He blinked several times. "I don't think with all our credit cards and pocket money that we could afford that. Even if we could, we wouldn't have money left to get us home."

Looking down his nose, the clerk said, "Not my problem, Sir. However, checkout time is still 11 o'clock."

Coach spears nodded. As he handed out the keys, he said, "Get as much sleep as possible, guys. Tomorrow looks like a long day."

***

The next morning, the phone in my room rang. One of the other guys answered it. "Jake, for you."

I took the phone. "Hello."

"Jake, this is Dad. The incident at the game was all over the news and is burning up the social media. How are you doing?"

"I'm doing fine. The trainer wrapped my hand and gave me some painkillers in case I need them. I'm okay so far."

"It must have been a concentrated effort to do that to your bus so quickly. Has your coach found a way to get you home?"

"Not as far as I know."

"Okay. I'll see what I can arrange. Let him know I'm working on the problem."

"Will do, Dad. Hope to see you soon."

***

At breakfast, I told Coach Spears about my conversation with my father.

He pushed his food around on his plate. "I hope he can come up with something. I don't fancy all of us sleeping on the street."

Later, we collected our gear and met in the lobby.

"What do we do now, Coach?" several of the guys asked.

He sighed. "We wait for a miracle." He went to the desk clerk glad it wasn't the same one as the night before. "Can we stay in the lobby at least until it gets dark? I promise we won't get in anybody's way and we'll leave after dark."

The clerk said it would be okay if we found a corner out of the way.

Coach found a spot away from the entrance and out of the mainstream of traffic. We had just settled down when a policeman entered and asked the desk clerk for the coach.

When Coach saw him approach, he mumbled, "Crap. What have we done now?"

The officer approached, took off his hat, extended his hand and said, "Coach Spears, I'm Captain Reeves. I have two busses waiting outside to take you and your team to the airport."

"How . . . how did you know?"

"Jake's dad called me and told me you needed transportation. He and I spent a few years together in the Air Force. We're both still in the National Guard on reserve duty." He looked at his watch. "Let's get going, guys. Time's a wasting."

We all gathered our bags and followed the Captain outside to the waiting busses.

When the doors were closed, the bus took off with all of us wondering what would happen next.

***

At the airport, a C-130 transport stood waiting with the rear cargo door open. We were all amazed. This thing looked like it could hold several large SUV's. Several guys in military uniform hustled us in, stowed our bags and showed us how to buckle into the canvas seats.

Captain Reeves, Coach Spears and a man in a flight suit entered the compartment.

While Coach was getting settled in, the Captain said, "Guys, this is your pilot and Flight Commander. He's taking you to Las Vegas. Busses will be waiting there to take you to back to Franklin. Any questions?"

"Yeah," one of the players asked. "How did you guys arrange all this so fast?"

The Captain indicated the Flight Commander. "This is Lieutenant Colonel Stettler of the Las Vegas Air National Guard. He and a few others got together to solve your problem. Portland is buying you a new bus. It should be delivered in about a week."

I hadn't been paying attention. When he mentioned my Dad's name, I looked up. "Stettler? Stettler? Dad, is that you?"

He laughed. "Yes, Jake. It's me."

"Wow!" I said. "I knew you were in the Guard, but I didn't know you were an active pilot."

He just smiled. "Word spread about your situation. Gary, the guy with the pick-up, called Captain Reeves. He arranged for the busses and called me. I was in Minot on a training mission at the time and it was only a slight change in flight plan to get here. We train for all contingencies."

He and Captain Reeves shook hands and Reeves departed through a side door.

Stettler went up to the flight deck.

Within minutes, we were on our way.

As promised, buses were waiting for us when we landed.

***

A cheer went up the moment we entered Franklin. The main street was lined with people all the way to the stadium.

We were astounded by what we saw. Inside the stadium, the town had set up tables and filled them with all types of food and desserts. Tubs with iced drinks stood nearby.

A gentleman I didn't recognize said, "We would have had a banner made, but we didn't have time."

The team thanked him and everybody else for all they did.

***

I enjoyed myself and almost, like the rest of the team, ate myself sick.

The townspeople kept urging us to eat, eat.

Out of politeness, we ate until we were almost sick, then the towns people packed good for us.

Even with all I took, I felt like it wouldn't be enough. There was something missing.

I sat on my couch for a few minutes, then decided to go to bed. I lay there with my hands behind my head, my eyes open. Sleep would not come. *Maybe fresh air will help.* I got up, went to my car, got in and stated driving. I didn't know where I was going and didn't care. I just needed fresh air.

***

After a while, I pulled off the road into a small parking lot. Another car pulled into the far end, only three spaces away. It was a low, slung jobbie with the top down. I saw the guy look over at me. He guy got out of his car and came over to mine.

"You got a problem, Buddy? We're not giving a show. Move on."

When I didn't respond, he banged on the roof of my car.

I opened the door and got out. "That wasn't necessary. Good thing you didn't dent my car."

He pulled himself up to his full height, pushed out his chest and flexed his arm muscles. "Maybe I should. What would you do about it?"

Not smiling, I said, "Hurt you."

He threw his head back and laughed. "You would hurt me? You couldn't even pull the hair off my chest."

I took a step closer to him and lashed out with my fist, hitting him in the throat. He gasped and collapsed in a heap. Without thinking, I squatted over him and took his head in my hands. His mouth hung open, gasping.

Not knowing why, I put my mouth on his. My tongue started stretching. I kept still, wondering what else would happen. My tongue kept getting longer and longer. It went up the back of his throat and then I felt and tasted the most exquisite sensations. I held his head and moaned as this new phenomenon invaded my body.

Suddenly, it was over. My tongue retracted and I rolled off him. I lay panting beside him.

His girlfriend came over and looked down at us and screamed. "What have you done?"

I raised myself to a sitting position, then slowly stood up. Facing her, I said, "I think I killed him."

She stared at me, then knelt beside him. She took him in her arms and cried as she rocked him.

I was still standing there, watching them.

After a short while, she got up and looked at me. Suddenly, she was yelling and screaming, "You killed him. You killed him!" The she came at me kicking and with arms swinging.

I barely had time to protect myself. I put my arms around her and with my lips on hers I pushed my tongue into her mouth. As she bit down, there was a brief, sharp pain and then my tongue expanded until I heard a 'crack' and she went limp in my arms.

Still standing and holding her, I felt my tongue elongate. *Here we go again.* I couldn't wait. It was better with her. Her brain was softer and sweeter.

Finally, it ended. I relaxed and let her go. When she hit the ground, I blinked. I couldn't believe what I saw. It wasn't enough that I took her brain. I also broke her jaw and crushed her body. From what I remembered hearing about June, I knew the woman's ribs broke and punctured her lungs and heart and her collar bones punctured her neck.

I stood looking at the two of them. *What kind of monster am I?* I shook my head, ran to my car, got in and drove as if the Devil was chasing me. I didn't look back. I was afraid of what I would see.

***

Back in my apartment, I stripped down, took a shower and wished I could drink alcohol without getting sick. I almost envied alcoholics. The exertions of the previous night gave me what I needed to sleep.

***

When my alarm clock woke me the next morning, I felt really good. Refreshed and, will wonders never cease, stronger. Oddly, I felt great. There was no remorse for the couple I'd killed. I didn't worry about fingerprints or DNA. I wasn't in any system so there was no way to identify me. Last night I was a monster. Today I was just Jake. I gathered my gear and took off for the stadium.

***

Practice went very well. We all played our hearts out as though it was a real game.

Coach Spears was well pleased. "Play like that on Saturday and we'll annihilate our opponents."

We did and he was more than happy. We beat the LA Dolphins 5-0.

Their coach grudgingly congratulated Coach Spears. "Where would you be without your goalie?" he asked.

Coach Spears shrugged. "Probably at the bottom of the league, where we were before."

The other coach nodded, turned and walked away.

Of course we celebrated. Coach took us to a restaurant and paid half the price for the meals. "I'm not in the big league yet," he said smiling. He told the waitress, "Everybody gets one beer on me."

"Just one?" a few of the guys asked.

"Yes, just one. If you want to get drunk, do it on your own nickel."

I gave mine to our striker. He deserved it since he scored a hat trick (3 goals).

***

A month later we hosted the Vancouver Rockies. All went as expected. We beat them, but only by 2-0. It didn't do much for their dispositions.

A few of their guys got yellow cards for illegal tackles. They were careful enough not to have any player get more than one. That would have meant a red card and dismissal from the game with no substitute, and they needed all the help they could get.

After the game, Coach Andrews asked Spears, "Don't you ever learn? We need to win against you. We've beaten every other team in the league. Why do you have to be stupid?"

Coach Spears shrugged. "I guess we don't know any better. We only know how to play to win. My team doesn't know how to play to lose."

Andrews snorted, shook his head and walked off. "Have it your way."

We thought everything would be okay. We were wrong.

As we were coming out of the stadium, their players met us. They had clubs and bats. We only had our gear.

The fight started. More than a few of us were hurt seriously by the time the police got there swinging clubs and screaming orders. In an instant, some of the players had wrenched the clubs loose and were hitting the police. Several of them were injured too, some badly.

I did my share to put some of the other team out of commission. I grabbed an arm that was on its way to Coach Spears' head, twisted it behind the owner and pushed up until I heard a crack. I let him drop to the ground and grabbed another guy that was pounding his fist into Kyles face. I squeezed the fist, until I could feel the bones crumble. A broken jaw, a caved in chest, a crushed throat, I did my share to protect my team. I couldn't hear any screams. There was too much yelling and screaming by everyone involved.

I don't know how long the fight lasted. It seemed to go on forever. It finally ended when the fire department turned hoses on us. Our EMT personnel had more than they could handle. The police, those who were still able to function, used plastic tie wraps instead of handcuffs to cart the worst offenders off to jail.

Of the twenty-three of their team members, fourteen were arrested. The rest were taken to the hospital with various injuries.

Unfortunately, more than half of our team had been injured. I even let myself get a few bruises, just to make it look good.

Coach Spears and Marty Wilson, one of our forwards, were the worst injured. Coach had a broken collar bone and cracked ribs. Marty had three cracked ribs, a broken jaw and a cracked femur. Their coach came through totally unscathed. He just stood back and watched the mayhem. He was arrested for inciting a riot. As he went quietly, we heard him say, "It was worth it."

***

Both teams had to cancel the next two games. We didn't have enough players fit to make up a team. What surprised me was how calm I felt, both during the melee and afterwards.

I sat in my apartment and replayed the scene over and over in my head. The next day I went to the police station.

"What's up, Jake?" the officer on duty asked.

"I just want to get a look at the idiot who decided this was the only way to beat us."

He nodded, got his keys and walked toward the cells. He unlocked the gate and said, "Call me when you're done."

"I will."

I walked down the hall until I came to Coach Andrews' cell. I folded my hands behind me and leaned against the cell across from him.

He looked at me for a few moments, then got up and walked to the bars. With his hands wrapped around the bars, he said, "You're the goalie, Jake something or other."

I nodded. "Jake Stettler."

"What do you want?"

I only stared at him.

"What the fuck do you want?" he screamed.

I didn't move, didn't speak, just stared.

He started pacing back and forth from his cot to the bars and back again. Finally, he decided, "Two can play this game."

He sat on his cot and returned my stare.

As I looked at him, I thought about my tongue moving through his mouth to the back of his throat. It expanded until his air was cut off. Then it crept up into his skull until it contacted his brain. I could almost taste the sweetness of his brain matter.

Then someone was shaking me.

"Jake! Jake!"

I blinked myself back to reality.

"What the Hell is going on?" the officer demanded.

I shrugged. "Nothing on this end. Is there a problem?"

"Yeah. I came because he was screaming. What did you do to him?"

I shook my head. "Not a thing. I just stood here and stared at him." I looked through the bars. Coach Andrews lay on his cot whimpering and holding his head.

"What's wrong with him?" I asked.

"Don't know. I'll get the medics in to see what's going on."

I nodded and headed toward the main office and home.

CHAPTER SEVEN

Later that evening, as I lay in bed, that "feeling" came over me again. The last time I'd felt it, I'd gone out into the night and killed two people. I was bound and determined not to do that again. Even if it meant no sleep, I wouldn't go out. At least, that's what I promised myself.

After an hour, I got up and made myself a cup of lemon tea. *When did I get a craving for this? When did I even buy lemon tea?* When I finished, I went back to bed and woke up the next morning when my alarm went off. *I keep learning new things about myself. I'll have to keep a supply of lemon tea on hand.*

***

A month later, with Coach Spears in bandages. We faced the Vancouver Rockies with our new forward, Kyle Simmons.

Their coach, Mr. Andrews, told Coach Spears, "If we don't score at least once, your goalie will be in serious trouble. I won't vouch for his safety or wellbeing. Let a word to the wise be sufficient." He paused and moved closer to Spears. "You do understand English, don't you?"

Spears smiled. "Of course I do. I even understand Spanish, French and German. Foreign languages come easy to me."

Andrews didn't smile when he said, "Being a wise ass seems to come easy. Think about the health of your goalie." He turned and walked away.

Coach Spears came over to me and let me know about the threat. "Thanks, Coach. I'll worry about it after the game."

He shrugged and walked off.

***

We beat them 2-0. Coach Andrews first congratulated Coach Spears, then came over to me. "How many times do you think you can die?" he asked.

I blinked. "Only once, as far as I know."

"I guess we'll find out." He sneered and walked off laughing.

Several of my teammates heard his comment.

"Are you afraid?" one of them asked.

"Not really. I have my bodyguards."

Another asked, "Do you think two will be enough? Remember the riot."

"How can I forget it? Yes, I think two will be enough." Then a thought occurred to me. Once the owner's find out about the new threat, they'll probably double the guards.

I was right. Two were with me in the car on the drive home and two were waiting outside my building.

Everything was going well until the next evening.

It was just past 9 p.m. when my doorbell rang.

"Yes?"

The voice on the other side said, "Mr. Stettler, we have a problem. There's been a breach in security. You need to come with us, now."

I didn't recognize the voice, but I didn't know the voices of the two new men.

When I opened the door, all I saw was a smiling face before it felt like my chest caved in. I fell backward and hit the floor, gasping for breath. Looking up through hazy eyes, I saw a barrel supported by a pair of legs. The smile on the square face was full of malice. "I am your worst nightmare and I've come to send you to hell. How many times would you like to die?" it asked.

Unable to breathe, I just shook my head.

"Well, I'll make that decision for you." He grabbed me by my belt and throat and threw me across the room.

I don't know what I hit, but it hurt.

He walked over and stood looking down at me. "Maybe I'll just start breaking things." He raised his foot.

I barely had time to move my leg before his foot hit the ground. He waggled a finger at me. "Naughty, naughty. You were not supposed to move." He reached down, grabbed my belt and lifted me up. It seemed I was light as a feather to him. "I'm not getting paid by the hour, so, I'll do you a favor and end this now." He put a fist the size of both my hands around my throat. "I'll do it slowly so you can enjoy it."

He started squeezing.

I couldn't move and I couldn't yell. All I could do was hang in the air with his hand slowly crushing my throat. It didn't take long for me to black out.

***

Surprise, surprise! I was alive and, on my stomach, and I could feel the hard surface of my floor beneath me. I could even smell the oil in the hardwood. I opened my eyes, slowly. My whole body hurt. *Where was the monster? Why am I still alive?* I slowly became aware of a loud banging. When I raised my head, I could see the legs of the monster beating on the floor.

"What the Hell?"

Ignoring the pain that shot through every part of my body, I raised myself to my hands and knees. The monster's legs slowed in their beating on the floor. They got slower and slower, then finally stopped.

I crawled over to the couch and started to pull myself onto it. In the process I looked over at him and immediately fell to the floor. I didn't even feel the pain when my butt hit. I was speechless. I couldn't believe what I was seeing. *How could this have happened?* I shook my head, closed my eyes, then opened them again. The scene didn't change. The monster lay on the floor with his arms and upper body covered in what looked like white, silk rope. *What is that stuff?*

Where did the stuff come from? When did it come? How did it get on him? These questions spun around in my head for what seemed like forever.

I sat there on the floor, looking at him. "What the hell do I do now?" The walls wouldn't even echo my question, much less answer it.

***

Still sitting on the floor, I debated what to do next. I watched as the white rope slowly dissolve into brown dust. *If this is a dream, I hope I wake up soon.* If I called my dad, it would take him two and a half hours to get here. Coach Spears would be sleeping since it was well after midnight. With a sigh, I dragged myself off the floor, found my phone and called 9-1-1.

"9-1-1, what is your emergency?"

"My name is Jake Stettler. I live at 1435 Sunset Way, Apt 2. I have a dead man on the floor of my living room. At least I think it's a man."

"Meaning?"

"He's built almost like a man, but his chest is huge, and his legs are thin and spindly. His arms look to be about as big around as my legs."

"Are you sure he's dead?"

"Yes. His legs were kicking and now they've stopped. Please send the police right away." I hung up before she could say anything else.

Five minutes later, I heard sirens. When I looked out the window, there were two police cars with their lights flashing in front of my building. A few moments later, there was a knock on the door. "Franklin Police," the voice said.

I went and opened the door. The man who entered first was in a suit.

"I'm Detective Walsh. I understand you have a dead body here."

"Yes. He's over there." I turned and pointed to where the monster lay.

He and a uniformed officer headed in that direction.

"Holy Shit!" Walsh exclaimed.

The officer crossed himself several times while mumbling.

"How the Hell did you subdue him?" Walsh asked, his eyes still on the corpse. He had a pen in one hand and notepad in the other. Both hung suspended.

"I let him choke me until I passed out," I informed him. I wasn't smiling.

His head moved back and forth between the dead man and me. To the officer, he said. "Coroner."

"I think he's already on the way," the officer said. He made sure his eyes were turned away from the monster.

Walsh nodded. "Of course." He looked at me and said, "Let's sit."

He took the chair. I took the couch.

"From the beginning." His pen paused above his notepad.

I took a deep breath. "About 9 p.m., there was a knock on the door. The person said there had been a security breach and I was to be taken to someplace safe. When I opened the door, a sledgehammer hit me in the chest. This 'thing' came over, picked me up by the belt and throat and threw me across the room. He picked me up again and said, 'I'm going to send you to hell.' I couldn't fight back as he started choking me. I passed out and woke up, I was surprised that I was still alive. He was lying on the floor, the way you see him now." When I stopped talking, I realized I had been twisting my hands. *No way am I going to tell him about the white rope.*

He nodded. "I understand you have bodyguards?"

"Yes. I had two but, because of an incident at our last game, our owners increased it to four. I don't know where they are."

He coughed. "Two were across the street in their vehicle. It was upside down. The other two were found alongside the building. Their necks were broken. I assume *that*," he indicated the dead body on the floor, "was responsible for their deaths."

I nodded. "Makes sense. He would have had to take care of them to get to me."

I didn't realize the door was still open until two men walked in pushing a gurney.

The older one, Dr. Hoag, the coroner, said, "Detective Walsh, we meet again. Where . . . Holy Shit!" His eyes caught sight of the body. "Is that real?"

Walsh shrugged. "Don't know, didn't check."

Hoag walked over to the corpse, knelt beside it and checked for a pulse. He stood up. "It's real and very dead. I guess we can thank our lucky stars." He knelt again and checked the temperature. "He's been dead less than two hours." He looked at Walsh and me. "When did all this happen? I don't usually get called so soon after a death. Is this your place, son?"

I nodded. "Yes, it is."

He looked at the body again, then back at me. "How did you subdue him?"

"Like I told the detective, I tried to fight back and he choked me, but he was so strong that I passed out. When I woke up, he was dead."

"Hm. I guess you didn't know what you were doing while you were unconscious."

"Is that a question?"

"Not really. Just thinking out loud." He turned to his assistant. "Let's get this, uh, guy, out of here."

They tried to put him in a body bag. It was a tight fit. He was really wide.

"First time for everything," Hoag said.

When they tried to lift him onto the gurney, they could barely move him. In the end, it took four men to accomplish that task.

"Autopsy ought to be interesting. Care to guess what this guy's made of, Detective Walsh?"

Walsh shook his head and snorted. "My wildest dreams probably wouldn't come close."

Hoag nodded and he and his assistant rolled the gurney out the door. "By the way," Hoag said. "Thanks for living on the ground floor." He was gone before I could make a comment.

I turned to Detective Warren. "Do you need anything else from me?"

He looked around the room. "I don't think so. If I do, I'll call. We'll notify the owners that you need new bodyguards." He said goodnight as he closed the door on the way out.

***

I decided I should try get some sleep. Tomorrow was another day. It would slowly fade into the background, I hoped.

***

After having breakfast, I called Coach Spears.

"Hi, Jake. What's up?"

I tried not to sound stressed but, I failed. "I need to talk to somebody. There was a problem at my apartment last night."

"What? What happened?" he demanded.

"Someone tried to kill me." I choked up slightly as I said it.

"I'll be right over."

Before I knew it, the line was dead.

It was normally a twenty-minute drive from his house to my apartment. He made it in fifteen.

I was at the window when he drove up. I opened the door before he could knock.

His eyes searched my body as he entered the room.

"What happened?" He put both hands in my shoulders.

"Sit down. I'll tell you all about it."

He sat on the edge of the couch and waited.

I got him a cup of coffee and put it in front of him on the coffee table.

With my own cup cradled in both hands, I sat on the chair facing him. I took a sip and watched him. I knew he was getting anxious.

Finally, I said, "A man tried to kill me. He killed my two security people and disabled my other bodyguards. I'm still trying to figure out why I'm still alive. He choked me until I passed out. When I woke up, he was on the floor, dead."

Spears took several sips of coffee while his brain processed my story. Finally, he put his cup on the table and looked straight at me. "Do you know who he was? Had you seen him before?"

I shook my head. "No, to both your questions."

"What about the police? Did you call them?"

I nodded. "They told me about the guards. The security men were found dead on the side of the building. Their necks were broken. The bodyguards were in their vehicle. It was upside down."

He blinked several times. "Their car was upside down?"

"That's what the detective said."

He leaned back and folded his hands in his lap. "Let me get this straight. This person upended a vehicle with two people in it, then killed two others before coming to you."

I nodded. "That's right."

He tilted his head to one side. "How did he get in?"

I sighed. "I opened the door for him."

His jaw dropped. "Didn't you recognize his voice?"

"No. I never heard the two new people speak, so I didn't know what they sounded like."

He sat looking down at his hands as he folded and unfolded them. Finally, he looked up. "Do the owners know about this?"

I shrugged. "I don't know if the police informed them. They should know since two of their people were killed."

He nodded. "I guess I'll be hearing from them some time today." He bit his lip and looked at his cup on the table. He took a deep breath. "Obviously this guy was hired to take you out, permanently. Do you have any idea who would be responsible?"

"I think I know." I wasn't smiling. "I'd put my money on Coach Andrews. He made no bones about veiling his threat." I nodded. "I'm sure it was him. I don't have any doubt."

Spears nodded. "He was the first to come to my mind, too. I thought only the South Americans went so far. Come to think of it, they only try to kill the ref, never a player. At least not that I've heard of."

He leaned back and rubbed his thighs. "What do we do now? Other coaches will make the same threat. Some will even try to carry them out." He stopped, seemingly at a loss for words.

I nodded. "I know what you're thinking. Protecting me will put the whole team at risk."

"Jake, I . . ." He shook his head.

"It's okay, Coach," I interrupted him. "The same thought is going through my head. I don't want to see others get hurt because of me." I picked up my cup, took a few sips, then put it back on the table.

We both sat looking at our hands for a few moments.

Finally, I said. "We're two-thirds of the way through the season. Losing a few games won't seriously hurt our standing. I'm assuming we won't lose *every* game from now on."

He sat up straight, took a deep breath and looked straight at me. "Are you suggesting what I think you are?"

I nodded. "I think I am. I'm going to take three weeks off. You have two other goalies. They're pretty good. They just need a chance to show it. I'm sure they'll make you proud, if you give them a chance." I thought about the other goalies and how their lives would change if they help the team win.

He put his hand on his knees and closed his eyes. Finally, he opened them and sighed. "You do realize I'm thinking about the other guys, right?"

"Yes, I realize it. I have to think about them too." I could see him hesitating.

"What do you think I should tell the guys?"

I leaned forward and put my arms on my legs, "I'm sure, by now, they've heard of last night's incident. I guess you can tell them I'm lying low for my own safety."

He sighed. "I'll talk to the owners and see what they say. There shouldn't be any problems. The other goalies will be thrilled to get to play again." We both stood and walked to the door.

"What will you do?" he asked with his hand on the doorknob.

"Just lie low too. I think I'll spend some time with my Dad and just relax. I'm sure he'll be glad to have me around for a little while."

He opened the door and stepped out. "Take care of yourself. Call me a day or two before you're ready to come back."

I stood with my hand on the door for a few seconds. I nodded and went to get the cups. On the way to the kitchen, I thought *Coach Andrews, I'm going to give you what your goon promised me. A trip to hell.*

CHAPTER EIGHT

I had a dilemma. I needed to visit Coach Andrews. I couldn't do it from Franklin. As long as I was in town, I would be expected to be with the team. By the same token, I couldn't be in Milton. Dad and Mrs. Burns would expect me to be home.

I sat on the couch trying to decide how I was going to accomplish my goal.

I have to disappear. Coach Spears has to think I'm in Milton. Dad and Mrs. Burns have to think I'm still in Franklin. After a few minutes, I decided, this would be easier than I thought.

I called Coach Spears and told him I was going home to Milton. My dad said he would take me hiking. Then I called my dad and told him I would be staying in Franklin, but I would be laying low, not playing or practicing with the team. I was sure he wouldn't have a reason to call.

***

I packed a few clothes and filled my backpack with stuff I thought I'd need. I then drove to the seedier side of town and found a motel. The clerk asked, "How long you need the room?" He looked like he hadn't changed clothes in a month and hadn't bathed either.

"I'll need it for three weeks."

"I'll need a credit card." He lit a cigarette and blew smoke in my direction.

"I don't have one. I'll be paying cash."

He blinked several times. "Cash?" he repeated.

"Yeah. Cash. Can you handle it?"

He put out his cigarette and started typing on a computer keyboard. When he finished, he said, "That'll be $333.75. A hundred per week for the room plus tax." His eyes glistened as I pulled a wad of bills from my pocket. The more I counted, the bigger his eyes got.

I pushed $350 toward him. "Keep the change."

Licking his lips, he counted the money twice. When he was satisfied it was all real and correct, he reached under the counter and pulled out a key. "Room 107. Out the door, turn left. It's on the other side of the parking lot."

I picked up the key and stood waiting.

"What?" He looked annoyed.

"Don't you want me to register?"

His mouth fell open. "Oh. Oh, yeah." He retrieved a blank card and put it on the counter.

I stood waiting,

He looked up from his counting. "Now what?"

Very calmly, I said, "I don't have a pen. Do you?"

"Of course, I do. What kind of place do you think I run?"

"May I borrow one?"

With his mouth open, he blinked several times, then looked at the blank form. "Oh." He found a pen and laid it on the counter. I guess he didn't want to touch me.

As I filled out the form, I listed my name as Art Samson from Las Vegas. I made up an address. I didn't list my car.

***

In my room, I put my backpack on the only chair in the room. I checked the bed for bed bugs. I didn't find any. What a surprise. The cleanliness of the room really impressed me.

Convinced that everything was in order, I left to go to the bus station. I started driving away then remembered my phone was in my backpack. When I entered the parking lot, I could see the door to my room closing. Parking a few rooms down, I got out, went to my door and waited.

It wasn't long before the door opened. The desk clerk was looking into the room as he exited. As he stepped out pulling the door shut, he turned and came face to face with me. He stopped and gasped.

I put my hand on his chest and gently pushed him back into the room.

Fear contorted his face. The way his mouth moved reminded me of a fish.

When we were next to the bed, I said, "Empty your pockets."

"I didn't . . ." he started to protest.

I cut him off. "Empty your pockets. NOW!"

He whimpered and mumbled as he turned his pockets inside out. Among the items he put on the bed was my phone, my razor, my toothpaste, a rosary, a gold chain with a cross, a bracelet and two rings.

I picked up my razor. "Do you know how to use this?" I demanded.

"Please, sir, I'm sorry," he blubbered.

I put both hands on his shoulders, looked him in the eye and said, "Return all these items. I'll know if you don't."

He nodded. "Yessir. Yessir I will, I promise."

I let him go, stepped aside and picked up my phone.

Three seconds later, he ran out the door.

I shook my head and left to go to my car. I took my backpack with me.

***

At the bus station, I bought a round trip ticket to Vancouver. I had a two-hour wait, so I went to the nearest restaurant and had lunch. I decided to put my car in the long-term lot. As a precaution, I took out the registration, insurance card and anything else that had my name and address on it. If someone decided to break into my car, I didn't want them to know my name or where I lived.

***

As if a two-hour wait for the bus wasn't enough, it would be a five-hour trip to Vancouver. It was well past midnight when we arrived. Since I slept most of the way, I was well rested and wide-awake when we stopped. It was just as well because I had to walk four blocks to the nearest cheap motel. I didn't need a Holiday Inn or a Marriott or any place on that scale. I needed to remain incognito and watch my finances at the same time.

At the Super Eight motel, the clerk didn't know what to do when I told him I didn't have a credit card.

"How am I supposed to charge you?" he asked, a confused look on his face.

I smiled. "Can you accept cash?"

Another guppy. Finally, he said. "Uh, yes, I suppose so. Just a minute."

I waited while he consulted someone on the phone and made entries on his computer. After a few moments, he looked up and smiled. "No problem, Sir. I can accept cash."

"Wonderful," I said and counted out enough to pay for the room for two weeks. I hoped I wouldn't need more time than that.

***

Since I'd spent most of the night on the bus, sleep was the last thing on my mind. The room didn't have a phone book, but it did have a folder with items of interest. There were advertisements for just about everything in town, including restaurants, bars, beauty parlors, department stores and places where one could rent almost anything. There was a bike rental shop not far from the motel. *I should be able to ride to almost anywhere.* I found listings for sports clubs and gyms. There was even a listing for the Vancouver Rockies, listing the officers, coach and location. I smiled when I read Coach Andrew's number. I thought that using my cell phone I could come up with an address. I could wait until after breakfast. It was still dark outside.

With just the lamp on, I lay back with my hands behind my head, and just relaxed. I set the alarm for eight, just in case I fell asleep. I did drop off and the alarm woke me up. I splashed water on my face and went to breakfast.

***

I had a full stomach when I went to find the bike shop. Even so, I still had that funny feeling in my stomach. *Can't be hungry. I just ate.* I put it out of my mind and concentrated on reaching my destination.

At the shop, I rented a mountain bike. It would be fine riding the streets and would be perfect if I wanted to go off road. I hoped a week would be enough.

***

Back at the hotel I got a map from the desk clerk.

Then I had an idea. Sure that coach would be at practice, I called his house. His wife answered the phone.

"Mrs. Andrews, my name is Art Sampson. I'm supposed to have an interview with the coach about joining the team. He said it would be better if we met at the house because he would be too distracted at the stadium."

"Okay, son," she said. "Do you have a pen and paper?"

"Yes, ma'am."

She gave me the address. It was 1283 Acorn Way. I was almost jumping for joy when I hung up. Looking up the address on Waze, it was about 14 miles from the motel. I smiled, piece of cake. *I'll see you tonight, Coach Andrews, but I doubt you'll see me.* My laugh sounded sinister, even to me.

***

I took a short nap after lunch, then prepared to take a ride. I first rode around the streets by the motel to get my bearings and accustom myself to the bike.

After a few minutes, I headed for the coach's house. It was an easy ride. The city was mostly flat. The neighborhood was upscale with lawns in front and on the sides of the houses. *This place smelled of money.* Only one or two houses had a car in the driveway.

His house was easy to find. I smiled at the location. It was at the end of the street and shared a circular driveway with another house. At night, it would stand alone.

I rode through the surrounding neighborhood to see if there would be any problems. There were none.

***

On my way back to the motel, I stopped in a thrift shop and bought a pair of black pants and a black, long-sleeved sweater. I then went to a sports shop to get a ski mask and gloves.

The clerk looked at me questioningly.

"I buy my winter stuff in the summer and my summer stuff in the winter," I told him. "It saves me a lot of money."

He pursed his lips and nodded. "Makes sense." He went and rang up my purchases.

I was set. I already had black shoes. The stuff I bought would make me virtually invisible.

Back at the motel, I just happened to notice security cameras in the halls. "I like the idea of the cameras," I told the desk clerk. "They make me feel safer."

He looked around. "Not real," he whispered.

He walked away before I could say anything. What more could I ask for? I would be able to come and go, anytime of day or night and no one would know. I tried not to laugh on the way to my room.

***

Just past midnight, the alarm woke me up. That strange feeling, almost like a hunger, had invaded my body again. Tonight, it was stronger. I tried to ignore it as I prepared for my trip. That just made it worse. "Okay, whatever it is, I'll take care if it when I get back." It didn't help but made me feel better.

***

I rode to Coach Andrews's house with no lights. No need to advertise. If I got stopped, I'd say I forgot to turn them on. I didn't get stopped.

I parked the bike at the side of the house far enough back so anyone passing wouldn't be able to see it. I found the main fuse box.

Just like in most houses, it wasn't locked. I threw the main switch and waited.

It was almost ten minutes before Coach Andrews came out to check. As he reached for the fuse box, I grabbed his hand.

"Wha . . .?"

I grabbed him by the throat and held him against the building. I took off my mask. "Hi, coach. Remember me?"

He clawed and kicked, trying to escape.

"Time for you to precede me to Hell."

I brought him close so his face was level with mine. Afraid that his kicking and thrashing would draw attention, I let go of his throat and wrapped my arms around him. I turned and lowered him to the ground. With my arms around him and my legs intertwined with his, he was completely immobile.

He gasped when my mouth covered his.

"Please," he cried.

While his mouth was open, I entered it with my tongue. He was really strong, but I was stronger. As my tongue reached up into his skull, I realized what the odd hunger meant. I needed brains from someone. I needed to empty their skull. I had to kill somebody.

While I was with Coach Andrews, it was just something that had to be. It was part of my makeup. That it was retribution for what he had done was secondary.

I really felt wonderful when I finished with him. I didn't put the mask on when I rode back to the motel. I didn't think I'd need it.

About two blocks from his house I turned on my lights. No need to be careless.

Back at the motel, I kicked off my shoes and lay across the bed. I felt wonderful. I felt great. First, I had finally figured out what that strange feeling meant. Second, I had dealt with the person who had orchestrated the attack on my team. I was sure his team would be looking over their shoulders for some time to come, wondering who would be next.

***

I turned in the bike the next day and was strolling along wondering how much longer I would be staying in Vancouver. Not paying attention to anything, I was surprised when someone called my name.

"Jake, hey Jake."

I realized I'd made a mistake when I turned to see who was calling. I was supposed to be Art Sampson, not Jake Stettler. "Shit!" Too late now.

A small group of five or more guys came toward me. I realized they were part of the Vancouver Rockies.

"Hi, Jake," the apparent leader said. "I guess you heard about Coach Andrews."

I feigned ignorance. "No. What about him?" I noticed they started to surround me.

"Don't tell me you didn't know he died last night?" He crossed his arms over his chest.

I was completely surrounded by now. "No, I didn't know. How did he die?"

He cocked his head to one side. "How long have you been in town?"

I shrugged. "I just got in yesterday. Does that make a difference?"

The leader, a guy about my height with a crew cut and a scraggly beard, hooked both thumbs on his belt and jutted his jaw forward. "I think you know damn well what difference it makes. You come to town, probably under an assumed name, and the coach winds up dead the next day. I guess you'd call that a coincidence, huh?"

I nodded. "Yes, I would. I don't even know where he lives, and I have no transportation except my feet."

Crew cut sighed and dropped his hands to his sides. "I think you need to come with us so we can discuss this further. The public doesn't need to get involved."

"Suppose I don't want to go with you?" I turned my head from side to side. I was completely surrounded and they were moving in closer. The guys on either side of him raised their arms.

Each one had brandished a knife. "I guess I don't have much choice."

The leader smiled. "No, you don't." He gestured toward the curb. A van waiting there with the side door open and the engine running. "If you don't mind."

I nodded and moved to the van. Inside, the rest of the group crowded around me. "How come I have to sit on the floor? Everybody else has seats."

"Don't worry, you won't be down there long."

After a few minutes, I asked, "How did you know I was in town?"

"We didn't. It was just by chance we saw and recognized you. Just luck, ours good, yours bad."

I nodded and waited to see what would happen next.

CHAPTER NINE

We rode for quite some time. From the way the van turned, I felt like we were going in circles.

When we finally slowed down, it seemed like we were going into a tunnel. The van was shut off and the interior lights came on. I looked up and saw six guys pointing knives at me. We were in a horse barn.

The van doors opened and there were four more guys. They didn't brandish weapons. The leader of the van group greeted the apparent leader of the barn group. He nodded. "Glen."

He raised his hand in salute. "Seth."

"Step out," Seth said.

When I was out, Glen said, "Hands." He was about my height with brown hair and a mustache.

I held my hands out. "You sure are a talkative bunch," I said.

One guy on each side held my arms just above the wrist. The one standing next to Glen started wrapping and knotting a rope around my wrists. When he felt I was secure, he stepped away. The two holding my arms raised them. The knot was put over a hook and a few seconds later I was dangling with only my toes barely touching the ground.

The group stood around laughing and spinning me.

"Not so tough, are you, Jake?" Seth, the leader from the van, a blond with a square jaw, scowled at me.

A few minutes later, I was left with two guards. They stood apart, watching me.

"Can you let me down a little? My arms are starting to hurt."

They smiled but said nothing and didn't move.

***

After several minutes, the rest of the group came back. My two guards left.

I asked, "Are they going to get something to eat? I'm hungry too."

"Where you're going you won't need food," Glen said.

"Can I at least know who I'm talking to?"

Seth said, "We all have the same name, your Executioner."

"Cute. Your mommy and daddy must have been really busy to produce the bunch of you. Is Executioner your first or last names?"

"Aaah," I yelled. Something hit me on my back, right about my kidneys. I closed my eyes for a few seconds. When I opened them, the whole group held what looked like half a broomstick.

Seth said, "Spin him."

Someone reached out and started me spinning.

Glen said, "Now the fun begins."

As I hung turning, I was hit across my legs, back and stomach. How long it lasted, I couldn't say. It seemed to go on forever. I was glad when I finally passed out.

***

I don't know how long I was out, but when I woke up, my whole body was a mass of pain. All I could do was spin and hurt and groan.

A few minutes later, the group came back. Glen asked, "You killed Coach Andrews, didn't you?"

"I didn't even know he was dead." Whack! I was hit across my kidneys.

"You're lying. You are the only one with a reason to want him dead. How did you do it?"

"It wasn't me," I protested.

Whack! Another hit to my kidneys.

"It doesn't matter. You are here and the Coach is dead. They fit. That means you have to die to avenge his death."

Before I could say anything, Glen nodded to the group and they all turned and left. They turned out the lights as they left.

"See you in the morning," one of them called.

I need to get out of here before morning, but how? I hung slowly turning, trying to think of a way out. My arms hurt from hanging and my body hurt from the beatings. The pain made it hard to think. A few moments later, I remembered the monster that had tried to kill me. His head and shoulders were wrapped in what looked like white rope when I woke up. *Could it be I have that ability too? Could I generate what I believed to be spider webbing? If so, how do I produce it?*

I tried everything I could think of. Nothing worked. *There has to be a way.*

I closed my eyes and concentrated. Suddenly, a stream of white flew across the room and attached itself to the far wall. *Great! I did it! Now what. I can't suck it in, and I can't reach it.* I opened my mouth and my end fell to the ground. I watched in dismay as it turned dark then disappeared into the dirt.

"Of course." I looked up, closed my eyes and concentrated. I shot a stream of what I thought was spider webbing straight to the ceiling. Somehow, I could tell when it stuck. Before I opened my mouth, I managed to grab hold of it. I held on, willing strength into my arms. I waited a few moments until I felt I was ready, then started pulling myself up. When I was free of the hook that held my hands, I let go. It hurt like hell when I hit the ground, even though it wasn't very far.

I lay groaning, not worried about being found out. They said they'd be back in the morning.

After a while, I started looking for a way to get the rope off my hands. A few feet away, there was a rack of tools hanging on the wall. I crawled toward it and managed to get the shovel to the floor. I held it between my legs as I used the edge to cut my ropes. It took a long time, but I got it done.

Too weak to stand, I crawled to the door. There was a water trough a few feet away. *Please let there be water in it.* There was. I pulled myself up and started scooping handfuls of water into my mouth.

After a few moments, I felt rejuvenated. I sat with my back against the trough thinking of my good luck, so far. "Wait a minute. There's no moon and no light in the barn. How could I see everything so clearly?" There was no one to answer.

***

Now that I was free and my strength had returned, I had to start thinking of how to get back to my motel. It would be a problem since I had no idea where I was.

If and when I escaped, these guys, how could I be sure they wouldn't come after me again? I didn't need to be looking over my shoulder for the rest of my life. I had to somehow convince them to let me be. *Fat chance of that happening.*

I got up and walked around the property. It was pretty isolated. There was only a house and the barn. I couldn't see any other buildings in any direction. The road was dirt and the only way to the property. *They must all be in the house.*

***

In addition to the van, there was a car. Of course, they had taken the keys. I walked to the front door of the house and found it unlocked. I was supposed to be hanging in the horse barn. I wasn't. The house was quiet and dark. It was a two-story house. I guessed all the bedrooms were on the second floor. I wandered through every room downstairs. It was as clean as if the maid had just finished cleaning.

I stood at the bottom of the stairs thinking. Finally, I shrugged. Might as well get it over with. I walked up the stairs, trying to be as quiet as possible. I didn't want a creaky step announcing me. The carpet helped me keep quiet.

At the top of the steps, I decided to go left since there were fewer rooms in that direction. There were two single beds with the occupants who were snoring quietly. I entered and searched for a set of car keys. No luck.

I stood with my back to the door and shut my eyes. I pictured strands of webbing crisscrossing the room. When the picture in my mind was completed, I opened my eyes. What I had imagined came to be. These two would have to go out the window to get out of the room without encountering the webbing.

I did the same to the next two rooms. They both had two beds with sleepers in them. No visible car keys here either.

With only two rooms left, I figured Glen and Seth occupied them. Since they were the leaders, they probably didn't have to share.

***

Wait a minute, I thought. Five rooms, ten guys. I found six guys so far. Glen and Seth must be sleeping with the other two. How cozy. I found out later I was wrong. When I entered the next to last room, there was only one bed and only one person in it. I figured it was Glen because the van keys were on the dresser.

Outside his room I thought, one room left, three men not accounted for.

Seth's room also had only one bed with one occupant. I took the car keys and exited. All the rooms were laced with spider webbing. There were still two men missing.

***

I crept quietly down the stairs, my ears on alert. At the bottom, I stood still, listening. No voices, no footsteps, no sounds.

I was about to open the front door when I heard voices.

"Heard or seen anything?" one voice said.

"Nah. It's dead out here," the other answered.

"Should we check on him?"

A laugh. "What for? The way he was tied and the condition we left him in, I don't think he'll be going anywhere."

"This last half hour is going to last forever."

"Don't look at your watch. Wait for the alarm to go off. Think about something else in the meantime."

I could hear them walk away from each other. I waited a moment, then went out. I hoped neither would hear my footsteps until it was too late.

As I approached one, he stopped and started to turn. "What's up? It's not time . . ."

I hit him in the face. He crumpled and I watched him fall. My mouth started to water as I stood over him. It was almost like a reflex. I knelt and straddled him. Taking his head in my hands, I forced his mouth open.

When I was finished, I stood and stretched. I felt wonderful.

I could hear the footsteps of the other guy approaching.

I moved to the shadows of the house and waited.

He came around the corner and yelled when he saw his buddy lying on the round. "Hey! What happened? You all right?"

He bent down and shook the shoulder of the man lying on the ground. When there was no response, he felt for a pulse.

"How the hell can you be dead? I just talked to you less than a minute ago."

After a few seconds, he stood, drew his knife and started looking around. I stepped out of the shadows. "Looking for me?"

"How the fuck did you get out?" Pointing to his buddy, he asked, "Did you do this?"

I nodded. "Yes, I did. You guys had decided I should die. I thought it should be the other way around."

He brandished his knife. "Maybe we'll go back to the original plan and you die now." He lunged at me with the knife.

I sidestepped and grabbed his wrist with one hand and his neck with the other. I squeezed until he dropped the knife. I let go of his wrist and slammed my fist into his throat.

With a soft gurgle, he crumpled.

Not wanting to play favorites, I treated him the same way I did his buddy.

When I was finished, I looked up at the house. "Come and get me, if you can."

It was very quiet, too quiet. I stood stock-still and listened. Nothing. No birds, no bugs, no insects, nothing. It was if the world had died and I was still in it.

Then on the horizon, the sun started painting the sky in bright red/orange to announce the coming of a new day. As if on cue, birds started welcoming the day with song, insects and bugs picked up the melodies.

I smiled and reentered the house.

CHAPTER TEN

I stood in the hall, listening. No one was stirring as yet. *Time to get them up.*

I went to the kitchen and found a large metal spoon and a large pot. Reclaiming my position in the middle of the hall, I started banging on the bottom of the pot with the spoon.

"Wakey, wakey, wakey! Time to get up and get moving. Dawn is almost here and you're wasting daylight. Wakey, wakey, wakey."

I stood still and listened. The commotion and screams of pain were like music to me. I had spread webbing in every room from floor to ceiling, wall to wall, floor to wall and wall to ceiling between the beds and the door. The only way to get out of the room was through the window. That was if they hadn't already run into the webbing. Some had. I could hear cries of, "What the hell . . .?"

"Son of a bitch. What is this stuff?"

"Hey, somebody help me. I'm stuck."

I turned and went outside to the back of the house. Two of the guys lay on the ground. One had landed on his head and lay unconscious. I could see bare skull in places.

The other lay groaning. "Help me. Help me." He had broken both knees.

Then I heard a muffled cry. Looking up I saw another guy hanging sideways along the side of the building. It looked like he tried to get out and dragged the webbing with him. While it was holding him up, it was also enveloping him.

I went back into the house and got a glass of water. Listening and watching the mayhem made me thirsty. I waited until I couldn't hear any more sounds. I picked up the phone and dialed 9-1-1.

"9-1-1, what is your emergency?"

"I'm out here in the middle of nowhere. Some guys brought me to this house last night for an initiation party. Now they're all dead. Can you find me from this number?"

"Yes, sir, we can. Stay on the line. Help is being sent as we speak. What is your name?"

"Glen Chase. I was supposed to be joining the soccer team. How long will it take to get someone out here? I don't like being alone with a bunch of dead guys."

"Keep talking to me, Glen. That will help you remain calm. How do you know they are all dead?"

"I know because I killed them. They wanted to kill me, so I killed them first." I started laughing and hung up.

Then I thought. "Shit. Fingerprints." I went to the kitchen and moistened a dishtowel. I hoped I'd have enough time to wipe everything down.

I started with the doorknobs of the bedrooms, inside and out. Back downstairs, I wiped everything I thought I'd touched. The spoon and pot were wiped and put back from where I had gotten them.

Satisfied that I didn't forget anything, I hung the towel on a rack in the kitchen.

I took the car keys, wiped the doorknob, inside and out with my shirt, got in the car and started it. I drove down to the road. *Which way, left or right?*

After a few seconds, I found the car had a GPS system. I punched in the bus station. As I drove, I passed eight police cars, three ambulances and a Fire Department Fire and Rescue vehicle going the other way.

I followed the GPS prompts and arrived at the station twenty minutes later. I parked the car and left the keys in the ignition. After wiping everything down, I got out and walked the few blocks to the motel.

Because of the early hour, the streets were almost empty. The people I passed were too busy with their own agenda to notice me, I hoped.

I decided to stay in town a few more days. I had paid for the room for two weeks. I didn't expect things to go so fast. I had to be careful not to be recognized again.

It took two days for my escapade to get on the news. Coach Warren's murder was broadcast the day after he died. According to the newscaster, the FBI, because of the nature of his demise was, handling his death.

***

I had been out for a walk after dinner and just entered the lobby when the news came on.

BREAKING NEWS! "Good evening viewers. The police are searching for a man named Glen Chase in reference to a 9-1-1 call he made concerning the deaths of several people in a rural home. According to police, he told the operator he killed them all. Ten bodies were found in and around the property. Most died from asphyxiation. The main concern the police said they had was how one person alone could take the lives of ten men. The local police, the state police and the FBI will be working together to solve this crime."

I didn't stay to listen to any more. I knew how I did it. I just wanted to hear how close the police were to figuring out who I was.

In my room I celebrated by having a cup of lemon tea. *Where in the world did I get this habit from?* Lying in bed, I had a strange thought. *I'm becoming a regular Spider Man.* "That's not funny," I shouted to the empty room.

The next morning, I informed the desk clerk that I would be checking out early.

After a few seconds, he asked, "Is something wrong with the room or service, sir?"

"Absolutely not. Everything is excellent. It's just that I did what I came here to do. It's time for me to get back to work."

"I see. When are you planning to leave?"

"It will depend on my being able to rearrange my transportation. I should be able to let you know by tomorrow morning."

"That will be fine, sir." He took a deep breath and sighed. "I'll be awaiting your decision."

***

At the bus station, I found I didn't have to make any special arrangements for my trip back to Franklin. I just had to check in early to make sure I had a seat.

"There shouldn't be any problem, sir. That trip is never more than half full." He smiled broadly. "Guess not many people want to go to Franklin."

"Works in my favor," I said. I returned to the motel to update the clerk.

***

The bus trip to Franklin was uneventful. At least nothing happened while I was asleep.

I was happy to find my trusty VW Beetle, just as I had left her. I was happier to find no one had tried to steal her.

Back in my seedy motel, the clerk was surprised to see me.

"I didn't expect you back so soon." He started moving things around on the desk. There was no purpose to his movements. It seemed he didn't know what to do with his hands.

Tilting my head to one side, I asked, "What happened? Did you rent my room?"

"No. No." He held up his hands in defense. "It's still yours for another ten days."

"Good. Let me have my key. I need to take a nap."

He handed me the key and I left, wondering why he was so nervous.

***

The next morning, I made two phone calls. One to my Dad and the other to Coach Spears. I let them know I'd heard about Coach Warren's fatality and I felt I was no longer in danger. I told them both I could hardly wait to get back in the game.

Coach Spears said, "The other goalies won't be happy with your quick return. By the way, we won the last game."

"If you want, I can postpone my return for a little longer. It's up to you. I know the other goalies would like to show their worth and I don't have any problem with that. It's just that I love the game and my role in helping the team."

He was silent on his end of the line. "Why not as a sub for the next game?" Tim would like to show his skills. If he has problems, you could always rescue him."

"I can go along with that. At least I'll be with the team."

"Great! I'll let Tim know. See you Saturday."

***

The game Saturday was a good one. We won 3-2. I had to hand it to Tim. He was as good as he said he was. The other team was happy that they were able to score against us. That was twice in two games we had given up goals. I think the whole league rejoiced.

***

A week after our last game, Coach Spears approached me in the locker room.

"Jake. It appears you are famous. You're scheduled for an interview on the Marvelous Marvin Melchior show on Thursday at 10 in the morning. Wear a suit and tie and shine your shoes. Don't forget to shave and comb your hair. You'll be on TV in front of millions of viewers. You want them to see you in your best light."

I stood open mouthed for a few moments. "I'm to be interviewed on live TV in front of millions of people?"

"That's right. Don't worry. You'll be able to handle it."

"I'm shaking in my boots already. What if I get tongue-tied? What if I get so scared I can't talk?"

"What if you stop worrying and see what happens when you get there."

I sighed. "I guess you're right. No sense trying to dispel ghosts if you don't open the closet."

CHAPTER ELEVEN

I stood outside the news building. It was a ten-story structure of gray concrete and darkened glass windows. I hesitated, thinking, *here I am, eighteen-year-old Jake Stettler, about to be interviewed on National Television*. I took a deep breath, squared my shoulders and walked through the two sets of glass doors. As I approached the half-moon shaped counter, the woman behind it stood up. She was blonde with oval-rimmed glasses. Her bright pink lipstick covered a mouth, that when opened revealed straight, white teeth. Although she was very pretty, she looked very angry.

"Are you Jake Stettler?"

Taken aback, I stopped. "Uh. Yes I am."

"You're late," she announced.

"But . . .but my appointment was for ten a.m." I looked at my watch. "It's only a quarter to."

"Didn't they tell you that you have to be here at least thirty minutes before for makeup and briefing?"

"No. I was only told my interview was for ten."

She pointed past my shoulder. "Right elevator, sixth floor, turn right and go to the end of the hall. They're waiting."

I turned and headed for the elevator. As I waited, I read the directory on the wall display; the TV station was on the sixth and the radio station on the tenth. I guess it was up there to minimize interference. Offices filled the rest of the building.

I got off the elevator, turned right and walked to the end of the hall. There were two doors. Only one opened out. I pushed the other open and a young man with a clipboard hopped off a stool and asked "Jake Stettler?"

"Yes."

"I'm Craig." He took me by the arm and led me to a make-up table. I was pushed down on a stool and one woman arranged my hair while another started to apply makeup to my face.

I grabbed her arm and pushed it away.

She sighed and shook her head. "It's for the camera. We want to show you in your best light."

I released her hand and she continued.

When they were done, I was fitted with a chest microphone. It was tested for sound.

When everything checked out, Craig took me by the arm again and led me to a bank of cameras being organized by a woman, her name was Denise. She wore jeans and a long-sleeved blue shirt with the sleeves rolled up. White tennis shoes with no socks covered her feet. Her hair was dark blonde and tied in a ponytail. She was the epitome of the working woman. There was a polka dotted handkerchief hanging out of a back pocket. She would pull it out, wipe her brow then stuff it back in again. It was warm between the cameras.

Craig touched her shoulder.

She kept issuing instructions while she turned towards me. She raised one eyebrow.

"Jake Stettler," Craig announced.

"Denise." She said and turned and called out, "Marvin."

A short, pudgy man stood a few feet away. He looked up from a sheath of papers. He looked slim in a pinstriped gray suit over a white shirt and paisley tie. When he saw us he walked over. With an outstretched hand he asked, "Jake Stettler?"

"Yes, sir."

He took me by the arm and led me out of range of the cameras. When we were far enough away, he handed me several sheets of paper. "You'll be my only guest today. Your story is interesting enough to take up my whole hour. I normally have four guests that get fifteen minutes each, commercials included."

I scanned the sheets while he waited.

"Any questions? Anything too private? Anything you don't want to discuss?" he asked.

"No. From what I can see you want my life story from birth until now."

He smiled. "That's about the size of it."

"Twenty seconds," Denise called.

Marvin took me by the arm again and led me back to the cameras. There were four of them in a semi-circle.

Just before he went past the cameras, Denise took my arm. "Wait."

I wondered if she could talk in sentences longer than one or two words.

Out of the corner of my eye I saw a man raise his hand. He then counted down by lowering his fingers.

At the ten-second mark, music from out of speakers I couldn't see started playing Marvin's theme music.

Five seconds later a voice announced, "Ladies and gentlemen, please welcome the host of the Mid-Morning Meet-Up, Marvin Melchior."

Loud cheering and whistling started, making me jump. I hadn't realized there were people seated in the studio on the ground level and in a balcony.

During the cheering, Marvin entered the stage and waving, moved to behind his desk. He stood and waved to the crowd who cheered and whistled even louder.

He finally motioned with his hands, indicating to the audience to seat themselves. When they had settled down, he seated himself behind the desk and appeared to organize his papers.

Marvin looked straight ahead then started his spiel.

"Good morning ladies and gentlemen. This is Marvelous Marvin with your Mid-Morning Meet-Up." He waited for the applause of the audience to die down. "Because of his unparalleled achievements, I'll only have time for one guest today.

"Sports fans, the young man I'm going to interview just turned eighteen a few months ago. In spite of his young age, he has accomplished more in his field than any other player, bar none. He has been voted Goalie of the Year, Player of the Year and Most Valuable Player by panels of his peers, for the last season.

"He started off this season continuing his extraordinary feats of goal-tending. Without further ado, for all my fans of Major League soccer, let me introduce my guest for today."

He stood. "Ladies and gentlemen, please give a hearty welcome to Mr. Jake Stettler, goalie extraordinaire."

The audience stood and clapped and whistled.

Denise touched my shoulder.

I approached Marvin. Before I shook his hand, I wiped my sweaty palm on my pants leg.

He smiled, took my hand in both of his, then nodded to the chair at the side of the desk.

As I walked to it, I prayed my legs wouldn't collapse before I sat down. I made it and sighed with relief.

Marvin waited until the audience quieted.

I could feel the sweat running down my sides from my armpits, even though the studio was air-conditioned.

"Jake."

I turned my head toward Marvin.

"I imagine you're pretty nervous. Is this your first time on TV?"

I cleared my throat and swallowed hard. It didn't help. "Yes, sir, it is." I sounded like a frog.

He smiled. "Not to worry, you're safe with me."

I blinked several times. *What was he implying?* Then I caught on. He wouldn't let the audience harm me. I smiled back.

"Jake, you've accomplished something no other player has. As a goalie for the Franklin Thunder, you only allowed the ball to get past you once in 34 games. That's more than amazing. That's astounding. Other goalies count their success by minutes played. You count your success by games played. How in the world do you do it?"

I blushed. "I concentrate totally on the ball. I know where it is at all times and can determine where it's going, no matter who kicks or heads it toward the net."

Marvin shook his head. "I've watched all of your games. What I can't understand is how you can move so fast. Care to enlighten me?"

I shrugged. "I guess it's a natural ability."

He turned toward the audience. "For those of you who haven't seen this guy in action, we have a few video clips of him at work." He nodded towards the cameras.

The next three minutes were spent watching me perform as goalie on several large screens around the studio.

Oohs and aahs rose from the audience. When the clips were over, they broke out in thunderous applause accompanied by whistles and shouts.

In spite of myself, I blushed.

Marvin folded his hands together on the desk. "Is this natural ability inherited or did some magic fairy sprinkle you with magic dust?"

Giggles from the audience.

I shrugged. "I just grew up with it. As I got older, I got faster. I'm sure I don't know how or why."

He nodded. "Now, let's get to the other part of your story."

I took a deep breath, then slowly exhaled.

"I'll make it easy. Where did you grow up and how did you get interested in soccer?"

I cleared my throat again. This time it worked. "I grew up in Milton, Nevada. When I was in junior high school, my dad got tickets to watch the Las Vegas Lights soccer team play the Colorado Rapids. It was really exciting; especially since it was so different from every other sport I had ever watched. I kept waiting for the clock to stop, for any reason. It didn't. Also, I learned that once a player was substituted, that player was out for the rest of the game. It took me a while to wrap my head around that. I found it really exciting to watch twenty-two men kick a ball back-and-forth across a field, trying to get it in the opposing team's goal using only their feet and head. The only person allowed to use his hands to control the ball is the goalie. It really was thrilling to watch. When we were on our way home, I told my dad this is the game I wanted to play."

"What was his reaction?" He leaned forward on his desk with both forearms.

I shrugged. "He reminded me that I'd have to wait until high school since my junior high didn't have a soccer program."

He straightened up and asked, "What did you do in the meantime?"

"I ran track and played volleyball. I never really got into football or baseball. You could get hurt in football and baseball was too boring." I blushed. "I hope I haven't offended anybody."

"You say you ran track and played volleyball?"

"That's right."

He leaned back in his chair and looked hard at me. "What distances did you run?" He folded his arm across his chest.

I cleared my throat. "I ran the 100- and 200-meter sprints and the 3000-, 5000- and 10000- meter runs."

He sat still, looking at me as though I had grown a third eye in the middle of my head. He uncrossed his arms and leaned forward. "You ran sprints AND long distances?"

I nodded. "Yes, sir."

Marvin shook his head. "One or the other I could believe. You have to be extraordinary to be able to participate in both." He stared at me for a few seconds. "How did you do?"

I cleared my throat. "I hold the record in all five."

He sat back and shook his head, then leaned forward so quickly, it made me jump.

"That's impossible. Sprinters can't run long enough to complete a long run and long-distance runners can't move fast enough to win a sprint."

I looked at him, blinked and shrugged my shoulders.

"What is your time for the 100?"

"Officially or unofficially?"

"Let's start with unofficially."

"That would be 9.4, Sir."

He blinked several times. "9.4. You said 9.4. Did I hear you right?"

I nodded. "Yes, sir, you did."

He sat back again, shaking his head.

It was deathly quiet in the studio.

"That's impossible. The world record is 9.8 but, you say you did it in 9.4."

"That's right, sir."

He rubbed his face with both hands. "You do realize that makes you an anomaly, don't you?"

"I guess so, whatever that is."

Except for a few giggles, the audience still hadn't made a sound.

He leaned one arm on his desk. "How often did you get tested for drugs?"

"While I was in school, every week. Now it's only every two weeks."

"I'm not surprised." He paused. "I don't even dare ask what your times were in the other events."

I waited.

"What do you do for fun?" Marvin asked.

"I play video games, weight lift, run and go mountain bike riding in the hills around Milton."

"Do you ever go out with the team drinking?"

I sighed. "No, sir, I don't. Oh, I go out with them, but I don't drink alcohol. When I was seven, I took a sip of my Dad's beer and went into convulsions. My Dad said my body turned red and was too hot to touch. When I was fourteen, I drank a mouthful of wine. The same thing happened. I was on my back on the floor trembling and moaning. One of the guys grabbed my arms and wound up with third degree burns." I hung my head. "He still has problems with his hands."

"And you say that was because you had drunk some wine?"

I nodded. "That's right, Sir. It seems my body doesn't like alcohol." I put my hands between my legs and hung my head.

It was a long time before Marvin spoke to me again.

Somehow, during our conversation, the studio managed to get their commercials in.

Marvin and I waited patiently during the interruptions.

***

"I understand you've gotten numerous offers from clubs across the pond. The list is most impressive." He picked up a piece of paper. "You have offers from, Bayern Munich in Germany, Manchester City in England, Real Madrid in Spain and countless others. Why are you staying here?"

I sighed. "I promised my team I would take them to first place and win the End-of-Season Tournament. I haven't done that yet. I like where I am. It would be nice to travel and see other countries but, this is my home, I'm staying here."

"You say you live in Milton, Nevada?"

"Yes, sir. I live there with my Dad who is the coolest person in the world, and our housekeeper, Mrs. Burns."

"What about your Mom?" He tilted his head to one side.

"She died when I was two from breast cancer."

"I'm sorry to hear that." He took a deep breath. "From your comment, it seems you and your Dad have a great relationship."

I nodded and smiled. "That would be putting it mildly." I could feel my chest puffing up.

"What does he do?"

"He works for the DA's office in Las Vegas."

He paused, nodding and listening.

"Okay, Jake. That's all the time we have for today. There are a lot of questions I would still like to ask you. I'll have to get you back on the show another time." He stood.

Taking his cue, I stood too.

He reached out for my hand.

I took it and we shook, but he didn't let go.

He came around the desk and gave me a hug. When he let go, he turned to the audience. "Ladies and gentlemen, goalie extraordinaire, Jake Stettler."

There was thunderous applause and whistling.

I felt embarrassed but smiled anyway.

***

When I left the studio, I was accosted by a phalanx of reporters. Several security guards had to help me get to my car. I relaxed in the relative quiet of the vehicle.

On the drive home, I thought about the interview and wondered how many of my teammates had watched it. *Oh, well. I'll find out tomorrow at practice.*

My dad was waiting for me at home when I got there. "Dad. How come you're home? Is everything okay?" I rushed forward to hug him.

"Everything's fine. Because my famous son was on live, National TV, I got the rest of the day off. The day is ours. What would you like to do?"

I smiled. "I'd like to get out of this suit."

He laughed. "Go change, I'll wait."

Afterwards, I asked, "Can we go to a movie? I've had my fill of people for today."

"No problem," he said. "A movie it is."

We left the house with our arms around each other. It's a good thing we left when we did because we passed several TV vans heading for our house.

"I guess we'll have to see more than one movie."

"Fine with me," I said. I was with my dad, which was enough for me.

CHAPTER TWELVE

Things went well for the next few games. It seemed everyone in the league had seen my interview. There were a lot of questions asked and comments made. It let me know how interesting I was to the soccer world.

***

We were scheduled to play the Bakersfield Bombers the coming Saturday, on their turf.

Everything was going well. We scored twice. I kept them scoreless. Because of this, the Bombers stated getting rough. Coach Spears sent in a sub with the message to give as good as we got. He called them Bakersfield Bullies.

I felt sorry for the ref. He had to let a lot of the fouls go or there would only have three or four players on the field on each side.

***

During half time, the police came and talked to Coach Spears. After a few moments, he left with them. He wasn't back by the time the game resumed. We knew what to do. We played our game.

We were up 4-0 when coach Spears returned. He didn't look very happy.

After the game, Coach Burrows came over and very cordially, congratulated us on our win.

Of course this made Coach Spears very suspicious.

We gathered around our coach and peppered him with questions about the police visit.

"In the locker room," was all said, then turned and walked into the building.

When we were all assembled, he called for quiet. "Our bus caught fire. Although the fire department was on the scene quickly, they were not able to save it. We have to find other means of getting back to Franklin. At least we shouldn't have problems with Greyhound or Trailways. It's a good thing our hotel is not far from here."

One of the guys said, "Here we go again."

There was a lot of muttering.

"Will we have to fight our way to the hotel?" asked Tim, one of the other goalies.

Coach took a deep breath and shook his head. "I hope not. Lord, I hope not."

***

We had no problem getting to the hotel. The manager even asked if we needed help getting transportation back to Franklin. Coach told him we would only need a lift to the bus station in the morning.

"I'll arrange it," the manager said.

Coach thanked him, suspicious about his friendliness.

***

True to his word, the manager had the hotel shuttles take us to the bus station. When coach tried to tip the drivers, they refused to take it.

At the bus station, we were able to book passage to Franklin with no problem. It would be a three-hour wait for the next bus.

We settled down in the waiting area. Some read books they had brought with them. Some played games on their phones or tablets. A

93

few decided to explore the area around the station. That was a mistake.

They were waiting for us outside as if not wanting to cause a commotion in the terminal.

Four of our guys came back in with torn clothing. Bruises were starting to show on their faces. Tim was the worst affected. He walked in limping. There were bloodstains on his pant leg and dried blood on both his arms.

"What the hell happened to you guys?" Coach yelled.

One of the victims tried to speak, but his jaw was too swollen.

Wincing with pain, Tim told him. "We were walking along looking in store windows when a bunch of guys jumped us and beat us with fists and clubs. People crossed to the other side of the street. It was as if they didn't want to interrupt." He shook his head and hobbled to a nearby bench.

Al, a forward, said, "A police car drove by. It didn't even slow down."

Coach sighed. "I guess I'll have to wait 'til we get home to file a complaint. Pretty sure nothing will be done here. Probably nothing will be done from our end either."

About ten minutes later, they announced boarding for our bus was beginning.

***

I knew the attack was because of me. The rest of the team knew it too but, wouldn't say so. I planned to take care of the Bakersfield "Bullies" myself. Since they wouldn't all be in one place like Portland, I'd have to visit them individually.

***

When I got back to Franklin, it was easy enough to find a team roster that had pictures of all the players. I started looking up addresses. Somehow, things were going too easy. It took two hours, but I then had the names and addresses of the entire team, including the coach. Now I knew why he was so cordial to Coach Spears at the end of the game.

I wanted them to worry, to constantly look over their shoulders whenever they were in public.

There were twenty-three team members and the coach. I would take the coach out first.

Now that I had all the info I required, I needed to decide how and when I was going to carry out my plan.

I decided to sleep on it and see where my mind would go the next day.

***

In the morning, I got up, dressed and went to practice. The guys who had been hurt got to sit on the bench.

After practice, I asked Coach if I could take Mondays off. I didn't need to practice, but Tim and Jason did.

"Is there something going on that you don't want to tell me about?" he asked.

"No. I want to spend some time riding my bicycle. I found some mountain trails I'd like to try out."

He nodded. "Okay. We don't practice on Sunday anyway, so you can have Monday's off. You'll deserve an extra day off after Saturday's game."

"Thanks, Coach," I said and headed home.

***

I had another problem. All our games were not at home, which meant I wouldn't always be able to get to Bakersfield on a Sunday or Monday. *Oh, well. I'll have to deal with that when the time comes.*

***

It was two weeks before I could implement my plan. I drove to Bakersfield and went to Coach Burrows house. His house was in an upscale neighborhood. This made it easy. I wouldn't have to worry about the next-door neighbors. The electrical panel was on the side of the house. I opened it and pulled the master switch. The house went dark. It took a few minutes before he came out to check. When he did, I stepped out of the shadows and greeted him. "Hi, Coach. Remember me?"

He almost jumped back in surprise. "The super goalie. Did you pull my switch?"

"Of course. I wanted you out of the house so I could send you to Hell." I grabbed him by the throat and squeezed until he was half-conscious. His eyes bulged, his mouth opened and closed as if he were trying to speak. His hands tried to grab mine. I lowered him to the ground and put my mouth over his. It didn't take long. I felt great after I was finished.

I decide to try to take out as many as I could in one night. I headed to my next victim's house. He lived on a quiet street with houses close together and one-car garages. I shook my head and blinked as I drove by. *One-car garages? Wonder when these were built.* I parked three blocks away. I waited until the traffic died down, then I walked back to the house and rang the bell.

He was surprised when he opened the door. "I'll be damned. The super goalie. What the . . .?"

I hit him in the throat to shut him up. I grabbed him and lowered him to the floor. I listened for sounds of others in the house. I heard none. I looked down at him. He was holding his throat and gasping.

"You live alone?" I asked.

He rocked his head from side to side.

I nodded. "I'd better make this quick then." I squatted, took his head in my hands. His mouth was already open. I had to break his jaw because he bit me.

I looked at my watch when I finished. *Six minutes, not good. I have to be faster.* I got up and opened the front door. Not seeing anyone on the street, I left. I waved before I closed the door. Nosey neighbors would think I was saying goodbye.

There was a bounce in my step as I headed for my car and drove to my next victim's house.

***

When I drove by, I saw lights on in the living room. I checked my watch, almost midnight. Again I parked three streets away. I'd bought several burner phones for ten dollars each in a Wal-Mart. *Why not?* I walked back to the house and stood in the shadow of the garage.

I called my next victim.

"Hello?"

"Marty needs help! Get to his house ASAP!" I hung up and waited.

When he drives out, the car doors will be locked. I'll have to wait until he returns. It shouldn't be long when he realizes there's no Marty on his team.

A few moments later, the garage door opened. I waited until he turned to drive away. The door was on its way down. I had to rush to get in. *Don't take too long out there. I don't want to spend the night here.*

While the light was still on, I located a ladder. I would use it to disable the garage light.

While waiting, I noticed the garage had a side door. It was locked from the inside. *Cool. I can kill him in the garage and not have to raise the door to get out.*

***

I waited until the light had been out for a few moments, then used the ladder to remove the cover and unscrew the bulb enough so it wouldn't come on.

With that done, I sat on a toolbox to wait. It wasn't long, but it seemed like hours. I replayed in my mind how I'd taken out Coach Burrows. It was really satisfying, both the action and the remembering of it.

I was almost caught unawares when a car drove up and the door started to rise. I ran to a corner by the door on the passenger side of the car where I was completely hidden from his view as he exited the vehicle.

As he got out, I heard him mutter about the "damn light" being out again.

I started walking forward and said, "Maybe it's my fault."

"Who the hell are you and what are you doing in my garage? How did you get in anyway?"

"I am your worst nightmare and I've come to send you to Hell, so you can join your coach."

He hesitated and that was all I needed. I had him by the throat before he could turn and run into the house.

"Hard to yell when your throat is being crushed, isn't it?"

He gurgled.

Then I thought, *Why not?* I covered his mouth with mine and let my tongue do its work. I don't think I'll ever get used to the ecstasy of taking and tasting a person's brain.

When it was over, I released his head and let him fall to the ground. I felt wonderful. I walked over and unlocked the side door and was on my way to my car. *That's three.*

Back at my car, I looked at my watch. *I think I have time for one more visit.* I looked over my list. The nearest house was only five minutes away. I started the car and drove to it.

The neighborhood wasn't as nice as the last one, but it was presentable. The streets were clean and there were no cars or other items rusting on any front yard. The cars on the street all appeared to be serviceable. I walked up to the front door and rang the bell.

The guy who opened it recognized me. "What the hell do you want?" he demanded. He still had his hand on the doorknob.

"I'm just paying a friendly visit. May I come in?" I stepped forward and pushed past him.

Two other guys appeared from a room on the right.

Probably a living room.

They were each holding a can of beer.

Both registered shock when they saw me. Then one smiled. "'Super Goalie.' What brings you to our neck of the woods?"

I headed for the room they had come out of. Like I figured, it was a living room. There were two easy chairs upholstered in a "Post-Depression" floral pattern. The couch was a more modern dung-colored brown. I sat on one of the chairs.

"Gentlemen, please sit."

They had followed me into the room and, without comments, sat on the couch.

One of them asked. "What's this all about?"

"Why are you here?" another one asked.

The third one asked. "How did you get this address?"

I cleared my throat. "What this is all about is the beating some of my teammates got when we were in your town. I'm here to avenge my guys for their injuries. Getting your address was easy once I had your names. Welcome to the wonderful world of the internet."

"Do you think the one of you can take on the three of us and win?"

"No, I don't think so."

They all smiled.

"I know so."

Their smiles faded.

Already visualizing them dying together, I smiled. "A team that plays together . . . " I said as I stood up. With my arms by my side, I imagined the three of them being wrapped in spider webbing. When I opened my eyes, they were screaming and struggling while the webbing expanded and covered more and more of their upper torsos.

I whispered, "Hey, you guys have to stop making so much noise. Someone will think you're being killed."

They didn't listen. They kept screaming and struggling until the webbing covered their heads. This kind of quieted them down. They got quieter and quieter until they stopped struggling and lay still.

I sat down and waited a few moments. I wasn't sure if the neighbors had heard the commotion.

After about five minutes, I decided all was well. I didn't know how long the webbing would hold them. Didn't really matter. I got up and called 9-1-1. I gave the operator the address and informed him that there were three bodies on the premises. When he asked for my name and how I knew, I hung up. I couldn't help smiling on my way home. Tonight, I would sleep well.

CHAPTER THIRTEEN

Tuesday morning, as we were getting ready for practice, Coach Spears called for quiet.

He put one foot on a bench and leaned forward with one arm on his leg. "I suppose you all heard about what happened in Bakersfield over the weekend?"

All but four of us nodded. I was one.

"For you uninformed," Coach Spears said. "Five of the Bakersfield Bombers, along with their coach, were killed Sunday night or early Monday morning. The police don't have any suspects yet. According to the newscaster, because of the nature of the killings, the FBI has been called in to take over the case. The FBI Director, Anton Grabowski, will be leading the investigation."

"Wasn't he involved in the Black Widow cases?" Tim asked.

"I think he was. I'm not sure. I have other things to do besides follow murder cases." He straightened up and lowered his foot. "At eleven a.m. today, all teams in the league will observe a moment of silence for the victims." He waited to see if anyone had anything to say. "Okay, let's get moving."

We filed quietly out of the locker room.

***

At eleven o'clock, Coach blew his whistle and we all stood silent for a minute.

I was practicing with three others when Coach came over.

"I need a minute with Jake."

The others moved away out of earshot.

"What's up, Coach?" I asked.

"Do you know, or have any idea, about the deaths of those six guys?"

I put my hand to my chest. "Me? How would I know anything?"

He stood with his arms crossed, staring at me as though he could see into my soul. Finally, he said, "Are you sure?"

I shook my head. "Coach, I'm usually in bed by ten. What time were those guys killed?"

"Between ten p.m. and two a.m."

"There's no way I could make it to Bakersfield during that time and still get home in time to get some sleep. Why do you suspect I had anything to do with their deaths?" I was becoming irate with the veiled accusations.

He was quiet for a moment. "Call it a gut feeling. I don't have anything to base my suspicions on, but my gut says you were involved."

I shook my head. Quietly, I said, "I didn't even know they had been killed until you mentioned it before practice."

He nodded. "I hope you weren't involved." He turned and walked away.

When the other guys came back to continue practice, they asked what Coach had to say.

"He wanted to know if I had any idea who might have killed those guys."

"How would you know?" Larry asked.

I shrugged. "Maybe he thought I wanted to take revenge for the beatings our guys took."

"Wouldn't killing six guys be a little extreme?" Tim asked.

I snorted. "My thoughts exactly." I shook my head. "I could see beating up on a few of them but, killing. Way, way too much."

With that discussion over, we continued practice.

***

It was almost three months later before I could get back to Bakersfield. I still had my list. I knew they would have replaced the deceased players. I had no quarrel with the newbies.

My GPS took me toward my next victim's house. It was daytime which made it easy to see how the neighborhood was set up.

As I got close to the house, I started having stomach pains. I ignored them at first, but the closer I got to my victim's place, the worse they got.

I was almost doubling up with pain as I drove down the street. I almost hit a parked car and suddenly, several men in suits appeared. They watched me as I drove by. I could only surmise they were plainclothes policemen.

When I reached the corner, I turned and drove two blocks away from my quarry's street. The farther I drove, the less pain there was. When I was three blocks away, I stopped next to the curb. The pain was gone. It was as if it had never happened.

I opened the window and shut off the engine. I was relaxing for a few minutes thinking about my next victim, when my stomach started up again. It wasn't as bad as before but was very uncomfortable.

I was still wondering what the deal was when a uniformed policeman walked by. He paid no attention to my car or me.

Then I noticed the farther away he got, the less pain I felt. I shook my head. I had been in the presence of police before and hadn't had this kind of reaction. *What the hell is going on?* I asked myself.

"Time to experiment." I started the car and made a U-turn. Before I turned into the block, I started thinking of canvassing the neighborhood for a house to buy.

I made it through the entire street with no hint of pain.

***

Driving around, I stopped at a Mexican restaurant. I spent nearly two hours there taking my time and enjoying my meal. When I finished and left, I stopped at a gas station and filled up. I still needed the layout of my victim's street and how the houses were situated. I drove through the neighborhood again, thinking of how and when to approach the house. The pain started again. I immediately put revenge out of my mind and the pain went away. I noticed several men watching me as I drove by.

Once out of the street, I decided to try another victim's house. It didn't matter who went first or last. I intended to take them all out.

***

As I approached my next victim's house, the stomach pain started again. I managed to get through the street without passing out. I turned the corner and parked a half block away. When the pain had subsided, I got out and walked back to the street. I kept the thought of buying a house foremost in my mind.

As I walked, I noticed a homeless man rummaging through garbage cans. He watched me as I went by. I smiled and nodded. He just watched me.

Further on, there were four men playing cards on a folding table in a driveway. I could feel their eyes following me as I passed him.

That was it then. Policemen, or private security guards were guarding my victims. The pain warned me when I was in danger from the police. I smiled. Their presence in watching over the team members was enough to keep them alive, for now. I would have to find another way to kill them without the guards being there. No problem. I could wait.

***

It was Saturday morning and I decided to take a walk, hoping to somehow get a handle on my hunger. It wasn't working. It was three months since I'd fed.

I started through the parking lot of a large grocery store when I saw a woman pushing a cart with one hand and carrying a baby in the other.

I walked up to her and said, "Looks like you need help, ma'am."

At first, she frowned at me, then smiled. "Yes, I could use a hand." She pushed the button on her key fob to open the rear compartment.

I loaded her groceries into the car and pushed the button to close it

In the meantime, she had put her baby in its car seat and stood with the driver's door open.

"All safe and secure," I said.

"Thank you so much." She extended her hand. There was a folded bill in it.

"Sorry, ma'am. I don't want your money." I stood with my hands by my sides next to the open door.

"Are you sure? It would mean a lot to me."

I held up my hands. "No thanks. It was enough to be able to help you."

"Well, okay." She put one foot in the car and was about to step in when I hit her in the temple.

When she started to crumple, I caught her and placed her on the driver's seat. I closed the door and went around to the passenger side and climbed in. I leaned over and pulled her to me. Forcing her mouth open, I kissed her and let my tongue do its work. Just before the bliss engulfed me, I heard someone shout, "Get a room!" I almost smiled.

When I was finished, I put her seatbelt on and left the vehicle. On the way out of the parking lot, I saw a grocery store worker collecting empty carts. "There's a lady with a problem in a blue SUV that might need help."

He pointed to her car. "That one?"

"Yes." I turned and walked away.

***

Two weeks after the Bakersfield incident, Coach made an announcement. "Because of the deaths of the five Bakersfield guys and the attacks on us, several team owners have decided to hire bodyguards for the players. Our owners are doing the same thing. That means, in addition to Jake, every team member will have two bodyguards. They will be with you 24/7." The players all started asking questions at the same time. He held up his hand for silence. "No, it will not be the same two guys. They will rotate and be on duty for twelve-hour shifts. If you want to know what it feels like, ask Jake."

"I had gotten used to being on my own," I threw in. "But it's not as bad as it sounds."

***

As we went to the field, several of the guys asked me how it felt-- did I get used to being shadowed all day, every day and more.

I didn't have time to answer all the questions.

The news distracted me. I'd have to give up my plan for vengeance or try to find another way to accomplish it. By the time practice was over, I decided to give it up. None of our guys had died, so I could consider the debt paid.

The next day, we were all introduced to our bodyguards.

***

We finished the season in first place, as I had promised. The only time any team had scored against us was when I wasn't playing.

"Now comes the fun," Coach Spears said. "Every team we play against is going to try to take us down. Fortunately, only the top eight teams will be vying for the End-of-Season Trophy. The way it's set up, first place will play eighth place, second will play seventh and so on. I'm sure we'll be in the finals, unless, of course, Jake gets sick or takes off to get married."

Everybody laughed.

"I don't even have a girlfriend," I protested, meekly.

There was a lot more laughter.

"Are you gay?" somebody asked.

"Do you have a boyfriend?" someone else asked. He was grinning from ear-to-ear.

Those were some of the questions that were fired at me.

I stood up and waved my hands for quiet. "Hold on, hold on," I shouted. When all was quiet, I said, "On my eighteenth birthday, I went to Las Vegas and lost my virginity. It only cost me a hundred bucks."

"How did it feel?"

"Was she pretty?"

"How many times did you get off?"

"Come on, guys, you know a gentleman doesn't tell." I followed that with a lot of winks and smiles.

***

We made it all the way to the final two. Of course, nobody scored against us in our previous games. In the final game we were pitted against the Montana Miners. I was sure they would be glad to be able to play us again.

Coach Spears assured everyone that all would be okay.

We quieted down even though we didn't believe him.

The walk onto the pitch was everything but quiet.

Since both teams walk out side by side, there's lots of room to throw jibes back and forth.

Someone behind me whispered, "If we don't win, you're dead."

When I turned around, all the guys I could see were in conversations.

***

If I had seen a rough day before, it was nothing compared to this. We were fouled often and regularly and when the ref warned the culprit, one of his teammates smacked, punched or pushed one of our guys behind his back.

They were slick enough to keep the linesmen busy too.

When our guys hit back, the ref always caught us. Half our team wound up with yellow cards.

We ended the first half in a 0-0 tie.

On the way to the locker rooms, their captain told me, "We need to score at least once, or you die."

***

The second half started slow. Neither side committed a foul for the first thirty minutes, then one of our guys scored. Pandemonium erupted! Unfortunately, half the stadium was cheering while the other half yelled curses and threats.

Every once in a while, one could pick out an individual threat. They were against Coach Spears and me.

We ignored them as much as we could. I was just getting ready for a goal kick when one of the Miners was standing right in front of me. He was so close I could smell his garlicy breath.

"What do you want?" I asked him.

"I want the ball." He tilted his head to one side and smiled as he spoke.

It didn't matter which way I turned-he was right there. The stadium was quiet during the confrontation.

I was about to make a threat when the ref showed up.

"What the hell do you think you're doing? You know you have to be out of the box for a goal kick."

The ref pointed down field and shouted, "Go."

"Gee. I forgot," my shadow said. The guy nodded and turned and walked away.

Then I noticed he had a number on his jersey, but no name. Also, instead of joining the other team members, he walked off the pitch. Neither the ref nor the linesmen seemed to notice.

The play went on for another ten minutes when another idiot started shadowing me. This one, at least, stayed about three feet away.

Great! I didn't need another shadow.

He had me hooked. I thought I was safe from him. .

The next time someone kicked the ball to me, my shadow was right there. We were lucky. Because of my speed, we didn't collide.

I was becoming angrier and angrier. Then I decided, *if he wants the ball, let him have the ball.* My smile really stretched my face.

I watched from the corner of my eye while I prepared for a drop kick.

I started to throw the ball up when I saw him in the corner of my eye. He was moving fast. I threw up the ball, not straight up, but behind me. Not enough that he'd notice.

Then suddenly he was there. He was up in the air, probably trying to anticipate where the ball was going. I'm sure he planned to block the kick. Sorry to say, the only thing he blocked, and that not very well, was my foot, halfway between his belly and his crotch. *I'm not a complete monster. I could have aimed lower.*

He didn't fall. He just collapsed like a dropped cloth towel.

Suddenly we were in a crowd that came out of nowhere. My

shadow lay on the ground, unconscious. I stood looking down at him with the ball under my arm.

CHAPTER FOURTEEN

It didn't take long for the refs and the trainers to get to us. By then, both teams were separated by the security guards. I had the feeling that a major melee was on the horizon.

It took ten minutes to get everything under control and my shadow off the field on a stretcher. He was still unconscious as they carted him way.

We managed to continue the game without any major incidents. It ended with us winning 1-0. It didn't matter, 1-0 or 10-0, the outcome was the same: we got the three points for the win.

After the final whistle, we were surprised when the other team came and congratulated us on the win. Even their coach congratulated me personally.

Coach Strickland shook my hand and said, "Good game, kid." Then he put his hand on my shoulder, leaned close and whispered "You signed your death warrant today. I hope you have all your affairs in order." He was smiling as he walked away.

I didn't tell anyone about his second remark. No need to worry them unnecessarily.

***

We were startled when we stepped outside the stadium. A crowd had gathered and waited for us. They made a corridor to our bus. We shook hands and were patted on the back or shoulder all the way to our vehicle. We were flabbergasted at its condition. It had been scrubbed clean and decorated with streamers and banners.

When we were all seated, the driver started us on our journey home. He told Coach Spears he was worried when the crowd stormed the bus and pulled him off. "They needed me out of the way while the cleaned and decorated it. I was let back in when they were finished."

A gentleman in a suit and tie approached us. He introduced himself to Coach Spears. "I'm on the city council. We thought it would be a good gesture to decorate the bus to make up for the way your team was treated on the field."

Spears nodded, reached out and took the man's hand. After clearing his throat, said, "My team and I thank you."

They hugged and we boarded the bus.

***

Our entry into and through Franklin was incredible. The celebration lasted two days and everything was off the charts. We were all exhausted by the time it was over. I was afraid to relax too much. I couldn't get Coach Strickland's remark out of my head. I stayed in Franklin for a week, then drove to Milton to spend the winter with my dad.

***

We were having lunch one day when Mrs. Burns asked what I wanted to drink. I surprised her and my dad when I said lemon tea.

Mrs. Burns blinked several times, then nodded.

I looked up and saw my dad staring at me.

"When did you start that?" he asked.

"I don't really know. Several months ago, I got a craving for it and found I had bought some. I don't remember when. I really enjoy the taste of it."

He looked hard at me and nodded.

I waited for a few moments, then asked, "Is there something I should know?"

Still looking at me hard, he said, "Later."

His tone of voice let me know the discussion was over, at least for now.

***

On Thursday when Mrs. Burns had her day off, the discussion about the lemon tea continued.

Dad called me into the living room. We both sat on the couch slightly turned so that we could look at each other. I sat quietly, trying to read his expression.

He sat with one leg on the couch and the other on the floor with an arm over the back of the couch. His expression was very stern.

Finally, he said, "Do you remember getting stung by a Black Widow spider when you were five?"

I shrugged. My posture mirrored his. "I remember you telling me how I passed out and was in a coma for some time. I don't remember anything else." I knew my dad was going to tell me something important.

He nodded. "Did you notice how much stronger and faster you are than any kid in your school?"

"Yeah, I just put it down to good genes."

He took a deep breath. "Several years ago, there was a woman who went through the same thing you did. The difference was, she killed more than twenty men before she was caught. She was also faster and stronger than anyone had a right to be." He paused and looked down at his ankle as if gathering his thoughts. "After she was caught and killed, it was learned she had a daughter. The daughter inherited her mother's traits and abilities. She preferred women but, still left more than twenty bodies, both men and women, strewn across the country." He paused again and took a breath. "You're wondering what this has to do with you."

I nodded, not wanting to interrupt his train of thought.

"Neither of them could tolerate alcohol. Even the smell of it would make them sick." He let me digest that. "They both favored lemon tea."

I started thinking. I had drunk alcohol twice and went into

convulsions both times. My preferred drink at mealtimes was lemon tea. I could feel the blood drain from my face. Trembling, I ran my hand through my hair. If he knew those things about me, did he suspect the rest? When I met his eyes, I felt like he was reading my thoughts. There were a few murders where the brain had been taken, just as the Black Widow and her daughter had done. With what he had just told me, I was sure he knew I was the culprit.

He looked at me long and hard. "Revenge and vengeance, I can understand that. The couple in the desert doesn't fit. Explain."

I lowered my head and clasped my hands in my lap. I took a deep breath, then let it out. Not looking at him I said, "This feeling came over me that I didn't understand. I drove to the desert to clear my mind. I guess this guy was making out with his girl and didn't appreciate me being around. When he banged on my car, it made me mad. I got out of the car, we wrestled and fell to the ground. I wrapped my arms around him while I took his brain. I had finished with him when his date came over. When she saw me lying next to the guy, she dropped to the ground and cradled him in her arms for a few moments. She then came over to me and started kicking me, while yelling and screaming with each slash of her shoe. I rose while protecting myself and managed to put my arms around her. When I finished with her, I felt normal again and drove home." I had kept my head down looking at my hands while I talked. When I looked up, he was just sitting there, looking through me.

Dad pulled his arm from the top of the couch and held his wrist with his other hand. He stared at me so long I had to beg,

"Please, Dad."

He looked down and sighed. "Should I turn my son in as a murderer or keep quiet. You put me in a hell of a position. Working for the DA makes it even more of a problem. Turn you in or turn a blind eye?" He swung around and put both feet on the floor, leaned forward and placed his elbows on his knees and his face in his hands. He sighed. "I love you, Jake. You're all I have in this world. What you're doing is wrong but, I understand there's a need that has to be filled." He paused. "You said a feeling comes over you. How often does it happen?"

Because of his position, his voice was muffled, and I had to listen hard to understand him. "About once a month."

Finally, he leaned back, turned and looked at me. "Have you

received any threats lately?"

I swallowed hard. "Yes. Coach Strickland from Montana told me I signed my death warrant by not letting his team win the game."

He nodded, then sat back and crossed his arms over his chest. After what seemed like forever, he said, "Because of the threat, you're going to disappear for about two or three months. I have an idea that will still allow you to play with the team. I'll need to inform Coach Spears. I won't need his approval."

He got up and stretched. "I'm going for a walk. I need some fresh air and time to think."

He was out of the room before I could comment.

***

For the next month, I was on pins and needles. *What was he going to do? What did I have to do? What would it entail?* He acted as though our conversation never took place. I only had to think about what would happen if he turned me in and he'd give me a creased brow and a cold stare that shut me up before I could open my mouth. *Somebody once said, 'All good things come to those who wait.'* I just hoped I wouldn't go crazy waiting.

***

A week after the New Year, I found that Coach Spears had been invited to dinner. It would have been enjoyable if I didn't have to listen to a recap of most of my more spectacular saves. Since Dad hadn't been to any of the away games, he really enjoyed hearing about my prowess.

After dinner, we retired to the living room. When we were all seated and relaxed, Dad asked Coach if he knew about Coach Strickland's threat.

He moved forward to the edge of the chair. "What? He threatened you? When? What did he say?" He looked like he forced himself to wait for answers.

I told him when the threat had been made and what was said.

He sat open mouthed for a moment. "That S.O.B. I've a good mind to go see him and make him eat his words."

My dad held up a hand. "Chill. I have a plan."

Finally. I thought.

Coach Spears leaned forward, his elbows on his knees.

"Jake is going to take some time off. I think three months should be long enough. Of course, you'll use your other goalies during that time. I don't doubt they'll be glad to hear this." He paused to let that sink in.

Coach and I were just about to ask questions when he continued.

"You're going to get a new forward. Jake, you can decide on the name. He'll have to start at midfield, or defender, and work his way up. I don't think it will take long. This will only last until we can get Coach Strickland to forget his threat." He smiled. "Since I work for the DA, I'm sure he'll see things my way. I'll contact the owners to let them know Jake is going to Florida to stay with his aunt for three months and his bodyguards won't be needed for that time."

***

Later, I decided on Larry Walters as my alias. I almost screwed up and used Art Samson. The Bakersfield Police were probably looking for him in connection with the murders that occurred there.

We decided to dye my hair and eyebrows a dull red. It would be the easiest change since my hair was brown. Shaded contact lenses would be used to change my eye color to gray. I put inserts in my cheeks to make me look fatter. They took some getting used to but, I managed. I had to remember to walk with a slight bounce in my step. Mrs. Burns arranged my hair so that a few strands would fall over my face that I would have to move back.

Mrs. Burns was already aware of what we planned to do and she let us know that she would take care of everything.

"Not surprised," Dad mumbled.

She was as good as her word. She dyed my hair and eyebrows and gave me instructions on maintaining the color. "You can't shower for three days or the color will run."

I nodded.

***

When the season started, I was introduced to the team as Larry Walters. Coach let them know I would be starting at mid-field, unless

I could prove I was worth moving up. The team made me feel welcome with handshakes and pats on the shoulder.

To make things simple, I hailed from Prescott, Arizona.

One of the guys asked me the question I was expecting. "Since you're from Prescott, have you heard of Jake Stettler?"

"Are you kidding?" I said beaming broadly. "He's a hero. I'm sure everyone in the leagues has heard of him."

They all laughed.

Coach Spears interrupted. "Because of threats against his life, Jake will be taking a few months off. Tim, you'll be head goalie until he returns."

Tim looked about ready to jump for joy but managed to contain himself. He said, "Thanks, Coach. I know Jake is, or was, ten times better than I'll ever be but, I hope he stays out for the whole season."

Coach stared at him. "We'll see."

We hit the pitch for practice.

***

The season started better than was expected. Tim was outstanding as a goalie, even though a few balls got past him. In spite of that, we were still unbeaten after eight games.

I proved my worth by exhibiting my speed in getting away from the other players. No one could keep up with me. I had been secretly practicing my ball handling. I could outrun anyone on both teams, theirs and ours.

After the third game, I was moved up to striker. Everyone accepted my "promotion" without question. It was easy to dribble down the pitch past the other team and confronted their goalie. He was easy to get around. I scored three goals in the first half of our game against Colorado. I put the first one away when the goalie came out to meet me. I dribbled past him and leisurely put the ball in the net. When their goalie came out to meet me the second time, I kicked the ball over his head. Since he was so far from the goal, it went in while he was trying to catch up with it. The third one was almost identical to the first.

This was really cool, since the player scoring a hat trick would get the game ball at the end of the game.

Because our opponents couldn't stop me, they adopted a new

strategy. When I got the ball, the other team would head me off with four players. As I got closer to the goal, they would spread out. No matter which way I went, there would be two guys in front of me to block my way. I didn't always get past them.

Coach Spears came up with a solution to the ganging up on me. He stood in the locker room with his hands on his hips. "This is how we'll work it. Once Larry gets the ball, he'll slow down long enough for Kyle, and whichever midfielder is closest to him, to run down field.

"When the other guys start to spread out, Larry will kick the ball to the midfielder, who can then forward it to Kyle. If we can't go through them, we'll go around them. With four guys guarding Larry, we should have an almost open field." With his lips pursed h was quiet for a moment, his hands still on his hips,. "Anybody got any questions?"

"Yeah, Coach. Does it matter which one of us he passes the ball to?"

Spears chuckled. "In your words, yeah, it matters. He'll pass it to whoever is closest to him."

The next game we played was against the Washington Warriors. It only took twenty minutes for Coach Grimes to get upset with our new strategy. At the end of the first half, we were up 3-0.

When we resumed play, I still had four players to contend with. Kyle and two of the nearest midfielders each had two guys guarding them.

It was a problem until Coach Spears sent in a sub with new instructions. Since they had four players guarding me, two guarding Kyle and two in Mike Onslow, the midfielder, that left only two of their men to guard the rest of our team. Those two became frustrated trying to guard seven of us.

The new setup didn't last long. Coach Grimes realized his error after we had scored three goals in less than ten minutes. It didn't take long for him to switch back to a normal 4-4-2 formation. Four defenders, four midfielders and two forwards.

They managed to keep us scoreless for the rest of the game. Unfortunately, they didn't score either. Coach Grimes told Coach Spears, "Our turn next time." After a few seconds he asked, "Was it your idea to make that change?"

Spears told him, "You didn't leave me much choice. It was the only thing I could do."

Grimes nodded, then turned and walked away.

I was surprised when he didn't leave the field but instead, walked over to me.

He shook my hand then murmured, "I guess you'll need a broken leg. Or maybe both. We'll think about how bad we want to mess you up."

I didn't mention it to Coach Spears, we wouldn't play them again unless both teams made it to the End-Of-Season tournament. Entering the locker room, I got a lot of hard looks from his team. *Try me, guys. I would welcome the challenge.*

CHAPTER FIFTEEN

The threats against Larry built up. Coach Spears had a phone conference with my dad about bringing me Jake back. We made the switch easily. Spears told the team that Larry had a family emergency that would probably last past the end of the season.

A week after Larry left, I returned to the team. Although they'd maintained a winning season, the team was still glad to have me back.

***

I felt the need and decided to take a drive. It was aimless driving with no particular place in mind. Seeing a rest stop, I pulled in to empty my bladder. I was in the process when someone pulled my hand away.

"Let me do that for you." The stranger had more make up on than I've seen on most women. He was a bit shorter than me with wavy brown hair. *I wonder if it's permed?* I attempted to push his hand away, but he held onto me and began massaging. Against my will, I started getting an erection.

"I can take care of that too," he said. Still holding me, he led me to a stall. We went in and I closed the door.

While still massaging me, he asked, "Mouth or butt?"

My limited sexual experiences did not include either. I shrugged. "You're in charge."

He smiled and started to lower himself to his knees.

I hit him in the temple with both fists. When he started to collapse, I lifted him onto the seat. It didn't take any time at all to get my tongue into his mouth.

When I finished, I stood up and noticed a splotch of semen on his jeans, just below his belt. *Guess it was good.* I left feeling satisfied in more ways than one.

***

We only had two more weeks left in the regular season. Of course, we won every game. I was surprised when no threats were forthcoming.

Coach Spears asked me and the other team members daily if any threats had been received. He was more confused than happy when the answer was no. It seemed he worried more than when the threats were coming.

As expected, we were in the finals of the playoffs. We were to face the Colorado Cougars.

Their coach, Larry Grayson, met with Coach Spears and informed him that they were to win the Championship. "If we have to cheat to win, we will. I hope your guys don't plan on getting hurt too bad. We can be pretty rough if we think we're losing."

Coach Spears asked, "Are you threatening us? I hope not. You'll be sorry if you are."

Grayson laughed. "Your guys couldn't stand up to ours. We always play rough. The rougher the other team, the harder we play. I hope none of your guys end up in the hospital."

Coach Spears nodded and walked off.

***

As expected, the game got very rough. Two of our guys had to be taken off the field on stretchers. I must admit, the Cougars were careful. By the time the game had ended, the only man on their team not issued a yellow card was their goalie.

Four of our guys gave as good as they got and were carded. We didn't mind. We still beat them 2-0.

I overheard Coach Grayson when he approached Coach Spears. He was livid. He faced Spears with his thumbs in his belt. He pulled himself up to his maximum height, which put him a half-inch taller than Spears. Looking down his nose he yelled, "Didn't you understand what I said? Your team, especially your goalie, could be in for serious bodily harm. You'll be responsible." He stormed off the field.

Coach Spears advised the team not to be caught alone for the next few days. "They may come at us as a group or individually. I don't know. Just be careful. Stay in groups of three or more whenever possible."

After two weeks, nothing had happened. We didn't let that fool us. We stayed vigilant.

Soon after the game, Grayson got fired. Apparently, most of the owners had watched the game and some were even told of his threats toward us. The restraining order they filed didn't allow him to come within a mile of the team, no matter where they were.

We found out later that the restraining order only applied to *his* team. The owners were only concerned with his influence on the Cougars.

Of course, we found out by accident, if you could call it that.

We had all gotten complacent after we heard of Grayson's firing.

Not long after, Kyle got hit by a car one day while in a crosswalk. According to witnesses, the vehicle had no plates and didn't stop.

The vehicle was found later, abandoned. When the authorities traced the VIN number, they discovered it had been stolen.

A week after the Kyle incident, Mike Onslow, the midfielder, was stabbed in the stomach while walking on a crowded street. Of course, there were no witnesses. It took several operations before the doctors were certain he would recover.

***

We all suspected who the culprit was but had no proof. I went with Coach Spears to notify the police of Grayson's threat.

"Okay, we'll look into it," was all we got.

"Is that all?" Coach yelled. "My team is being disabled one-by-one and all you can say is 'We'll look into it.' Don't you plan on doing something? I told you who I think the culprit is. Won't you even check him out?"

The officer looked at Spears, annoyance showing. His nostrils flared and his eyes narrowed. "I said we'll look into it. We have a lot to do and not enough people, just like every other police department in the country. When we have someone, we can assign to your problem, it will be taken care of. We'll let you know what we find. Now, if you don't mind, I have other problems to take care of."

I thought he was about to come around the desk and either throw Spears and me out or put us in jail for harassment.

***

Not long after, Coach Spears surprised me with a visit in Milton. He was careful to pick a Thursday when Mrs. Burns had her day off, and my father was at work. He looked nervous when he entered the house.

"Are you sure we're alone?" He looked around the room seeming to try to see around the corners.

"Yes, I'm sure. What's this all about?"

He ushered me into the living room. When we were seated, me on the couch, he in a chair, he fidgeted for a moment. "Jake, I'm going to ask you to do something that's against all my principles." He looked at me, then lowered his eyes, all the time wringing his hands.

I cleared my throat. I think he wanted me to kill somebody. I still don't know where that thought came from. "Do you want me to take care of the problem, like . . . for good?"

His head snapped up and his eyes were wide open. "How . . . how did you know what I was thinking?"

"I didn't. I don't know what made me say that."

He took several deep breaths, folded and unfolded his hand. He cleared his throat and said, "That's exactly what I'd planned to ask."

I was in shock. I'm sure my coach was asking me to be a murderer. "This is a joke, right?"

He shook his head. "I hate to say it but, it isn't. Two more of our guys have had 'accidents,' if you want to call them that. I don't think it's a coincidence. I think it's Grayson, but I have no proof and the police won't listen to me."

I let all this sink in. "Why did you come to me?"

"With what happened to other teams' players after our incidents, my gut told me you were avenging the team." He held up a hand. "You were always unreachable when those guys were taken out. I know it was you, even though I can't prove it." He folded his hands and leaned back in the chair.

"What makes you think it was me? I know I have some extra abilities but, how could I break somebody's jaw? How could I do it? According to the reports, no hands or devices were used. At least that's what my dad got from the police." I waited. *This can't be happening. Does he really know my secret or does he only suspect? Should I honor his request? I've never been asked to murder anyone.*

He sighed. "My gut tells me it was you. I don't have anything else to go on." He looked straight at me. "I, we the team, need your help."

After a few moments I shook my head. "I'm sorry, Coach. I can't kill someone because you suspect him of harming our team. My dad works for the Las Vegas DA. What if he found out? Do you really want to put him in that position?"

Spears shook his head and leaned forward, resting his arms on his legs. He nodded. "I guess I didn't think about your dad." He got up. "Sorry. This was a bad idea."

He had made it to the front door before I even stood up. I didn't realize he could move that fast.

After he had gone, I made myself a lemon tea and went back to the living room. I turned on the TV and muted the sound. *I wonder how far it is to Denver.*

CHAPTER SIXTEEN

I woke up the next morning to the smell of coffee and other enticing aromas.

Dad sat at the table, reading something off his phone by the time I made my appearance.

"Good morning, sleepyhead. I take it you had a good night?"

"Slept like a log," I replied.

Mrs. Burns put a plate of scrambled eggs and bacon in front of me.

"White or wheat toast?" she asked.

"Wheat, please?"

She nodded and went to prepare the toast.

"What are your plans for the rest of your off-time?" Dad asked.

"I thought I'd use the upright bike and free weights in the gym to keep fit."

"Good. What will you do with the other twenty-three hours?"

We both laughed. Even Mrs. Burns chuckled.

"I guess I'll just take it easy and rest up for the next day."

"Right," Mrs. Burns said. "You don't want to wear yourself out before the season starts."

All three of us laughed.

***

Later that day, while I was thinking of Coach Grayson, that strange feeling came over me. *I guess I can't ignore it anymore. It's been three months since I fed.*

Somehow, I had to find a way to feed without alerting Dad and Mrs. Burns. It was going to be difficult since I had ignored the hunger for so long. *Why can't I ignore it forever?*

By the time we were all heading for bed, I decided on what to do.

"Dad, I'm going to watch a little more TV before I go to bed. I want to listen to the news to hear if any more of our guys have been hurt.

"Okay," he said. "Don't stay up too late."

I waited an hour until I could be sure he and Mrs. Burns were asleep. I set the alarm, then immediately disabled it. I snuck out and made my way to the nearest bus stop. I rode it to the end of the line. When I got off, I walked further out of town until I didn't hear or see any people.

I stood by the side of the road and waited. Luckily, it was only about five minutes until a car approached. I waved my arms. The car slowed and finally stopped. There was only one person in the car. He lowered the passenger window and asked, "What are you doing out here alone at this time of night?"

I walked around to the driver's side before I answered. 'I'm going to do what was done to me. I'm going to hijack your car."

His window was open, and I reached in and grabbed him by the throat. His hands beat uselessly against my arms. I squeezed until he lost consciousness. Once he had passed out, I had no problem moving him to the passenger side. I drove until I found a place where I could park without the car getting stuck in the sand. I pulled him out of the car and laid him on the ground. When I had finished feeding, I moved his body further into the desert. *I wonder if the animals will have a meal before he's found.* I shrugged and went back to the car.

I drove his car back to town and parked two blocks from a bus station. I wiped down all the surfaces I'd touched with my handkerchief. I had to wait less than ten minutes before the next bus took me home.

Back at the house, I set the alarm for real, listened for

movements or sounds from Dad and Mrs. Burns. Nothing. I went to bed feeling happy and sated.

***

The next morning, on the news, I heard that another of my teammates narrowly escaped being seriously injured by a car. *I didn't think Grayson would still be in Denver. I wondered when he got to Franklin and how long he'd stay?* By the time the season started, eight of my team members were suffering from injuries. This had gotten serious. I would have to stop Grayson before he disabled the whole team. I travelled to Franklin a week earlier than originally planned. I cruised the neighborhoods of my teammates, looking for signs of Grayson. Nothing. *He must be good at hiding in plain sight.*

Finally, I parked my car on a side street and started to wander. When I saw Nate Brunson, walking alone, across the street. I shadowed him. Sometimes, it became a little difficult because of the lunch crowd.

Then I saw a head of brown hair, graying at the temples. His height made him stand out and easy for me to recognize. *Grayson.* He was moving toward Nate. Dark sunglasses hid his eyes. I crossed the street pushed through the crowd until I was a slightly ahead of Nate.

As Grayson approached, he took his hand out of his jacket pocket and held it down by his side. I saw the quick flash of a knife blade.

When he got close, his hand came up to stab Nate. I grabbed his wrist and held on tight.

He looked at me, surprised.

I smiled and squeezed. His efforts not to scream were successful, even though his mouth dropped open, held taut for control.

I slipped the knife from his hand and palmed it. "Leave town, now!" I whispered.

Tears ran from under his shades. He nodded.

When I let go, he walked away rubbing his wrist. I watched until he disappeared into the crowd. Nate continued on, oblivious to what had happened.

***

The following week we were back at practice. I found time to pull Coach Spears aside and let him know I had spoken with Grayson.

"Are you sure we don't have to worry about him anymore?"

"Pretty sure. He seemed convinced when I spoke to him."

After a few moments, he asked, "What exactly happened?"

I shrugged. "I ran into him in town and told him he had to leave. He agreed without question."

"Just like that?"

I nodded. "Just like that. I can be very convincing when I want to be."

Another pause. "It seems too simple, too easy. Here's a guy that's been terrorizing our team and you have a few words with him, and it all ends?"

I shrugged. "What more can I say?"

He gave me hard look. "You can tell me exactly what you said and what you did."

I let my shoulders drop. "Okay. You win. I came to town a week early to look for him. I finally ran into him on Third Avenue. He was heading for Nate and concentrating so hard on him that he didn't see me. When he pulled his knife out, I clasped his wrist and took the knife. While I held him, I told him to leave town. I hoped by the tone of my voice and the pressure on his wrist that he knew I was serious. I was right. He nodded his consent. I released his wrist and he walked away. I'm pretty sure he won't be back."

"I hope you're right." He started to walk away, then turned back. "I'm glad you did it your way."

"Me too." I ran onto the pitch for practice.

***

Our first game of the season was against the Seattle Sounders. Their coach, Myron Davies, came to me and asked if I would let his team score.

"Not if I can help it," I told him.

He shook his head. "Haven't you caused enough pain and misery for you team? Aren't you afraid of getting hurt?"

I looked him straight in the eye. "Yes, I've caused my guys pain and misery. Anyone thinking of causing them more should think again. And no, I'm not afraid of getting hurt."

We stared at each other for what seemed like forever. He turned and walked away first. *I hope that lets you know I mean business.*

We won the game 2-0. Coach Davies shook hands with Spears, looked hard at me, then joined his team in the locker room.

Since we were the away team, we stayed in the hotel. The hotel security kept us safe during the night.

Coach Spears wouldn't let us go out and celebrate. "You can celebrate in Franklin when you get home. I don't want any more players on the injured list."

Nobody complained. We found things to do in the hotel. None of us stayed up late.

***

We were all surprised when we got back to Franklin without incident.

"Maybe they'll come at us later." Someone mumbled. More than a few heads nodded in agreement.

We used practice to get our minds off what hadn't happen.

Coach got really upset with us and read us the riot act every day.

"We have a game on Saturday against the Dallas Dynamo. They are NOT a pushover. They're only one game behind us in the league. We have to win to maintain our standing. For God's sake, get the Sounders out of your heads."

We somehow managed to get our act together. As Saturday approached, we focused more on our training.

***

Saturday night, the announcer had us stand for the National Anthem. The lady who sang it touched everybody with her rendition. Even the non-Americans put their hands over their hearts and stood at attention.

When that was over, I and the Dynamos' team captain met with the refs and decided who would defend which goal.

They were good, but we already knew that. It was a spirited first half with neither team scoring a goal. This was becoming a standard.

In the locker room, between halves, Coach Spears congratulated us for the way we played. "We almost didn't need Jake at goal." He

127

looked at Tim who had raised a hand. "No, Tim, you're not going in. The rest of you guys keep up the good work. Let's go out there and win this game."

We all cheered and made our way to the pitch. "I'll let one in if you will," their goalie suggested to me.

I shook my head. "Sorry, no deal. Do your best. Don't go slack on me. I don't want to lose respect for you."

He smiled and high fived me. We made or way to our respective stations.

Ten minutes later, we scored. Our team and the fans went crazy.

Less than five minutes later, the ball was heading in my direction. It would be an easy save. The ball was literally in my hands when a head appeared and deflected it into the net. I stood stunned while the crowd and the Dynamo players went ballistic. A ball had gotten past Jake Stettler.

Al stood in front of me, his head hanging, his arms by his side.

I finally lowered my hands.

Al said, "I'm sorry, Jake. I'm so, so sorry. I didn't think you had it."

It took more than a few seconds to tamp down my rage. I stood close to him our noses almost touching. "Do you realize what you've done? I've kept the ball out of the net against the best in the league and you, one of my teammates, puts the ball past me into the net. FOR THE OTHER TEAM! For two and a half years I've maintained our unbeaten record. Now, because you, for whatever reason, decided to help me . . ." I could feel my anger building, again. I closed my eyes and took several deep breaths. "Get the hell out of my sight."

When I opened my eyes, he was nowhere to be seen.

The next thing I knew, the ref was standing in front of me. He lifted the yellow card. "For delay of game."

I sighed and nodded in agreement.

The game finished in a 1-1 tie. Their goalie put his arm around my shoulder as we walked off the pitch to the locker rooms.

"Sorry about what happened. Try to put it out of your mind. It happens to most of us at one time or another. My team did it to me twice."

"That doesn't happen to me. My team knows no matter where the ball is, how it's sent to the goal or whatever, I will stop it or push it away from the net. Two-and-a half years I've been goalie. This is the first professional goal against me. It won't be easy to forget."

"I got over it. You can too."

By the time I got to the locker room, Al had showered, I think, and left. *Lucky for him it was a home game.*

CHAPTER SEVENTEEN

When I got to practice, the following Tuesday, Al wasn't there. Several people asked if I'd heard from him. He didn't show up for practice on Monday.

"I haven't seen him since Saturday," I told them. *I hope he fell in a hole somewhere.*

Practice went well. The passing was crisp and accurate. If we play like this on Saturday, when we host the Kansas City Eagles, it would be a win without my goalkeeping.

***

Saturday, after kick-off, we dominated for the first twenty minutes. Their coach, Lane Thomas, was using a 4-4-2 formation. Coach Spears set us up in a 4-3-3 formation. We found we were able to penetrate their defense with ease. I spent the first half watching the game from my end of the pitch. My guys kept the ball mostly in their territory. We were up 3-0 after the first forty-five minutes.

During the second half, I had to make two saves. *At last, I got to handle the ball.* Our team scored twice more to make it 5-0. This was the worst beating in their career. Coach Thomas was not happy, and it showed in his posture and on his face. While most coaches yelled and waved instructions to their team, he merely stood on the side lines with his hands in his pockets. His face was void of expression. I felt sorry for him. I'm sure his team would be read the riot act when the game was over.

Because I had little to do with their defeat, I didn't expect threats of any kind.

Coach Thomas hugged and congratulated our coach when the game was over. "Good game," he murmured, then left the pitch.

The way my guys acted in the locker room you'd think someone had flooded the room with one-hundred-dollar bills. It was loud and crazy with everyone hugging each other and dancing around the room. Coach had to finally blow his whistle to get our attention. When we were quiet, he said, "Congrats on winning a game without Jake's skills. You guys did it on your own and I'm proud of you." He held up his hand to quiet us before we could get raucous again. "Hit the showers, get dressed, go home. Rest up tomorrow. Monday is practice. We have the Houston Raiders on Saturday in their house. They have the home team advantage, so it will be a hard game. Texans love their athletes and will give them the support they need. Expect to get booed every so often. When they do boo us, it should encourage us. Again, get showered, get dressed and get out of here. The janitors would like to clean the place so they can go home."

We continued celebrating in the showers but, eventually, everyone was dressed and heading home.

***

We beat Houston 2-0. Of course, there was a lot of booing but, we used it to energize ourselves. Coach was right, it helped.

The next week, Al showed up while we were getting ready to go home after practice. He seemed nervous and wanted to talk to Coach and me alone.

We both wondered what was going on.

Standing in Coach's office, Al shifted from one foot to the other. He cleared his throat several times. He was obviously very nervous.

Coach and I waited patiently.

Finally, he spoke. "I was paid."

Coach and I looked at each other.

"Paid for what?" Coach asked.

Al cleared his throat again. "I was paid to score against Jake."

We were stunned silent.

I shook my head. "Who paid you?" I demanded.

Al sighed. "Coach Davies from the Sounders. He paid me five thousand dollars to score against you in the Dallas game."

Coach Spears moved behind his desk, sat in his chair and put his elbows on the desk with his head in his hands.

"Is this real?" I asked.

Al nodded. "I feel like I betrayed you and the team. It's only me and my mom and we're going bankrupt trying to keep up with her medical bills. I didn't think about you or the team. I only thought about my mom and me. After I did it, I was ashamed. I couldn't even face my mom. She finally convinced me to come clean with you."

Coach lifted his head and looked at Al. "You should have let us know. There are ways we can help. You and your mom are not in this world alone."

Tears were flowing down Al's cheeks. "I didn't know what else to do."

I told him, "It's okay, Al. We didn't lose the game. It finished in a tie. They were happy with the outcome." A thought went through my head, "Did the Dallas coach or players know about the deal?"

"I don't think so," Al said. "I think only Coach Davies and I knew."

Finally, Coach stood and came around the desk. He approached Al and nodded to me.

We gave him a group hug. We held him while his shoulders shook, and the tears flowed. His sobs were heartbreaking.

"I'm sorry. I'm so, so sorry," he cried.

Neither Coach nor I could find words.

When he finally calmed down, we realized we'd been in the office for a half hour.

Finally, Coach held Al by the shoulders. "Come see me after practice tomorrow. I'll have information on getting help for you and your mom."

Al wiped his face with the back of his hand. "After practice tomorrow?"

"Of course. We didn't fire you and you haven't officially quit. Practice tomorrow at ten. Tell your mom the team is looking into ways to get you help."

I thought he was going to get on his knees and kiss Coach's hand. "Thanks, Coach. My mom will be happy when I tell her the news." He looked at me.

"It's okay, Al. It's okay. I understand. Go home, hug your mom and be safe. Welcome back to the team."

When he started to turn away, I stopped him.

"You are a very special person. You can tell the world that you scored against Jake Stettler. It should make you famous. Even though we're on the same team."

The three of us laughed.

He thanked us again and left.

When he was gone, Coach looked at me. "I guess we have to watch out for Coach Davies. I didn't think he'd stoop that low."

"I didn't either." I was about to leave when Coach called me back.

"Don't go after him, Jake."

I could tell from the tone of his voice that he was very serious.

I sighed. "Okay Coach. I won't. I promise."

He nodded and I left.

It was good to have Al back on the team. The rest of the guys welcomed him as though he was a long, lost brother. In a way, he was.

Our next game was against the Santa Fe Saints. Their coach, Oscar Holdridge, held Coach Spears hand a bit long. "We've heard about your goalie."

"Who hasn't?" Spears replied.

Holdridge snorted and adjusted his glasses. "Don't be an asshole. Tell your goalie we don't mind losing if we score at least once."

Spears shook his head. "I don't think that's going to happen. It would be like asking him to throw the game."

"I don't want him to throw the game. Just let us score once."

Spears shrugged. "I'll mention it to him." He turned away, effectively dismissing Holdridge.

***

It was a very spirited game. We were ahead 2-0 at the half. On the way to the locker room, several of the Saints made comments, such as, "Let a ball through, asshole."

133

"Take a break, Dumbo. Let us score."

"Do we have to break your arms to get the ball in the net?"

I ignored them, as did the rest of the team.

Coach Spears didn't say anything while we rested up for the second half. He just sat on a bench and watched us interact.

Finally, our fifteen minutes were up. We headed back to the pitch, energized, knowing this game too, was ours.

Of course, we won. We scored twice more to make the final score 4-0-.

The Saints and Holdridge half-heartedly congratulated us on the win.

Holdridge asked Spears, "Do you expect to be at the top of the league at the end of the season?"

Spears smiled. "Naturally. With Jake as goalie we can't lose."

Holdridge snorted and walked off. On his way, he looked at me and pointed two fingers at his eyes and then at me.

I got the message. *I hope you're not making a threat. It could backfire.* I headed to the locker room, to celebrate with the rest of the team.

***

The rest of the season was no different from the other seasons. We finished at the top of the league. The Vancouver Rockies finished second, the Minnesota Miners finished third and the Kansas Eagles finished fourth. In the playoffs, we were pitted against Minnesota for our first game. We won. Vancouver beat Kansas like they owned them. The score was 8-1. We only won our game with a 3-0 score.

This meant we would face Vancouver for the top spot.

Coach Andrews told Spears, "Prepare to finally lose a game."

Spears was man enough to not laugh in his face.

***

It was a rough game for us. The refs called three personal fouls against our team. The Rockies were outstanding as divers. They would have made the National Diving Team proud. We only had to pass by one of them and they would fall and roll, holding a leg or ankle, as if they'd been tripped.

We were worried the game would be awarded to them because of our unnecessary roughness. We were glad when the game finally ended with the score at 0-0. Bad because it was a Championship Final. The game didn't end there. An extra thirty minutes were added to the game. That meant we would play for fifteen minutes, switched sides and play another fifteen minutes. Whatever score was on the books at the end, would stand. If at the end of the overtime there was still a tie, a penalty shoot-out would ensue.

We smiled at the end of the overtime. We knew the game was ours.

Andrews' smile was so wide, Spears thought his face would split.

I wished it would.

Five men from each side would go against the goalie from the other team.

The penalty shootout ensued. We went first. Marty placed the ball high and wide to his right. The goalie went the wrong way.

It was my turn. I waited. The ball was kicked, I lunged and caught it. We were up 1-0. Kyle was up next. He got the ball past their goalie into the net.

My turn again. I shifted right and left in rapid movements. Since most goalies try to anticipate where the ball will be going, they move before the ball is kicked. I waited and the ball was kicked right to me. We were up 2-0.

Al was up next. He also got the ball into the net. Their goalie went one way, the ball went the other. That meant if I stopped the next ball, we would win. Since we were up 3-0 and they only had three men left, if the next man didn't get the ball in the net, the game would be over, and the Championship would be ours.

The next man kicked the ball high and wide. I almost missed it, but I managed to get enough fingers on it to deflect it past the net. That was it. We won.

The fans went crazy and the confetti machines flooded the air with a shower of man-made colored snow.

If they hadn't gotten the second-place award, we would have forgotten they were there. We'd won the other Championships by scoring more than the other team. This was the first time we had to go into overtime and finish with the penalty shootout. It didn't matter how we won. It only mattered that we won.

We now had two weeks to prepare for our match against the winners of the Eastern conference.

***

Since we'd had no threats for a few months, I convinced Coach that I no longer needed bodyguards. It took some doing but I finally got him to agree. It was even harder for me to get him to convince the owners, but he did.

I was so glad when the bodyguards left. I needed to get out. Having them around seriously curtailed my *other* activities. The hunger was driving me crazy. I got in my car and headed out of town. I let my body take the car while my brain thought of how and where I would feed.

I wasn't paying attention because I almost went into a ditch. My brain took over just in time. Then ahead I noticed a lone cyclist. *I guess you wanted to get my attention,* I told the car.

As I drove past, I got close enough to cause him to crash. I braked and ran back to him. "Oh, my God! I'm so sorry. Are you all right?"

After a few seconds of shooting daggers at me, he said, "I don't think anything is broken but I'll probably have a few bruises. I think I'll live." He had untangled himself from the bike and raised himself off the ground. After brushing off the dust and gravel, he took off his helmet, stared at me, then took a step back. He almost fell when his leg collapsed.

I grabbed him just in time to keep him off the ground. I had my arms around him.

"Thanks. I suppose it's the least you could do." He looked at me sideways as if there were something more on his mind.

"No. I can do more."

He struggled to break my hold. When he opened his mouth to speak, I planted my mouth on his and inserted my tongue.

He struggled, trying to pull away.

I held him tighter.

It was sweet. I don't think I'll ever get tired of tasting human brain. I laid him gently on the ground by the side of the road, next to his bike. "Someone will find you and take care of you."

I got in my car, turned it around and drove home.

CHAPTER EIGHTEEN

During the winter break, I went with my dad to a Christmas party given by the District Attorney. It was very festive with Christmas decorations and a table with lots and lots of food. The drink table held beer, wine, champagne and a punch bowl. I didn't know if the punch had alcohol in it. I had poured a little in a cup when a voice said, "Are you sure you can drink that much?"

I had just enough for a sip. I turned to see who had spoken and was struck dumb by her beauty. Her face was the softest milk-chocolate I could remember ever seeing. A mass of soft-looking, black curls surrounded her face down to her shoulders. I felt like I could drown in the dark brown pools of her eyes. To say she was beautiful would have been an understatement.

"I . . .I just wanted to see if it had alcohol in it. I can't do alcohol," I managed to finally say.

"You don't or you can't?" she asked, smiling. Her white teeth seemed to reflect the light.

"I can't."

She tilted her head to one side and looked at me for a few seconds. "Okay. I won't ask what your problem is, that's your concern. What's your name?"

"Jake, Jake Stettler," I stammered.

"Do you work in one of the offices here?"

"No. My father works for the DA. Do you work here?"

"Yes. I work in the Public Defender's office. I'm a lawyer." She extended her hand. "I'm Greta Schwartz. Glad to make your acquaintance, Jake Stettler."

"Greta Schwartz. Isn't that an odd name for an African-American?"

She smiled. "Yes, it is. My grandfather was in the army stationed in Germany. My mother visited him during a break in college. While there, she met Karl-Heinz Schwartz. They hit it off and spent a lot of time together during her two months' visit. She had been back in the states for three months when Karl-Heinz showed up at her apartment. She was both surprised and pleased. They spent as much time as possible together until his visa ran out. A year later, she went back to Germany, but this time, only reason was to visit Karl-Heinz. Two months later, they were married. When they returned to the states, she continued in college and he got a job as a German teacher. I was born four months after my mom got her degree. They both agreed to name me Greta, after his mother. If they would have had a boy, he would have been named after my father. Didn't happen. I'm an only child."

During her dissertation I had poured both of us a cup of punch and we drank while she talked. I thought we were getting along good when she dropped a bombshell on me.

She took me by the arm and said, "I want you to meet someone. Oh. I'll need another cup of punch."

I poured it and we made our way through the revelers and came to another beautiful woman with a pale complexion and raven hair that hung to just above her breasts. One ear was exposed, and a gold cross hung from her earlobe. A short way from the cross was a diamond stud. Her green eyes sparkled in the light. I was transfixed by her beauty until Greta introduced her.

"This is my wife, Annika. Annika, this is Mr. Jake Stettler."

Annika beamed a bright smile that showed lots of sparkling white teeth. She held out her hand. "Glad to meet you, Jake Stettler."

I shook her hand and tried not to show my astonishment. "Glad to meet you," I managed to get out. "Annika sounds like a Swedish name," I said.

"It is. My father was Danish, and my mother was Swedish. She got to choose my name. He had grey eyes and hers were blue. I gave up trying to figure out how grey and blue combine to make green."

I decided to leave that one alone and just enjoy the view.

They both stood looking at me and smiling., enjoying the expression on my face.

Greta wore an off-the shoulder dress of dark blue. The sleeves were short, showing flawless brown skin.

Annika wore a sleeveless gown of a green silk that matched her eyes.

Both ladies' dresses were long, almost reaching the floor. While their garments accented their shapes, they didn't make them look overly sexy.

Annika smiled. "Do you live here in Las Vegas?"

I cleared my throat. "I play soccer and during the winter break I live with my father in Milton. During the season, I live just north of Las Vegas in Franklin, where my team is based."

"What position do you play?" Greta tilted her head to one side. .

"I'm the goalie."

Annika pushed her hair behind her right ear.. "You said, 'I'm the goalie.' Don't soccer teams have more than one goalie?"

"Yes, but only one plays at a time. I wear number one."

Greta snapped her fingers. "Of course. Now I remember. There was a news article about how one of your own teammates scored the first goal against you in more than two years."

I blushed. "I got angry with him but I apologized."

Annika said, "That must be some kind of record."

"It is." I felt my chest swell.

They looked at each other. It was if they had a secret language in their nods, looks and smiles.

Greta asked, "What are your plans for the rest of the time you're here?"

"I don't have anything special planned. When I get home, I'll go to the gym or go for a run to keep in shape. Other than that, I'll just spend time doing whatever."

She held out her phone. "Your number."

I punched in my number.

"Good. You'll be hearing from us before you go back to Franklin."

"That would be nice," I said, lamely.

They both smiled. Each squeezed one of my arms, and then they were gone.

***

The following Monday, as my dad was getting ready to leave for work, he gave me a nod.

I followed him to the door.

He put a hand on my shoulder. "Be careful. They think they're getting close."

I nodded. "I will Dad." I knew he was talking about the FBI.

When he was gone, I went to my room to think about what he said. *I'll have to be more careful about my fingerprints and DNA. They don't know who I am yet. No sense giving them clues.* Dad had mentioned, and I'd heard on the news, that FBI Director Anton Grabowski and Las Vegas Metropolitan Chief of Police, Dan Stroberg, had teamed up to head the investigation into the strange deaths. They were instrumental in bringing the Black Widow and her daughter to justice. I couldn't let that happen to me. *Just be extra careful when you feed. Don't break the jaw. If you do, they'll look into the skull and know you were there.*

***

Two days later, I got a call from Greta. She asked if I could meet her and Annika at their place in Las Vegas.

Curious, I said I could.

She gave me their address and we decided on the following day. I would meet them for dinner.

They lived in Summerlin, a suburb of Las Vegas. The house was a ranch-style in an upscale neighborhood. *They may not be rich, but they seem to be well off.*

They both greeted me with hugs. I had to admit even though I knew they were lesbians, the hugs felt good. Their house was tastefully furnished with modern furniture. Everything was in light brown or pale blue. I was surprised not to see pink. *Probably only in the bedrooms and bathrooms. If there's more than one of each. Or maybe my thinking was old fashioned and I was thinking of children.* Sheer curtains and dark drapes covered all the windows. The meal consisted of salmon steak on a bed of white rice and a green bean casserole.

"What would you like to drink?" Annika asked.

"Lemon tea," I replied.

She nodded.

***

After dinner, they cleared the dishes and put away the leftover food while I was told to sit and drink my tea.

When they had all in order, they sat across from me at the table.

I started to get nervous as they sat and looked at me with nods and looks at each other.

Finally, Greta asked, "Is there someone special in your life?"

Looking at them in turn, I finally said, "No." I waited.

"Have you ever thought about being a father?"

I looked at Greta and blinked several times. *Where the hell did this come from?* "No. The thought never crossed my mind."

They smiled at each other.

Greta smiled. "I'd like you to be the father of my baby. Annika and I talked it over and we thought you'd be a good candidate."

I sat there dumbfounded. It took a few seconds to realize my mouth was open. "Why me?"

"Like I said, we thought you'd be good." She held up a hand. "I don't want you to be a Dad, just a father."

I shook my head. "I'm confused. Why do you think I'd be a good candidate?"

Greta sat back and smiled. "You're young and single and you don't have any commitments to get in the way. It's the way you carry yourself, the way you speak and something else that we haven't been able to put our fingers on."

Annika said, "If you agree, we'll go to a sperm bank where you'll donate your sperm. Greta will use your, uh donation, for want of a better word, to fertilize her egg. If it takes, and I'm sure it will, then you'll be the father of her child. Your name will be on the birth certificate as the father, but that's the only claim you'll have."

I sat quietly for what they may have thought was forever. *Me. A dad. What would my dad say?* "Can I tell anybody?"

"We'd prefer you didn't," Greta said. "For all practical purposes, you'll be the father on paper only. You'll have no claim to the child."

"That's kind of harsh, isn't it?" I asked.

141

"Not really," Annika answered. "This is happening all over the world, even as we speak. Women want to have children without the burden of having a husband. The world is changing."

I sighed. "I guess it is." After a few seconds I said, "Okay. I'll do it. Just tell me when and where I have to be."

They both got up, came around the table and hugged me.

"We'll let you know as soon as we've made the appointment. We'll try to make it before you have to go back to Franklin."

We spent the next hour talking about what the baby would look like and whether it would be a boy or girl. They would prefer a girl. I thought a boy would be better. We debated the pros and cons for the next hour.

Finally, our gathering broke up and I made my way back to Milton. A lot of the conversations ran through my mind as I drove home. *I'll just tell Dad I was invited for dinner by the two ladies.*

***

The next day, I got the call from Greta. "Can you be here Friday? I've made an appointment for you at the bank at two. Would that be all right?"

"I don't see any problem. Should I come to your place first?"

"I think that would be a good idea. That way I can make sure you don't change your mind."

"Thanks for the vote of confidence."

She laughed. It sounded like silver bells tinkling.

After I hung up, I thought, *why me? Why did she have to be gay?* I wasn't in love, but it would have been an easy fall. That she seemed older than me didn't matter. *Oh well, such is life.*

***

The trip to the sperm bank was an experience I'll never forget. We signed in and waited a few moments. A woman in a nurse's uniform called my name.

When I got up, she handed me a small plastic jar. "Put it in here."

I guess the confused look on my face indicated my ignorance.

"Your sperm goes in the container. Do you need a magazine?"

"I don't think so. What would I do with it?"

Greta and Annika were trying their best not to laugh out loud.

"Some men need it to help them get in the mood."

I blinked. "Oh."

Exasperated, she put her hands on her hips. "Young man, do you know how to masturbate?"

I could feel the blood rush to my face. "Of course, I do."

"Go in the bathroom and masturbate. The sperm goes in the container. Do you think you'll need help?"

I could feel my face burning. "No ma'am."

Greta and Annika were doubled up laughing.

Five minutes later, I handed the nurse the container.

She looked at it closely.

I couldn't decipher the look in her eyes.

"We only needed a sample. Were you planning to start your own army?"

I blushed. "No ma'am."

She snorted then walked over to a desk. After putting down the container, she came back to me with a large hardcover book in her hand and handed it to me. "Hold this."

I took the book.

"Raise it higher. Hold it with both hands."

I complied. Then came a loud whack and I felt excruciating pain in my groin.

She caught the book as it flew from my hands. "How you can still have an erection after all you put in the container is beyond me."

I doubled over in pain and slowly sank to the floor on my hands and knees. The pain radiated from my groin down to my knees and up to my chest. I could hardly breathe.

The nurse sneered. "A ruler always brings men under control."

Greta and Annika were almost on the floor, doubled up with laughter.

After a few minutes I was able to straighten up and got in to chair.

The nurse came over and said, "You'll be okay in a few minutes." She crossed her arms and gave me a hard look. "Do you have a girlfriend?"

"No, ma'am."

"Best get one or at least find a way to empty the sac. You'll feel much better. Trust me," she snorted as she turned away. "Men."

She turned to Greta. "Come in tomorrow at 9."

"Very good," Greta answered.

"Thanks a lot for the support," I said.

Still smiling, Greta said, "You have to forgive us. It wasn't like that when Annika visited the sperm bank. The donor wasn't there. I didn't know what would happen with you being here to donate on the spot."

The two ladies had composed themselves and I was sure they would be able to get me back to my car without incident.

***

I got a call six weeks later, Greta was pregnant. I was as happy as she was. She let me know that Annika had visited the clinic a month earlier and she was pregnant also. Her baby would be a girl.

"You guys are going to be busy."

Greta laughed. "Yes. Isn't it wonderful?"

"Yes, it is. I guess it's too early to tell if it's a boy or girl."

"I should know in about two weeks. Should I call you?"

"Yes, please. Even though I won't be involved, I still would like to know the sex."

"I can do that for you. Bye for now."

I sat holding the phone for a few minutes after she hung up. *I'm going to be a dad. I wish I could tell my Dad.*

CHAPTER NINETEEN

The season started just as we thought it would. We won every game we played. Coach Spears and I were surprised that there had been no threats against me or the team. I got the expected call from Greta three weeks later. The baby would be a girl. She planned to name her Heidi. She sounded ecstatic. I felt happy too. That I'd have a daughter. I wished I could tell the world. *Oh well. A promise is a promise.*

Two months into the season, I received a nice surprise. I had been selected as goalie for the Men's National Team. The whole team was happy for me. It did mean I would miss some games with the Thunder, but a few here and there wouldn't stop us from having a winning season.

*****

I met with the coach of the men's team a week after the notification at his office in Loren, Missouri. It was in the lower part of the stadium, not far from the locker rooms. He was middle-aged with graying temples and piercing gray eyes. He was taller than me by half a head.

"I'm Coach Lindermann." He extended his hand. "Glad to meet you."

We exited his office and went out to the pitch where the team was practicing. They stopped when we approached.

"Gentlemen, this is Jake Stettler, our new primary goalie. I'm sure you've all heard about his accomplishments. We should have had him on the team earlier, but the owners dragged their feet. Something about death threats. We still need to complete some paperwork, but, you can expect him to start practicing with us in two weeks."

After the team welcomed me, Coach Lindermann and I headed back to his office. There we completed the necessary contracts and he gave me a copy of the practice and game schedules. It would mean a lot of traveling because they did a lot of their practice, and played most of their games, in Florida. When we were done, he walked me to my rental car.

"How long will you be staying in town?" he asked.

"Just today. I have a flight back to Las Vegas tomorrow, right after lunch."

He nodded. "You have the schedules. See you when you get back."

We shook hands and I drove back to my hotel.

I spent the rest of the afternoon thinking about how things were working out for me. If there were people who had never heard of me, they soon would. I promised myself I'd take the team all the way to the World Cup Finals. We would win that too. *Don't get too cocky. You'll be playing against the best in the world.*

As it worked out, the national team practiced and played during my winter break, and I was able to spend time practicing with them. I was glad to learn the team would be moving to Orlando, Florida where the weather was warmer. It was also where we would play most of our games against other teams in the CONCACAF (Confederation of North Central American and Caribbean Association Football) for the Nations Cup or, the Gold Cup. They were the equivalent to the European Nations Cup and Champions League. The winners of these tournaments would play in the World Cup. At present, there were thirty-two teams from around the world.

***

A few of my team members had doubts about my abilities. Coach Lindermann set up a practice session for penalty kicks, not one ball got past me. That made believers out of them.

Aaron Sondberg, one of the strikers, asked "How do you move so fast? Do you have some kind of magical powers?"

I laughed. "No. I just have the ability to know where the ball is at all times and can move quickly to catch or deflect it."

The whole team was impressed. Harry Adams, another striker, said, "With your talents we should be able to win the World Cup. Nobody can beat us if they can't score against us."

***

I had been living in hotels and motels during my time with the national team. Although I was making good money, it was starting to get expensive, especially with the flights to and from the practice fields. While the team was at home, it was our responsibility to take care of our own expenses. That's why we were paid. During away games, the owners took care of our hotel and transportation costs. Meals were usually include in the hotel costs. Therefore, I was surprised when Louis Westerfield, a mid-fielder, offered me a solution.

"Hey, Jake," he said one day. "I have houses in Loren and here in Orlando. Each has a spare bedroom I'll rent you for fifty bucks a week. We can work out arrangements for the food with the other guys."

"Wow! That sounds great! How soon can I move in?"

He laughed. "Get with me after practice and I'll show you the room."

I asked, "Will it be a flat two hundred a month?"

"No. If you're not there, you don't pay. I know you'll still be playing for the Franklin Thunder every now and again. You won't have to pay while you're with them."

We shook hands on the deal.

After practice, we went to his house. The room was on the second floor. It had a twin bed and there was a bathroom and toilet accessible to my room and another one on the floor below. He couldn't have made me happier.

I met with the two other guys renting from him. We sat around and made plans for who would supply food and who would cook when we were there. These plans would carry over to Loren when we were there. Those guys also rented rooms from Louis there.

How convenient, I thought.

***

It would be a month before our next game. This gave me time to fly back to Franklin to help the team get ready for their next game. The day after I got back, I had two visitors. They showed FBI credentials at the door.

When we were comfortable in our living room, they introduced themselves. "I'm Agent Townsend," the one said. "This is Agent Clay." Agent Townsend had a folder with him.

Of course, they both wore dark suits with white shirts and dark ties. I was surprised their ties didn't match.

Townsend opened the folder in his lap said, "Mr. Stettler, I'm sure you've heard about the attack on the Portland soccer team last spring."

"Yes, I heard that some of the members were killed."

"Where were you during that time?" he asked.

I blinked several times, then stared at them as if in disbelief. I shook my head. "Let me think." I paused with my hand on my chin. "You say it happened in the Spring?"

They both nodded.

"As I remember, I was here in Franklin during that time."

They both looked hard at me.

Clay said, "We checked, Mr. Stettler. You took time off and no one in Franklin can confirm your presence in the city for three weeks during that time. Can you explain your whereabouts?"

I sighed and hung my head. "I was having emotional problems and needed to get away. I rented a room in a motel on the other side of town and kind of hibernated. I didn't want anyone to now I was having problems. That's why I told my coach I was spending time with my father and I told my father I would be taking a break from games and practice but would still be in Franklin."

They both stared at me hard for what seemed like forever.

"What was the name of the motel?" Townsend asked.

I told them. They both looked at each other and nodded.

"We'll check it out," Clay said.

Townsend turned a page in his folder, his gray eyes piercing me. "Where were you during the second week of July last year?"

I rubbed my chin. "As far as I can remember, we had an away game that week in Minnesota. May I ask why?"

"Several of the Bakersfield team were killed during that time. The method of their demise is consistent with murders in other states, including this one."

I sat up straight. "What has that got to do with me?"

Clay said, "It seems wherever you go, death follows. I suppose you haven't noticed that, have you?"

I shook my head. "I try not to listen to the news. I have to concentrate on my skills and don't need the distraction."

They both nodded.

Townsend closed his folder and they both stood up.

I stood too.

"We will be in touch with you from time to time to ask about your whereabouts during certain periods." He handed me a business card. "Expect to hear from us soon."

I took the card and watched them leave. *Dad said they were getting close. I'll have to be more than careful.*

***

Things were going exceptionally good for me. I wasn't receiving any threats and I wasn't getting hungry. Or so I thought. I went to bed one night thinking it had been almost four months since my last feed. I felt I was getting it under control.

When I awoke the next morning with severe stomach cramps and a dry mouth, I knew I had to feed.

After getting dressed and having breakfast, which didn't ease my hunger pangs, I left the house and started driving, not aware of where I was going. A pinging in my head started very low and slowly increased in volume. It was not very loud but, bordered on distracting. I pulled into a public parking lot and waited for it to subside. It didn't.

When I started driving again, I noticed a black sedan pull out not far behind me. I made several random turns to see if it would follow. It did.

I could see two men in the other sedan. I guessed they were the FBI agents. I was about to make plans for them when they turned a corner and disappeared. The pinging stopped. *Maybe I wasn't who they thought I was and broke off the surveillance.*

I continued driving and the pinging started again. It sounded like a truck reversing, but at half speed. This time my tail was a blue sedan with two men inside. After ten minutes, they broke off and the pinging subsided. *I guess they realize I've spotted them. I'm sure another car will take up the tailing.* I was right. This time it was a large, green pickup truck. *No pinging. Hm.*

I headed out of town sure they would follow. They did.

When we were about ten miles out of town, the pickup increased its speed and got really close. No matter how fast I drove, it was right with me.

Then came the bump. *They hit me!* I couldn't go any faster and they bumped me again. *These guys are NOT with the FBI. I need to do something before they run me off the road.* Since I couldn't outrun them, I put on my emergency flashers on and started to slow down. They did too.

I stopped and waited. Nothing happened. *You want to play, do you?* I got out of my car and waited.

Four men got out of the vehicle and approached me. I stand tall at five-ten. These guys made me feel small. I think the shortest one was about six-one. As they approached me, I backed up. They all wore leather jackets and had blond crew-cuts. Two were smoking while a third one chewed a toothpick.

When I had my back against my car, they surrounded me. "What can I do for you guys?" I tried to sound brave.

The one with the toothpick said, "We came to warn you to stay away from the school."

I blinked. "I don't know what you're talking about."

"A likely story." One of the smokers said.

The one without anything in his mouth, said, "We've been seeing a car just like this hanging around the school our kids go to. We don't like pedophiles." He took a step closer. "Do you understand?"

I nodded. "I don't like them either. What has pedophiles got to do with me?"

Toothpick said, "We figure you're one. Was there any one kid you had your eyes on, or were you just waiting to catch one alone?"

I shook my head. "I don't have any interest in kids. Especially not the way you think. I find what you're telling me disgusting. I have absolutely no desire to do anything to anybody's kid."

"I suppose you expect us to believe that," Toothpick said.

I figured he was the leader of the group.

He continued, "We're going to convince you to stay away from the school."

They started to move in on me. I closed my eyes and pictured them wrapped in spider webbing.

A few seconds after they started yelling and screaming, I opened my eyes. They were struggling to unravel themselves from the webbing. I nodded and waited.

When they were all sufficiently immobilized, I bent down and fed on them, one by one, remembering not to break their jaws.

When I was done, I leaned against my car, basking in the wonderful feeling of satisfaction. It didn't take long to realize I couldn't stay there. I opened the back doors of the pickup and, after disentangling them from the webbing, I put two of the dead bodies inside. I piled the other two in the front.

I would be good for at least three months, I hoped. I got back in my car, turned around and started to drive home.

Oh shit! We're just about ten miles from Franklin. I can't leave them there like that. It's too close to home. The FBI will know for sure it's me. I shut the engine off, put my hands on the wheel and leaned my head against my hands. *What to do? What to do?*

After a few minutes, I realized I had to somehow get rid of the vehicle. I got out of my car and went back to the pickup. Not really knowing what to do next, I made sure they were all seated with their seatbelts on. When done, I stepped back and waited for a solution to come to me. After a couple of minutes, I knew what I would do.

To my right, I could see the outskirts of Franklin. To my left, there was nothing but desert. I got in and sat in the lap of the driver. I started the vehicle and drove toward the desert. When we were moving at a steady pace, I engaged the cruise control. I hoped it would work below the recommended thirty-five miles-per-hour. It did. After a few seconds, I opened the door and stood on the running board. When I was sure all was good, I jumped off. I had to run like the Devil was after me to keep from falling and tumbling.

When I had gotten control of myself, I stopped and watched the green monster rumble slowly over the desert. *Keep going, please. Don't stop until you run out of gas, please.* It kept going. Then suddenly, it disappeared. *What the hell!* I blinked. *They must have run off a cliff. I didn't know there was one there.* I ran to the edge of the cliff and saw the vehicle at the bottom of a crevice. As I watched, it burst into flames, emitting black smoke. The black smoke continued to rise. I looked up at it and thought of Aladdin and the magic lamp. I almost expected a Genii to appear out of the smoke. Nothing of the sort happened. The smoke kept rising until it caught a breeze high up and started to dissipate.

Time to get out of here. I returned to my car, got in and drove home knowing I would be safe, for a little while, anyway. When I stopped in front of my house, I thought about the first two cars that followed me. *Were they FBI and why did they break off? Will they follow me again? I'm pretty sure they will. I'll just have to wait and see what happens next.*

***

The next day, I'd barely settled down after my evening meal when the doorbell rang. It was agents Townsend and Clay.

After I let them in, we went in the living room. They sat on the couch and I sat in a chair.

"What is it this time?" I asked.

Townsend asked, "Where did you go yesterday?"

I shrugged. "Just for a drive. I felt restless and needed to get out of the house. Why?"

He ignored the question. "I thought your team's owners had provided you with bodyguards."

"Since I haven't received any threats lately, we agreed they were no longer needed."

"Who is we?"

"The owners, Coach Spears and me. Is there a problem?"

Townsend gave me a hard look. "Not that I'm aware of."

I wondered if Clay knew how to talk. "Then why the visit and the questions?"

"Now that you've been selected for the Men's National Team, your safety is important."

I stared at the two men. "Is it normal for the FBI to get involved with soccer team members?"

He shook his head. "Not normally, but you're a special case because of your abilities."

I leaned back in the chair. "Wow! I'm a National Treasure! I'll be famous."

Both of their faces turned sour.

I moved forward. "Just what is the purpose of your visit?" *I was sure it wasn't to tell me I lost their tail.*

Townsend cleared his throat. "No one knew where you were. We just wanted to make sure you were safe."

I cocked my head to one side. "Was someone looking for me?"

The men started to fidget. "Um, not really. We decided to check on you, and you weren't here."

I nodded. "As I said before, I just went for a drive. Should I find a way to let you know when I leave the house and where I'm going?"

Townsend cleared his throat. "I don't think that will be necessary."

"By the way, what happened to the third car? After the black and blue sedans, I expected another car to follow me."

His mouth popped wide open. Clay was looking at his hands.

He coughed into his hand. "Someone hit the car and left the scene." Townend blinked several times. "How did you know you were being followed?"

"I noticed the vehicles making the same turns I did. Even though they were four cars back, after a while it was pretty obvious."

"Did anyone else follow you?"

"No. I drove for a while and wound up out of town. After a few miles, I turned around and came back home."

He nodded. "I see."

I stood. "Now, if you don't mind, I need to get some sleep. I have practice early in the morning."

They both looked at their watches, stood, nodded and headed for the door. Neither looked back as they went out the door, leaving it wide open.

CHAPTER TWENTY

As we neared the end of the season, everyone on the team knew we'd be in the regional finals. In first place, of course. We just had to wait to see who we would be playing.

As it turned out, the other three teams in the finals were the LA Dolphins, the Phoenix Arrows, and the Salt Lake Bison.

We faced Salt Lake first and bet them 3-0. LA bet Phoenix 2-1. That meant we would play LA for the finals. Piece of cake. We had beaten them before and would again.

Coach Thorne of LA wasn't happy with the outcome. He was a bald man who stood six-feet-one. When he confronted Coach Spears, we expected to see him pounding Spears into the ground. At least, that's what we got from the look on his face.

He surprised everyone when he shook hands with Spears and wished him good luck.

***

The game was very spirited with a few minor fouls by both sides.

We managed to score twice against them. We could see that Thorne was not pleased.

154

During half-time, I heard him tell Spears that he expected his team to lose to us because of me. He didn't looked forward to facing any of the teams from the east.

"Why is that?" Spears asked. "With the team we have, especially with Jake as goalie, we are virtually unbeatable."

Thorne smiled. "We'll just have to wait and see."

Spears aid, "Could you be a little more explicit?"

Still smiling, Thorne said, "Most of the East coast teams have hired coaches and managers from Europe. Their style of play is different from ours. Every time we played them we got trounced. It was 8-0 the last time we played New York and 9-0 when we played Philly. Most of the coaches here on the west coast have been studying their manner of play, but it doesn't seem to help. We still get beat." He paused and sighed. "I wish you good luck. I really do." He turned and walked away.

***

We got the news later that we were to face the NY Rebels. We were to play them in Philadelphia, the City of Brotherly Love. What a laugh. As the bus took us from the airport to the hotel, we passed streets lined with people. They just stared at us as we drove by, then Coach Spears said, "This feels like we're in a funeral procession."

There were murmurs from a few of the players.

We didn't know what to expect when we got to the hotel. The staff surprised us by going out of their way to make us welcome and comfortable.

"Could be a ruse," Coach Spears said. "They may have something planned for us. Stay alert."

It was hard to relax not knowing if there would be trouble coming.

***

The night in the hotel ended without incident. Friday morning came and we were glad that we got a good night's sleep. At breakfast, the manager asked coach what time the bus should be ready to take us to the stadium for practice.

He checked at his watch. "Can it be ready for ten?"

"Ten it is. I'll inform you when it's here."

Coach nodded as the manager walked away.

After breakfast, Coach gathered us all together. "Something doesn't feel right. Everything is going too smoothly."

We all nodded in assent.

"Anyway, the manager said the bus will be here at ten. Be ready."

We went to our rooms to gather our gear.

***

Coach Spears paced nervously in the lobby when the manager approached him.

He had a concerned look on his face. "Mr. Spears," he said. "The bus is outside waiting. Would you be so kind as to usher your team on board as soon as so you can. The lobby will get really crowded in a few minutes, and it will be more difficult for your players to get through. We wouldn't want you to be late."

"No problem." He turned to me. "Jake, get the guys moving."

"Will do, Coach."

I started the team moving as fast as I could. I let them know we had to clear the entrance as soon as possible.

They all headed out the entrance and were all on the bus in record time. I'd never seen them move so fast.

The manager looked at Coach and me. "I'm impressed. Maybe I should hire you to get tour busses loaded."

We all laughed.

***

As the bus wound its way through the streets to the stadium, we noticed a lack of people on the sidewalks.

"Hey, Coach," Nat called. "Is there something going on that we don't know about? Philly is a pretty big city. I wouldn't have thought the streets would be so empty."

Spears shrugged. "It's Friday. People have to work."

We were all quiet as the bus made its way through what seemed like a deserted town.

At the stadium the Rebels' bus was in the parking lot along with two private cars. I figured they belonged to the coach and manager.

On the pitch, Coach Spears met Coach Ruggeri and Randy Daniels, the team captain.

We all shook hands.

"So, you're the famous Jake Stettler."

"That's me."

He smiled. "I understand you were tested for drugs last week and the tests came out negative."

I nodded. "I don't have any use for drugs. I frown on anyone that uses them to enhance their abilities."

He smiled. "Good sentiment." He paused. "Maybe later this evening, the four of us can get together for dinner. I'd like to learn more about you. I'm sure Randy feels the same way. What's your favorite drink?"

"Lemon tea."

"Lemon tea! You said Lemon tea? I would have expected a red wine or something fancy."

"I can't drink alcohol. It makes me sick."

"I see." He rubbed his chin. "There are a few drugs that cause an adverse reaction to alcohol." He looked at me hard.

I sighed. "When I was seven, I took a sip of my Dad's beer. I went into convulsions. Later, when I was fifteen, I had a mouthful of wine, the same thing happened. I haven't had any alcohol since, and I won't. I don't have any desire to put my body through that again."

He nodded. "I'm impressed. Its settled then. Randy and I will pick you guys up at 5:30. Is that okay?"

I nodded.

Spears said, "We'll be ready."

***

Spears and I met in the lobby at five. We plopped down in two easy chairs to wait. We didn't know what type of restaurant we were going to and were unsure of how to dress. I found that we both decided on semi-casual. I dresses in a pair of black slacks with a white shirt and no tie. On top of that I wore my blue blazer, glad I had decided to bring it with me. Coach was wearing a similar outfit with a pair of gray slacks, a peach colored shirt and a black blazer. He wore a gray tie with a gray paisley design.

"We could be over-dressed or under-dressed. What do you

think?" he asked me.

"Your guess is as good as mine. Since it's just the four of us, I think we'll be okay."

"What do you think of this dinner thing?" he sked.

"I don't know yet. I guess we'll just have to wait and see. What can happen in a public restaurant?"

Smiling, he said, "Maybe he'll pay the cook to poison us."

We both laughed. Just as we got control of ourselves, Ruggeri and Randy walked in.

We stood up to meet them.

"Great! You guys are ready," Ruggeri said, turned, and headed for the door.

We piled into his black Cadillac Escalade with heavily tinted windows. It made me wonder if he had something to hide or just liked his privacy.

"I hope you guys like Surf-N-Turf. We're having steak and lobster."

"Sounds good to me," Spears said.

I merely nodded.

It took twenty minutes to get to the restaurant. I didn't recognize the name. "Is this part of a chain?"

"No. It's a stand-alone. Two brothers had an idea and put it to work."

***

The restaurant was busy but, Ruggeri had reserved a table for us. I have to admit, the meal and surroundings were outstanding. It was the first time I had ever had lobster and it was an experience to be remembered. I thought I'd died and gone to heaven. We didn't talk much as we ate. I think the others were like me, wrapped up in the taste of the food.

When most of our meal was finished, Randy asked me about my abilities. "How do you manage to move so fast? You keep balls out of the net that would have gone past any other goalie. Do you have a Fairy Godmother that sprinkled you with magic dust?"

I laughed. "No. I just grew up being able to move really fast. Also, I concentrate on the ball at all times and don't move more than three steps from the goal line. I found the reason some scores are made is because the goalie is too far off his line."

He nodded. "I think you could teach our goalie a few things."

I shrugged and took a bite of steak that seemed to melt in my mouth. My taste buds would never be the same after this meal. I could see Coach Spears was enjoying himself as much as I was.

After the meal, we were back in Coach Ruggeri's vehicle. We were barely underway when I got the pinging in my head. *We're being followed.* I didn't mention anything to the others. If our pursuers were after anyone, it was me. No need to get them involved.

Back at the hotel, we all shook hands and said goodnight. We thanked them for the fantastic meal and the conversation.

"All gloves are off when the starting whistle blows," Ruggeri said. "We're looking to win tomorrow."

"That's good," Spears said. "So are we."

We all shook hands again and Spears and I entered the hotel and headed for our rooms.

***

At three in the morning, I found myself sitting up in bed, wide awake. The pinging wasn't there but the feeling in my gut told me there were police in the area, and they were there for my benefit. It surprised me that the hunger came back. Between the pangs in my stomach from being hunted and the dull throbbing from being hungry, I was very uncomfortable. I didn't think it'd been that long since I'd fed. I knew I wouldn't be able to get back to sleep but, what to do? I lay back and tried to think of somehow getting them off my trail. I needed to feed. It would be difficult. My room was on the fourth floor of the hotel. If I left by the door, they would be sure to know and follow me. I eased out of, put on my black pants and hoodie, and went to the French doors. They opened onto a balcony that would only hold two people. I was surprised when the doors didn't squeak or make any noise when I opened them. *They must oil the hinges and locks regularly.*

I stepped onto the balcony and closed the doors behind me. There was no drainpipe I could climb down and the room faced the street. No matter how I got down, I would be sure to be seen. There were balconies to the right and left of me. They presented the same problem.

I looked up and decided to try the balcony above. Using my webbing, I climbed up and found the door locked. Sixth floor, here I come.

On the sixth floor, the balcony door was unlocked. I eased it open and was accosted with loud snores. *With noise like that, he must be sleeping alone.* I approached the bed and was surprised to find a lone woman there. I shook my head, amazed. *No time to ponder this anomaly.* I headed for the door, unlocked it and eased my way out. *I'll have to be back before she wakes up.*

I decided not to take the elevator. I hoped I avoided the cameras in the hall.

On the ground floor, the door opened to the lobby, away from the check-in desk. There were pillars partially blocking my view of the lobby. I looked around for a side door and found one. It opened onto an alley. I wasn't far from the street. With my hands in my pockets and my hood up, I sauntered out to the street. I walked three blocks, then turned a corner. The street was deserted. I kept walking for several blocks. Not finding anyone, I turned around and headed back in the direction of the hotel, then I got lucky. A few blocks later, a man stepped out of the shadows brandishing a knife, and said, "Your money or your life."

I smiled with relief.

He looked at me quizzically. "What's so funny?"

"I don't have my wallet with me, but I'll take your life. That's if you don't mind."

He tilted his head to one side. "Are you drunk or stupid or what?"

"Neither. Just hungry."

Before he could say another word, I hit him in the throat. As he was collapsing, he dropped his knife. I caught him and lowered him to the ground. Since his mouth was open, I had no problem satisfying my need. *Don't break the jaw!* When I was done, I pulled him into the shadows. I rested a few minutes, then headed back to the hotel. To my chagrin, I found the side door could only be opened from the inside. *DAMN! Why didn't I notice that before?*

This meant I would have to chance being seen when I entered the lobby from the street. I stood outside for a few moments. Girding up my courage, I pushed the hood back on my jacket and entered the hotel. Walking straight to the elevators, I didn't look at anyone and hoped no one would pay too much attention to me. At the elevators, I waited for someone to call and ask me who I was and where I was going. No one did. When the elevator came, I took it to the sixth floor and reentered the room with the loud snorer. The woman was still sawing logs, sounding like a buzz saw. I didn't think anyone could snore so loudly. I was surprised she didn't wake herself up.

As I was about to enter the balcony, she stopped snoring and coughed several times. *Please don't wake up yet!*

She didn't. She snorted a few times, then continued her raucous noise. I was glad when I was out of the room. I had no further problems getting back to my room and into bed. I sighed as I lay down. The sharp pangs of being under observance were back but, I didn't care. I'd accomplished my goal. I was content and sated. Tomorrow would be the big game. I let myself drift off to sleep.

***

The next morning, chatter dominated breakfast about a man was found dead not far from the hotel. The police didn't reveal how he was killed. I listened to the many theories around the table.

When asked what I thought, I said, "I have a game to think about. Can't be worried about some unknown man being killed on the streets of Philly. Let the cops worry about him. That's what they get paid for."

Kyle looked at me with a creased brow. His eyes narrowed into slits. "Get much sleep last night?"

"As a matter of fact, I slept like a log. I felt really refreshed when I woke up this morning." I flashed my best smile.

A few minutes later, we were on the bus heading for the stadium, we passed crowds with flags and banners chanting for the Rebels.

Mike asked, "I wonder if we have any supporters here?" His face scrunched in dismay.

"Probably only a few brave souls," Tom said. "People around here would probably get tarred and feathered if they showed support for us."

"I don't think it would be that bad," said Coach.

Just then, we pulled into the stadium parking lot. A heavy police presence guarded the doors to the locker rooms.

The bus driver didn't open the doors until a uniformed policeman appeared. He waited for the cop to nod and then the driver opened the door.

The police formed a corridor to the building. We walked down it and were glad when we arrived safely. We could hear the crowd chanting and playing instruments. Mostly drums that continued a steady beat, almost matching our steps as we walked into the locker rooms. I felt like we were going to our doom instead of getting ready for a soccer game. I wondered if any of the other guys felt the same way.

After we'd dressed, we went out to the pitch to warm up and saw more banners and flags for the Rebels scattered all over the stadium.

Coach scanned the array. "I guess our supporters are afraid to show themselves."

I nodded. "The way this crowd is acting, I don't blame them."

After ten minutes, we went back to the locker room to await for the official start of the game.

When the call came, we filed out of the room and walked down the hall. We stood side-by-side with the Rebels.

"One of them said," 'Good luck, guys.'" They all laughed.

We didn't.

CHAPTER TWENTY-ONE

The game was more than a little spirited. There was a lot of shoulder shoves and accidental stepping on toes in addition to shirt pulling. A couple of our guys almost lost their shorts. In spite of their efforts, we were ahead 2-0 at half-time.

Needless to say, the fans were not happy. I thought we'd get booed off the field.

None of the Rebels spoke to us on the way to the locker room. We didn't mind. We were used to it.

Coach Spears didn't say a word as we waited for the second half to start. Of course, we were all talking about the plays we'd made. Several of the guys even made mention of some of my saves. I took it in stride. It was my role in the game.

On the way back out to the field, one of the Rebels stopped me. "Hey, man. Can we score just once? You guys have the game won. It would make the fans a lot less antagonistic."

I shook my head. "Sorry, not in my nature. I couldn't let the ball by even if I tried."

He looked at me hard. "Understood."

I wondered if he did.

***

About five minutes into the second half, the Rebels managed to get the ball into our penalty zone. I was ready.

When the ball came my way, I reached out to grab it and got an elbow in my stomach for the effort. Of course, the ref didn't see it. We were lucky. Al was close enough to divert the ball out of the net. Mike headed it out of bounds. They asked me if we should tell the ref.

"What for? He didn't see it and wouldn't believe us. They're supposed to be impartial, but if he didn't see it and the line refs didn't see it, it didn't happen."

They nodded.

"I guess you're right," Al said.

We got ready for the corner kick.

When it came, I knew one of their strikers would try to head it in. I was ready.

The ball made a long arch past the net. Their striker was there. He jumped, met it and sent it toward the net. I couldn't stop it, but only had to stick out my hand to direct it over the net.

He looked at me with disbelief written on his face.

When we got ready for the next corner, he came to me and said, "You're probably the only person in the world that could do that."

I shrugged. "Could be."

When the next ball came, my guys were there to block it and send it upfield.

Both teams made a mad dash to gain control of the ball. My guys won and we scored again. The crowd was quiet.

I figured we were in trouble and would probably have a tough time getting back to the hotel.

***

After the game was over and the trophy awarded, we stayed on the field to celebrate. The Rebels congratulated us and most of them shook our hands. Coach Ruggeri also shook the hands of every member of our team. Most of the Rebels did too.

When Loren came to shake my hand, I said, "No hard feelings, I hope. You guys had a good run."

"Yeah, we did. This is only the second time in the last six years that we've lost. You guys are the only team to beat us in the finals. Congrats."

I shook his hand. "Thanks. Good luck to you guys. If things go like I think they will, we'll be doing this again next year."

He laughed. "At least I'd know what to expect. Have a safe trip home."

"You too." We shook hands again then headed to the locker rooms.

When I got there my team was dancing and singing. The police in the halls only smiled.

***

We started the trip back to the hotel celebrating but the deserted streets changed our attitudes. I could almost hear each guy wonder what would happen at the hotel tonight and on the way to the airport tomorrow, their faces lined with worry.

I prayed the hotel staff would be as good to us as they were when we first arrived. The slow pinging in my head told me I was being followed. *Are you here to keep me safe or catch me in the act?* I shrugged and welcomed the escort.

I had nothing to worry about. Several police cars stood in front of the hotel. Inside were almost as many uniforms as the number of our team. We were all escorted to our rooms. I'm sure the other guys felt as safe as I did.

We stayed up and talked for some time. Finally, I asked, "Are you guys afraid to go to sleep?"

They all nodded.

I smiled. "Don't worry. We're being adequately guarded. I don't think anything will happen to us tonight. With all the blue uniforms around, anybody would be stupid to try anything. Go to sleep. Tomorrow is another day." I crawled under my covers and relaxed. I didn't let the pain in my stomach bother me. I wasn't going anywhere tonight, anyway.

***

The next morning was uneventful. We ate breakfast and prepared to take the bus to the airport. Half-again as many blue uniforms around us as we ate and our guys relaxed. I didn't feel the dull pain in my gut.

When we had all eaten, we strolled back to our rooms to collect our gear. I was amazed when the cops stayed in the lobby. I was surprised again when I saw uniforms and men in suits on our floor. *Things must really be bad to warrant all this protection.*

On the way to the airport, some of the streets were lined with people. They just stood on the sidewalk and watched the bus go by. I guess the motorcycles in front with flashing lights and the vehicles behind us let the people know safe passage was expected.

During the flight, the trophy got passed around so many times I thought the engraving would be rubbed out.

The usual crowd waited for us as we disembarked. How they were allowed on the tarmac was beyond me. Then I saw the mayor. *His doing, I bet.*

An open limo led our bus into town. Again, they had decorated the stadium and prepared tables held food for us. They even had the high school band play.

Since we arrived before noon, the celebration lasted for several hours. It was starting to get dark when the mayor called for an end. It was just as well. We had almost run out of food. Plus, everyone was getting tired.

When it was over, being worn out from overeating and the long flight, I happily found my trusty Beetle and made it home. Although it was still early evening, I stretched out on my bed.

I must have dozed off because I woke up to a dark bedroom. Getting up, I made myself a cup of lemon tea. Holding it, I went to the living room and turned on the TV. According to the newscaster, the police were still puzzled by the death of the man in Philly. I was glad I remembered not to break his jaw and wondered if they'd found his knife.

***

The next morning, I went to the local grocery store to get a few items. In the check-out line, as I put my items on the belt, the cashier said, "Did you find everything, Mr. Stettler?"

It surprised me that she knew who I was. "Yes, I did. Thank you,

166

Marla." I cheated. I read her nametag. "How did you know my name?"

"You're Jake Stettler, the goalie for the Franklin Thunder. The whole town knows who you are." Her warm smile and her brown eyes shone as she spoke. She stood about six inches shorter than I was and wore her black hair in a ponytail.

"Are you familiar with the game?" I asked.

"Yes, I am. My father was a midfielder for Real Madrid before he retired. Football was his life. He came to the US to coach high school teams. That's what he's doing now. We could have stayed in Spain but the money is better here. We live in Franklin."

The man in the line behind me said, "Get her number and move on. Some of us want to get home."

We both smiled. She wrote her number on my receipt and I took my groceries and moved on. I waved to her before I left the store.

***

I called my dad later that day and told him I'd be saying in Franklin an extra week. He didn't mind, as long as I came to Milton for the holidays. I said I'd be there.

I guess I should have told him I was staying on so I could get to know Marla a little better. I knew a week wasn't much but, it was at least a start.

Two days later, I went back to the store for a few items that I didn't need. They were just an excuse to revisit the store to see Marla.

When she saw me, she lit up like a Christmas tree. I have to admit, I was more than pleased to see her again.

"Jake. Stettler. Good to see you again."

"It's just Jake." I cleared my throat. "Are you free Friday night?"

She batted her eyes. "What did you have in mind, just Jake?"

I swallowed hard. "I thought we could take in a movie and have dinner."

"You'll have to come by the house to pick me up. My parents will want to meet you, so you'll have to come early. Since you are who you are, my dad will have no objection to you. I'll be ready by five on Friday. We can decide on which movie during dinner."

I stood with my mouth open, blinking. It was as if she had expected me to ask her out on a date. "Right. Five on Friday. I guess you'd better give me your address."

She handed me a slip of paper. It had her address and phone number on it. "Just in case you forgot the number." She handed me another slip of paper and a pen. "Your number. In case you're late." She shook her head. "No. I won't be calling to cancel."

While I wrote my address and phone number on the paper, she rang up my purchases.

"Do you do your own cleaning and cooking?" she asked over her shoulder.

I wondered if I was mistaken. Maybe she only wanted to work for me. Or, maybe, she might think I was married or had a girlfriend. "Don't have much choice. I live alone."

"Are you a good cook?"

"I haven't killed me yet."

We both laughed.

"I guess I'll let you cook me a meal one day."

"I think I'd like that. Is there anything you prefer?"

She nodded. "As long as it's fish, fowl or meat and has at least two or three vegetables or a salad to go with it."

I laughed. "I think I can handle that. When I get back before the start of next season, I'll see if I can please you."

"That would be nice. Gives me something to look forward to."

A voice behind me said, "You can make the marriage plans during dinner. In the meantime, can you speed it up?"

I turned to the man behind me. "Sorry, sir." I picked up my bag and moved toward the door. "See you Friday."

She waved.

***

That Friday, I showed up at her house at a little before five. She answered the door the second after I rang the bell.

"You'll have to come in and meet my parents."

"Of course." I entered and she guided me to the living room.

A middle-aged couple stood up and approached me.

"So, you are Jake Stettler, the famous goalie," the man said. He was the same height as me but had gray hair and a gray goatee.

The woman, slightly plump, and wore a one-piece flowered dress. Her eyes moved between me and Marla.

I shook hands with Mr. Santo-Dominguez. Mrs. Santo-Dominguez whispered something to her husband. He looked at her and smiled.

"How long have you been playing *futbol?*" he asked.

"Three years," I answered.

He grinned ear-to-ear. "I thought you call it soccer over here."

"We do," I said. "That's only because we already have a game by that name. I don't think many people here would be able to tell the difference between football and *futbol.* To add to the confusion, the Germans call it Fussball and the English call it football. It can be confusing."

He nodded. Then he turned to his wife, he said, "I like this young man."

She smiled.

Marla touched my arm to get my attention. "Ready to go?"

I nodded. "Nice to meet you both." I held out my hand and Mr. Santo-Dominguez clasped mine in a warm but tight handshake.

"You must come for dinner," Mrs. Santo-Dominguez said.

"I'll look forward to that." I nodded and we left.

"My dad likes you. You said all the right things."

"I didn't really say much."

She just smiled.

I opened the car door for her.

"Where are we going," she asked.

"I thought Applebee's would be nice. Have you eaten there before?"

"Oh, I love that place, especially their two-for twenty. My mom and dad almost always get that when we eat there. Sometimes I share mom's portion."

"I wouldn't take you there if it wasn't."

***

In the parking lot, I finally looked at her and the way she was dressed. She had on a pink blouse with a square neckline and elbow length sleeves. He skirt was full and swished when she walked. *A country girl if ever I saw one.*

It was the first time I'd worn a tie and jacket since the Christmas party in Milton. I hoped I wouldn't choke myself while I ate.

I suggested the Two-for-Twenty-Five with the spinach dip.

She thought the idea neat. "I'll have to remember this when we have our girls-night-out."

"I'm sure they'll enjoy it."

After the meal, we headed to the theater. We stood in the lobby and looked at the posters, trying to decide what to watch.

"Your choice." I said.

She looked at me and smiled.

My heart thumped. My breaths became short. *And I thought she was only beautiful.*

She decided on a *Jack Reacher* film. "I like thrillers," she said, flashing that warm, lovely smile.

I decided that she could have anything she wanted, as long as it was within my power. *Am I falling in love? Except for my need to feed, it wouldn't be a problem. Would she understand if I told her? Something to think about later.* I bought the tickets and asked if she wanted anything from the concession stand.

She laughed. "After that wonderful meal, how can you even think about eating more?"

I grinned. "Dessert?"

She laughed again and it was like music. "No thanks. I don't think I could hold anymore."

Wow! This woman is fantastic! I think I'm going to be seeing a lot of her.

***

During the show, she reached over and took my hand, her palm felt soft and warm. Our fingers interlaced. Her touch distracted me from the movie. She kept me on track with squeezes and the occasional giggle.

When the credits were playing, she put her hand on my arm and said, "Wait."

We sat together and watched the other patrons leave. When we were the last two in the theater, she stood.

When I stood up she put her arms around my neck and kissed me deeply. We were both breathless when the kiss ended.

"I hope you don't mind. I've never been this forward with a guy before. Please don't hold it against me."

It took a few seconds for me to find my voice. "The only thing I envision holding against you is me."

She smiled and kissed me again.

We held hands and exited the theater. Once outside, I put my arm around her waist. She rested her head on my shoulder. When we reached the car, I opened passenger the door. She turned, took me in her arms again and kissed me long and deep.

I was glad when the kiss stopped. I started getting excited. *Not on the first date, Dude.* "I better get you home, while I still can."

She laughed. "You'll have to cook a meal for me next time." Her hand rubbed my arm. "Do you have any wine at home?"

I hoped I could get her back to her house before I did anything stupid. "No, I said, I don't do alcohol."

"I guess I'll bring a bottle of wine so you can get me drunk and take advantage of me." Her smile invited or dared me. I couldn't figure out which.

"I get the feeling I'll be the one being taken advantage of."

She laughed and my heart skipped a beat. "That wouldn't be so bad, would it?"

"I think it would be a wonderful experience." When we pulled up in front of her house, I got out and opened the door for her. Her skirt had shifted and showed her legs half-way up her thighs. A moan escaped my lips.

She rubbed against me when she got out of the car. She breathed into my ear, "Call me soon, Jake Stettler."

She had reached her door by the time I recovered. I hoped her parents wouldn't think less of me for not escorting her to the door.

CHAPTER TWENTY-TWO

I called Marla the next day. "I hope you enjoyed our date."

"I did and I'm looking forward to the next one."

"That's why I'm calling. It looks like it might be some time before I can see you again. I have to fly to Florida tomorrow. We have a friendly game against Mexico on Wednesday. Then, on the following Saturday, we have another friendly game against Venezuela. We'll be playing every Wednesday and Saturday for the next month. All the teams are getting ready for the CONCACAF Gold Cup. It'll keep me pretty busy. I'll call you when I can."

"I'll look forward to your calls and look forward even more to your return. I have my bottle of wine picked out. I just need to know what you're going to cook to go with it."

I swallowed hard. "I'll have to decide that when I get back. In the meantime, I have to concentrate on my skills. I know the upcoming games are friendlies, but they can get pretty rough. We'll all be looking for the other team's weaknesses. If we can beat them in friendlies, we should be able to beat them in a regular game. At least, that's our hope."

"Are the games going to be televised?"

"I'm not sure, but I think they will be."

"Good. I'll look for them on the sports channel. It'll be keen seeing you play."

"Gotta go now. Take care. See you when I get back."

She blew me a kiss. "I'll be waiting. Take care."

***

Coach Lindermann asked if I'd ever seen the Mexicans play.

I had to admit, I hadn't.

"Be prepared for some pretty rough play. That goes for all the South American teams. They take their game more seriously than the Americans and Canadians. To say they want to win at all costs would be an understatement. Be careful out there."

"I will, Coach."

We all hit the pitch and waited for the national anthems to be played. When done, we shook hands with the refs and then the other team.

When Coach Lindermann said they played rough, he wasn't kidding. I thought we'd had rough games before, but they made the previous games seem tame. It surprised me that we weren't awarded penalties for the fouls they committed. At half-time the score stood at 0-0. Coach Lindermann told us they were careful not to commit fouls in the penalty area. He hoped one of them would get careless and we'd be awarded a penalty. He shook his head. "Wishful thinking."

Ten minutes into the second half, I went up to catch the ball and my legs were knocked out from under me. I landed on my back and the ball went into the net. The Mexican fans went ballistic. Fortunately, the ref was right there. He disallowed the goal and carded two of the Mexicans. That meant a penalty kick for us. One of the culprits decided to argue with the ref and got a red card for his efforts.

Coach decided that Arnie would take the penalty. He kicked it high and to the left. The goalie didn't have a chance. We were up 1-0. Of course our fans went berserk. The shouts of "USA, USA, USA" could probably be heard miles away from the stadium.

Coach Lindermann sent in a sub with instructions to be extra careful. It would get nasty. Boy, did it ever.

One of the Mexicans accidently bumped into the ref and

distracted him just enough to give his teammates time to take Arnie out. Since the ref didn't see what happened, he could only call for the trainer. Arnie had to be carried off the field on a stretcher. Of course the linesmen didn't see what happened either.

Without a doubt, these guys were slick. When I had the chance, I told my guys to give as good as they got but be careful. They got the message, and so did the Mexicans. They started complaining to the ref about the way we were playing. I guess they were upset that we were just as rough as they were.

When the ref didn't do anything, things got really bad.

Louis had the ball and as he moved downfield, a Mexican ran up to him and hit him with his shoulder. It caught Louis off guard and he went down. The Mexican started to run off with the ball but the ref stopped him. Another red card. That meant they were playing with only eight men on the field. It didn't make it easy but allowed us to score another goal. We were glad when five minutes later, the ref blew the whistle, ending the game. They congratulated us individually, shaking hands and, in some cases, giving hugs.

Their goalie came up to me and I could see he wanted to talk. "Hey, man. How the hell do you move so fast. We had to put two men on you to take you down so you wouldn't get the ball. Too bad they got caught. What the hell are you?"

"I'm just a guy who is quick on his feet. I've always had that ability. I was born with it."

He shook his head. "The rest of the league is going to go berserk when they run up against you. Good luck and take care."

"Thanks, I will." We hugged and went our separate ways.

***

Before the next game, we got two new guys. A German named Hans Stichler took Arnie's place as striker. The other, a black guy named Mohammed el Said, an Islam convert, would take Louis's place in mid-field. Although they both held dual citizenships, they were born to American parents overseas.

It pleased Coach Lindermann. Just before practice, he introduced the newbies. "It's going to be a good game on Saturday. These two guys are not unknown in the league. Stichler had played for Bayern Munich in Germany and Said had played for Manchester City in

England. There's not a lot we could teach them, but we can learn a few things from them. The Germans and English play differently from the way we Americans play."

We were concerned that they wouldn't know our moves and would have problems working with us. We shouldn't have worried. They both had played overseas for at least three years and knew all the standard formations used by the teams. By the next game on Saturday, they'd already worked out moves with the other guys.

***

The two new guys made quite a difference in our next game. We were up 3-0 at half-time against Venezuela.

In the locker room, Coach Lindermann said, "I guess Venezuela either heard about or saw the game against Mexico and decided to play it cool. Don't let them give you a false sense of security. Play like you mean it. We're here to win, not be nice to the other team. The object of the exercise is to score enough goals to win. I don't care if it's by two or ten. Score goals. Let them know we are serious. Now, get out there and make me proud."

We went out of the locker room fired up. Although we wanted to shout USA, USA, but we let the spectators do it.

***

We won easily. There were no really bad fouls by either team. We finished 5-0 against them. Their coach told Lindermann, "You guys would be easy without your goalie. Maybe we'll think about a way to neutralize him."

Lindermann said, "I wouldn't even think about it. Anybody that can move that fast would be a threat to his attackers."

The other coach nodded and walked way.

***

We would be against Panama on Wednesday. We heard they weren't as bad as the South Americans, but still could be rough. They were.

We gave as good as we got and beat them 4-0. It would have

been more if not for the "almost" fisticuffs around the penalty box. We were as careful as they were to not commit fouls in the box. No need to give grounds for a penalty kick.

We faced Canada next. They were not as easy as we thought they would be, but we still prevailed against them.

We were about to hit the pitch for the second half when I got cramps in my stomach. *Damn! Why do I need to feed now?*

I told Coach I felt sick and didn't think I could play.

I lay doubled up on a bench.

He looked at me with shaded eyes. He called the trainers to have a look at me.

They found nothing wrong, gave me some antacid and told me to rest.

"Okay." He turned and shouted to our back-up goalie, "Peter! You're in. Go warm up."

Peter Grayson stood four inches taller than me, his body two-inches wider than mine. The other team would have a hard time getting a ball past him. When he got the call, his perfectly even, pearly white teeth shone through his full beard.

He came to me and asked, "You gonna be okay?"

"I think so," I rasped. "I just need to go someplace quiet and rest."

He nodded and followed the team out of the locker room.

Where and how am I going to feed? I lay on the bench and thought about what to do. I decided to change into street clothes and go hunting. It would be precarious because it was still daytime. I could get caught or be seen.

I left the stadium and started to wander. Once I got past the parking lot, the scenery changed. I walked through a neighborhood that looked poor. *It's probably full of transits. I don't think anybody from here would be missed.* As I wandered, I heard laughing and loud voices. I came upon a bunch of Mexicans celebrating their win over Argentina.

When they saw me, one or two recognized me.

"Hey, Dude! You the goalie for the US, right?" He weaved as he spoke.

"Yeah, I am." *Maybe my problem is solved.*

"Whatcha doin out here? Ain't you supposed to be playin?" one of the others slurred.

"I decided to give our other goalie a chance to play." *How will I deal with this bunch?*

One guy put his arm around my shoulder. "That's cool, man." Some of his beer spilled on my shoes. "You wanna drink, amigo?" He waved his beer bottle toward me.

"No thanks. I don't drink." His breath almost gagged me.

He let go of my shoulder, staggered back two steps and waggled his bottle at me. "What the hell, man. How you enjoy yourself you don drink?" Two of the others caught him as he tottered All three almost fell together.

"I have other ways to enjoy myself." *Oh, if they only knew.*

It was then I realized there were four of them. *Oh, well. Go with the flow.*

We wound up going to a bar. The sun didn't do a very good job of brightening up the place. The only lights inside were on the tables along the side and behind the bar, lighting up the mirror.

It got loud but the bartender didn't seem to mind. He fed them drinks as long as they paid.

Since I didn't drink alcohol, the bartender said, "I think I can make something you'll like."

He soon presented me with a dark, fizzy drink with a straw in it. "It's called a Roy Rogers. It's coke and Grenadine. No alcohol."

I tried it. It tasted sweet but nice. "I like it," I told him.

He nodded and went to serve other customers.

Now I could go to a bar with the alcohol imbibers and order something that wouldn't make me look like a teetotaler.

My other problem still persisted. My stomach started growling and I didn't know what to do.

They finally decided for me.

"Back to the hotel," one of them yelled. "We need to be ready for tomorrow."

I got invited.

They managed to get a cab that would hold all of us. They chipped in to pay the fare. I borrowed a sombrero and put it on before we all went up to their room. It hid my face on the way up.

In the room, I waited as they passed out, one by one.

I had to steel myself against the taste of the alcohol. My hunger helped me manage it. I felt much better after I'd finished. I sat on a chair and relaxed for a few minutes. *Time to vacate.*

Instead of taking the elevator, I took the steps to the lobby. *They have cameras in the elevators.* I had managed to keep my face hidden on the way up.

I walked a few blocks from their hotel, then hailed a cab and went to my hotel. In my room, I stripped down, took a shower and climbed into bed. I was supposed to be sick. I slept like a log until the rest of the team came back. By then, I told them I felt much better.

***

The next day we heard about the Mexicans. Of course the FBI had been called in to assist with the investigation.

I spent the rest of the games with the stomach pains from being watched and the pinging in my head from being followed. It helped that they were far enough away from the stadium not to cause me any real discomfort.

As we were preparing to head home, I got a visit from Agents Townsend and Clay in my hotel room.

"Hi, guys. Fancy meeting you here. Are you on vacation?"

Clay looked like he'd been sucking lemons. Townsend coughed into his hand to hide his expression. "It looks like you've been busy, Mr. Stettler."

I blinked. "I don't understand."

"Of course you do. The four Mexicans. How did you manage to subdue all of them before you killed them?"

With my eyes wide open I feigned surprise. "Do you really think I did this? I have problems with one-on-one and you think I took on four? You give me more credit than I deserve."

"We know you killed those guys we're just not able to prove it. Yet. Give us time. All criminals make a mistake sooner or later." His eyes were cold and they gave me shivers.

"So now I'm elevated to criminal. Thanks for that. Should I be proud?"

He snorted. "You can stop being a wise ass and confess your crime."

"Either charge me or leave me alone. Should I file a harassment suit against you?" I tried to be brave.

Townsend chuckled. "That would be an exercise in futility. You'd lose."

Clay stood with his hands in his pockets, rocking on his heels and smiling. His smile mirrored Townsend's in coldness.

I looked at him. "Do you know something he doesn't?"

He stopped smiling long enough to say, "No comment."

"If you gentlemen will excuse me, I have to pack and let the hotel have the room back."

They both nodded and left. I felt lucky we were the only three in the room. Didn't want the team thinking I went around killing people.

***

When we got back to Loren, an article on the news mentioned the four dead Mexicans. It seemed the forensics people managed to get the DNA of the killer and would be comparing it to that found in other unsolved cases. *Uh oh. I could be in trouble.* Then I realized the authorities didn't have my DNA. I supposed it wouldn't be long before Townsend and Clay, or someone else, would be around to collect it. I could think of no excuse for not giving it to them. *Jake Stettler, this could be the end of your career, and possibly your life as a free man.* Only time would tell.

CHAPTER TWENTY-THREE

We'd only been back in Loren a week when Coach Lindermann called a meeting of the Men's National Team. "Gentlemen, the World Cup qualifications begin next month. The groupings have been completed. There are four teams in each group. We only need to beat or tie every team in our group. We can't afford to lose any games. Next comes the knock-out stage. The winners of each group will play each other until only the four top teams will be left. The winners of the knock-out stage will qualify for the World Cup. The groupings for that will be done in December next year. In June the following year, the contest will begin. This time it will be in Russia. We didn't qualify last time. This time we will, partly because we have Jake and partly because you men are going to work your asses off. Jake can only keep the other teams from scoring. You have to . . . Jake, Jake, what's wrong?"

I lay doubled over, my gut in flames. *They're coming for me,* I thought. Then the floor came up and hit me on the head.

***

I woke up in a hospital bed and heard the beeping of the machine that monitored my vitals. I felt something in my hand. I picked it up and looked at it. The call button for the nurse. I pushed the button.

When the nurse came, she said, "You're finally awake. How do you feel?"

My mouth felt dry but, I managed to say, "Like I haven't eaten in a month. Could I get a glass of water then something to eat?"

"Of course." She moved toward the table next to the bed and picked up a glass of water with a straw in it. She held the glass while I put the straw in my mouth and drank. I never knew water could taste so good.

When I'd had enough, I sighed and said, "Thank you. How long have I been here?"

"Since yesterday. We were really worried about you. The doctor didn't know how to treat you since he couldn't find anything wrong. I'll see about getting you some food." She turned to walk away, then stopped and turned back to me. "Some of your teammates are here. Would you like to see them?"

"Yes, I think that would be nice," I whispered with a still hoarse voice.

She smiled and left.

A few minutes later, Coach Lindermann, Hans, Mohammed and Peter entered the room.

"You must be special to get a room all to yourself," Han said, looking around.

"Of course he's special. He's Jake Stettler," Coach Lindermann commented.

We all laughed.

"How do you feel?" Coach asked, his brow creased with concern.

"Other than hungry, I feel good. What happened?"

The other guys stood by the bed with their hands hanging at their sides.

"You passed out. We didn't know why. The doctors said they couldn't find anything wrong. Have you talked to them?" He crosses his arms over his chest.

"No. I've only seen the nurse. I'm sure a doctor will be in soon."

As if on cue, a doctor in the usual white lab coat with a stethoscope around his neck and a nametag on his left lapel entered. He picked up my chart from the end of the bed, glanced at the group, adjusted his glasses, then said, "Mr. Stettler, how do you feel?"

"Other than being hungry, I feel fine."

He harrumphed. "We couldn't find anything to explain why you passed out. Has this occurred before?"

"No, this is the first time."

He then asked a bunch of questions about my childhood illnesses, any current maladies, injuries and other possible symptoms. Afterward, he knew less than when he started.

Of course, I didn't mention the bites by the spider. No need to give anyone a clue about my abilities.

He consulted my chart quietly for a few moments. Then said, "We'll do a few more tests to make sure we haven't missed anything. We plan to release you tomorrow."

That made me glad. It worked for Coach and the other guys too.

The group stayed a few more minutes, then said goodbye. I thought they'd all gone, but Hans came back into the room.

"What's up?" I asked.

He pulled up a chair next to the bed. "I sat next to you when you fell. Before you hit the floor, you said, 'They're coming for me.' Who are they and why would they come for you? Did you do something you don't want us to know about? Are you in some kind of trouble?" He looked both worried and apprehensive.

I had to think fast. "I'm not in any kind of trouble. When I was a kid some friends and I went to play in a cemetery one night. We didn't know that some of the older boys knew about what we'd planned. They dressed up in sheets and chased us. I fell and became too scared to get up. One of the other guys yelled at me to come on. I couldn't move. All I could think of was them coming for me. I must have passed out from fright because I woke up later with the guys standing over me. When they figured I didn't have a real emergency, they sent me home but not before making me promise never to play in the cemetery again. I don't know why that came back to me. Maybe because everything went dark before I fell."

He sat and looked at me for what seem like ages. Then he nodded, got up and said, "See you tomorrow. Will you be able to practice?"

"I think so. The doc didn't mention any restrictions."

He nodded again and left.

I hoped he believed my story and could persuade the other guys.

***

The following day, when I had recovered, Coach Lindermann picked me up after I got discharged. A week later, I thought we were going to my room instead, we stopped at a restaurant and got coffee and tea to go. We next went to his office. He motioned me to sit in the chair across from his desk. He sat on the edge of it sipping his coffee with one arm across his chest. After a few moments, he asked, "Jake, what are you into?"

I shook my head. "I don't know what you mean."

"About two minutes after you passed out, four FBI agents came looking for you."

I feigned ignorance. "The FBI, looking for me?"

He just stared at me.

"I'm sure I don't know why. I haven't done anything illegal. There are no crimes in my past. I've been a law-abiding citizen my whole life. Never even got a Jaywalking ticket." I tried my best to be convincing.

"You must have done something to make them come looking for you. Especially four at one time."

I shook my head. "I'm as confused as you are."

"It must be bad if the FBI, and not the police, came after you." He sipped his coffee as he watched me.

"I really don't know what they might have wanted. Honest." I hope the confused look on my face would convince him. I closed my eyes, then raised my hand. "I do remember them following me and coming by my place while I was in Franklin. The lead agent said now that I'm an asset, I had to be protected. I wonder if it's the same thing?"

He stared at me for a few moments more. He finished his coffee and threw the container into the waste basket. My tea had gotten cold.

He stood up and walked behind his desk. "Go change and hit the pitch."

I nodded and went out the door.

***

The guys were all glad to see me. I couldn't wait to get back in action. It would get my mind off the FBI and my hunger. *The hunger I can deal with. The FBI is another story. I wonder what they have on me? It must be critical if they sent four agents. I guess I can expect them to show up at any time.*

We were busy enough to take my mind off them. On the way back to the house after practice, Louis asked me about the FBI.

"I had two of them visit me in Franklin. It seems I'm important enough for them to take an interest in protecting me. It could be what the guys who showed up after I passed out were there for. I'm surprised they didn't talk to Coach."

"They did but, we don't know what they said since they met in his office. He didn't say anything to you?"

"Only that four of them came looking for me. Maybe they had something else on their minds. I'll try to remember to ask him what went on when I see him tomorrow."

When I saw Coach the next day I asked him about the FBI visit. He said, "They only asked for you and were surprised when they heard you'd passed out. None of them said anything about why they wanted to see you."

***

Since we weren't scheduled to play for next three weeks, I went back to Franklin. I'd only been home an hour when Townsend and Clay showed up.

"Hi, guys. Did you miss me? I didn't miss you. What's on your mind today?" I gave them my cheeriest smile.

Clay sneered.

Townsend said, "Always the wise guy."

I shrugged.

"We have a court order to collect a DNA sample from you." He pulled a folded sheet of paper from his pocket.

"Can I read it?"

"Of course." He handed me the paper, smiling as he did so.

When I finished reading it, I asked him, "What's it for?" Of course I knew.

"We think it's you who's been killing people. The four Mexicans, for instance. Getting your DNA is going to prove it's you." He smiled. "I have to admit, you're the most openly available serial killer

I've ever had to deal with."

My head snapped back I raised my hands to my chest. "Me! A serial killer! You must be joking. How have I been doing these killings?"

His smile narrowed into a thin line again. "Somehow, you've strangled your victims. We don't know with what, but that doesn't matter. We only have to prove it's you."

I sighed. I had to comply. I didn't expect my life to end this way. "Let's do it," I said.

Clay took the sample. Surprise, surprise. And here I thought he was a mere shadow.

When he finished, Townsend said, "We should get the results in about three days. We'll tell the lab it's high priority, everything else has to wait." They got up to leave. "You're not going anywhere for the next week, are you?"

I shook my head. "I'll be here for the next two weeks, then I go back to Loren."

He laughed. "I don't think you'll be making that trip." I could still hear him laughing as they headed for their car.

What the hell am I going to do? I can't run. No matter where I go, they'll know. So much for being famous. I sighed. *I guess I'll have to wait and see what happens.*

After they had been gone a few minutes, I picked up the phone and called my dad. He wasn't surprised when I told him what had happened.

"I saw the request for the court order. I couldn't warn you. I had to let you handle by yourself." He paused for a moment. "What are you going to do if they figure out you are the culprit?"

"I have no idea. I'll just have to wait and see what happens." I took a deep breath. "I'll be on pins and needles until they let me know what they've found."

"Do they have fingerprints?" he asked.

"They didn't mention anything about fingerprints." I shook my head. "It's going to be hell waiting to hear what they found. I hope I can concentrate on my game. The guys and Coach Lindermann will know if something is wrong by the way I play."

"I don't know what advice I can give you. You'll have to try to be normal until they give you the results."

"Easier said than done." I rubbed my forehead. "I'll do what I can to seem normal. That's about all I can do."

"Good luck. I'll be praying for you." He hung up.

I sat with the phone in my hand for what seemed like hours. *What will I do? What can I do? Will they arrest me when they come to tell me the results? What will the team and Coach Spears think of me? What will Marla and her parents think of me? What will Coach Lindermann and those guys think of me? Will I be just a common criminal to them? I can see it now. As they parade me before the TV cameras as a serial killer people will start to hate me. All I've done for the game will mean nothing. I'll be just a common killer in their eyes.* I put the phone down, went to my room and lay across the bed. I didn't want to sleep, only think about what could happen and what I could or would do.

Somehow, in spite of myself, I dozed off.

CHAPTER TWENTY-FOUR

It took longer than I'd expected. My two FBI buddies finally showed up later the following week.

"Where have you guys been? I expected you last week. Did you run into problems?" I hoped I didn't look as nervous as I felt.

Clay immediately went to his favorite seat and glared at me.

Townend looked at me with so much hate in his eyes, it made me flinch. After what seemed like an hour, he finally went into the living room and sat.

I found my seat facing them, my hands hanging between my legs. "Okay, guys, what's going on? Didn't you get the results?"

Townsend grunted then cleared his throat. "Yeah, we got the results. It's not what we expected, that's why it took so long. We had the lab run the tests three times to make sure. Each time it came out the same."

"Well, damn! What did you find?" I tried my best not to yell.

Townsend looked at me with an ugly grin. "Your DNA matched with the killers."

I blanched. *I'm caught.* "Why did it take so long to come to this conclusion?"

He looked like he just swallowed a lemon. "There was only a four percent match. It seems you and eight others are the killers."

I shook my head. "That doesn't make sense. If I'm a match, then I'm a match. What has that got to do with eight other people?"

He sighed. "That's the problem. We ran the test and you and eight others matched that of the killer. Didn't I just say that?"

I sat and looked at him. *This didn't make sense. How could I be a match with so many others. I didn't think DNA worked like that.* I shook my head. "I'm still confused. I thought the only person I would be a match to would be my father"

"Apparently, that's not the case. Many humans have a small match with many other humans. It's just because we are human. Does that make it clearer?"

I thought about this for a moment. "I think so. How much did we match, me and the other eight?"

"Only by four percent." He shook his head. "And here I thought I had you."

"I'm sorry to disappoint you. Maybe you should find another way to identify the killer, or killers."

He picked up his briefcase and put it on his knees. Leaning on it he asked, "Is there something in your life we don't know about? Or maybe, something happened that you haven't disclosed?"

I leaned back. "Like what?"

He waited, looking at me hard. "Something that might have caused an illness or a change in your body?"

"Not that I can remember." I leaned forward. "What's this all about?"

He took a deep breath. "According to your DNA, you're not completely human."

I leaned back, my eyes blinking, my mouth open. "What the hell are you talking about?"

He cleared his throat. "According to the results, you are only 98-percent human. We don't know what the other two percent is. The lab is working on that."

I sat there dumbfounded. I didn't know what to say. *That two percent must be the spider DNA. It would seem my DNA changes to mostly Black Widow spider when I'm feeding. I'm sure the other thing he couldn't mention would be the empty skulls.*

He took a deep breath and shook his head. "Mr. Stettler, it seems we won't be bothering you anymore. We've identified the DNA of the killer or killers. Unfortunately for you, there's only a three percent match. Even one of the techs matched by that much. In other words, the test were nonconclusive. That does not mean we won't be watching you. I have a strong gut feeling that you're involved and I'm going to find out how. You may not see me but, I'll be there. Look over your shoulder every now and again. I won't hide from you."

We were all quiet for what seemed like ages. He tried to stare me down. He lost.

Curious, I asked, "Did you identify the DNA of the killer or killers?"

"Why would that concern you?" I didn't think you could sneer and talk at the same time.

"I'm just curious. I get the feeling it's, he or she, less than human. Am I right?"

This time he stared me down. Without answering, he got up. Clay did too. They headed for the door.

"Wait a minute," I called.

They stopped and turned back toward me.

"You said you won't be bothering me anymore. If that's true, why would you be watching me?"

Townsend smiled. They turned toward the door and Townsend said, "Be seeing you."

After they were gone, I sat still for some time, trying to digest what Townsend had told me. *I wonder if they'll find the spider DNA if they continue checking? Lord, I hope not!*

The only thing I could do now would be to wait and hope for the best. With the qualification for the World Cup coming up, I couldn't let it bother me. At least I could try to keep it out of my mind during the games.

***

When Marla answered the phone, she didn't sound happy to hear from me.

"How long have you been back in town?" The tone of her voice made me shiver.

I could almost hear the icicles shatter as they hit the ground after leaving her mouth.

"If you'd let me take you to dinner, I'll explain." I hoped I didn't sound like whining.

"What about my home cooked meal? When is that going to happen?" Her voice still had enough coldness in it to make me shudder.

"Let me take you to dinner tonight and I'll explain everything. Please?" Now I *was* whining.

After a long pause, she said, "I'll be ready in twenty." The phone went dead.

I sighed with relief. *At least she'll still see me.*

***

Twenty minutes later, I rang her bell.

She must have been standing near the door. She wore black slacks and a pink short-sleeved sweater.

She must really be mad at me. Normally, she would have worn a skirt.

She didn't talk or look at me as I drove to the restaurant. I feared trying to start a conversation.

When I parked in the Red Lobster parking lot, she sat and waited for me to open her door. Inside the restaurant, she waited for me to pull her chair out. *I guess she wants me to be the perfect gentleman.*

We both ordered water to drink with our meal. I asked what she preferred. She didn't even look at her menu. She merely nodded at me. *I guess that means I order for her.*

I ordered the shrimp platter for both of us along with the house salad.

Still the cold shoulder. She didn't even speak during the meal.

Several times I attempted to start a conversation but got cut off by a stern look.

After we'd eaten and the dishes had been cleared, she finally spoke. "Where were you?"

I sighed. "Last week the FBI visited me to get my DNA. It seems they suspect me of being a serial killer. I waited until they had the results before I called you. Apparently, I'm not the culprit."

"Why would they think you are a killer?" Her attitude changed. Her facial expression showed concern.

"It seems I wasn't at home or at practice when the killings occurred."

"Where were you?"

"I guess you also think I'm a killer."

190

She looked at me questionably. "I didn't say that."

I pushed my chair back and stood up. "Let's go. Time I took you home."

She didn't move. "Jake, I'm sorry. I wasn't accusing you."

I leaned forward with my hands on the table and tried not to shout at her. "Thanks for the vote of confidence, but I am not." I pulled her chair away from the table. When she got up, I walked toward the door, not looking to see if she followed.

After unlocking the car doors I looked to see if she had followed. She was. I slid in, started the car and headed for her house.

"Jake. I'm sorry," she said.

"Yeah. Me too." I kept my eyes straight ahead.

I sat with the engine running when we reached her place and waited for her to get out.

"Jake. . . ."

"I'll call you. Maybe."

She sighed and got out. I drove off before she reached her front door.

***

At my place I went to my bedroom and threw myself across the bed. I didn't become upset because she'd questioned me. It was because I had to lie to her. *What if we carry this relationship further? Will I have to let her know or will she find out another way? What will she think of me if and when she does find out? No time to worry about that now. The knock-out round starts Saturday. I have to be mentally and physically ready.* I slid off the bed and looked in the dresser mirror. "Get your shit together, dude. Your reputation and the team's success is on the line." I started packing my gear. I had to leave for Loren in two days.

***

Louis had waited for me and took me to the house. "Have a nice trip?"

"Actually," I said, "I had some stress with my girlfriend and we had an argument. We both were mad when we parted."

"Not to worry, buddy. Those things usually work themselves out. Trust me, you'll be back on good terms before we go to Russia."

191

"You think so?" I doubted it.

He turned to me and smiled. "Been there, done that. Just give it time."

***

We beat every other team in our group with no problems. Now, first and second place winners of each group would meet in the knock-out round. The top three winners would go to Russia. The fourth-place winner would have to play against a team in the Asian Confederation, which included Australia. My team would be counting on me for the win.

I put the FBI and Marla out of my head for the next five weeks. It surprised me that my hunger didn't surface. *Maybe I do have some control over it.*

We made it. We ended at the top of the heap and we were going to Russia. After the game, we all went out to celebrate. Harry asked what wanted to drink. I told him a Roy Rogers. He looked at me kind of funny, then nodded and went to get the drinks.

We were all laughing and having a good time when I sipped my drink. I felt something hit me in the head. When I woke up I lay on the floor on my back. A crowd surrounded me. My right hand hurt. I blinked a few times and asked what happened.

Several of the guys helped me to my feet. "You took a sip of your drink and crushed the glass as you fell."

I nodded. "It had alcohol in it." I rasped.

Everybody looked at Harry. He cringed. "I'm sorry. I didn't think anything like that would happen. I'm really sorry. I didn't know."

He looked like he would start crying.

"You dumb shit. Didn't you believe him when he said he didn't do alcohol?" Hans said.

"Yeah, but I didn't think it would have that effect. I'm sorry. I truly am." Harry stood and twisted his hands, his voice cracking.

Somebody took my hand and looked at it. "We've got to get the glass out."

Someone else wrapped it in a handkerchief. "Better get you to a doctor."

Next thing I knew we were in a car and were speeding to somewhere.

"My head hurts."

"Probably from when you hit the floor. You went down like a felled tree."

I nodded.

We arrived at the ER and a nurse spent the next few minutes pulling glass shards out of my hand. "Don't try to do too much with it for the next three or four days. It needs to heal."

***

Needless to say Coach Lindermann was not happy. It meant I couldn't play. He read Harry the riot act. "I ought to suspend you and eliminate you from the World Cup team. Do you realize what you've done?" He didn't wait for an answer. "Lucky for you we don't have any important games scheduled. Now get the hell out of my sight."

With his head hanging and tears clouding his eyes, Harry left the locker room.

Peter would be goalie until my hand healed. That made him very happy but he would have preferred it hadn't come at my expense.

***

That evening, I realized I hadn't fed for four months. *I thought I'd finally had gotten a handle on it. Now*, I had to feed. I couldn't go out the front door because Louis had turned on the burglar alarm. I decided to go out my window. Being on the second floor didn't present a problem. I used my webbing to get to the ground. A pathway ran between our backyard and the one across the way. It was barely wide enough for a bicycle. I went to the end of the street and turned away from our house. The moon hadn't appeared, which made things good for me. I stated running. After several blocks I slowed down and started walking. The first person to come my way would appease my hunger.

It seemed the whole town slept in their homes. *Doesn't anybody take walks at night?* Ten minutes later, which seemed like forever, a man with a dog walked toward me. The dog wagged its tail as I approached. Suddenly, it started barking and pulled away from the man and ran away. He looked at me with wide eyes.

193

First time that's happened.

"What the hell are you?" the man said, his eyes wide with fright.

I reached for his throat. "Your worst nightmare."

When I'd finished, I leaned against the nearest wall to get myself together. After a minute or two, I dragged his body into the nearest alley. Luckily, it wasn't far.

After resting for a few seconds more, I headed back to the house. Using my webbing again, I reentered my room, undressed and spent the next few hours in a restful, peaceful sleep.

***

Practice the next day bordered on boring. I wasn't used to sitting on the bench watching. Peter played great. He didn't allow any balls to get past him. *Do I have to worry about being replaced?* I didn't think so.

After practice I approached him. "You were really great out there."

He smiled, flashing his white teeth. "I took lessons from you. I tried to play the way you do. It makes a difference compared to how I used to play."

I cocked my head to one side. "Explain," I said.

"I notice you don't go more than three steps from the goal line. It makes defending a lot easier, especially when they come close with the ball."

I nodded. "That makes me feel good. With your size and my strategy, you should be a force to reckon with."

His smile got even wider. He squeezed my shoulder. "Thanks, man. That means a lot coming from you."

After practice, as we were heading out of the stadium I heard whistles and cat calls. *Must be a woman out there. A pretty one by the sounds of it.*

As I exited I could see what the guys were excited about. A woman stood facing the entrance to the hall. She wore a knee-length plain blue skirt and a waist-length gray jacket. *Marla! What's she doing here?*

She ignored the guys and their calls and comments but smiled when she spotted me. She had been standing with her arms across her body. When she saw me, she dropped them, then smiled even more. Although the sun still shone, it seemed the world got brighter.

It made me ecstatic. I walked up to her and put my arms around her.

w seconds to realize what he'd said. "Oh. Okay, thanks."

Marla smiled. "I have a hotel room booked. You're mine until tomorrow when you have to be at practice."

We were still hugging when a taxi blew his horn.

When we were seated, Marla gave him the name of her hotel.

"I have bad news for you," I said, trying to put on my saddest face.

She looked alarmed. "What's wrong?"

"I broke a glass and can't play for a few days. Peter is goalie until I can play again."

"Oh, honey. What happened? Is it serious?" She took my hand and gently held it, noting the bandages.

"Nothing serious. I fell with a glass in my hand and had to go to the ER to get the pieces out. I'll be back to normal in a day or two."

She still held and caressed my hand until we arrived at her hotel.

She had a room on the third floor. We managed to only hold hands in the elevator on the way up.

The room was tastefully furnished with all the normal stuff you find in hotels and motels, a dresser, king-sized bed, a small table with two chairs, a TV and a floor lamp.

The bed had been made, so she pulled back the covers.

I stood and watched her, wondering what I should do next.

Marla took off her jacket and put it on a chair. Underneath she wore a pullover sweater. That came off in one swift movement. *No bra.*

Next came the skirt. in one fell swoop, it hit the floor.

My mouth hung open as she stood before me, naked.

She climbed onto the bed, pulled back the covers and said, "Join me."

I couldn't get out of my clothes fast enough. As I got into the bed, she wrapped her arms around me and kissed me long and deep.

For a few brief moments I worried about holding her too tight. Somewhere, that thought got lost in the bliss.

Later, when we were resting, she said, "You'll have to marry me, Jake Stettler, so I can have your babies."

"Sounds good to me," I said.

She smiled and kissed me, then made love to me.

.

CHAPTER TWENTY-FIVE

Since we didn't have any games scheduled, Marla and I travelled back to Franklin. I decided not to call and let the team know I was back in town. They'd be concerned about my hand. I felt it should be good by Saturday.

I'll just show up and surprise them.

I arrived at the stadium at ten the next morning and saw that the gates were still locked. *I wonder where is everybody?* I decided to wait for a bit to see who would show up. After thirty minutes, nobody showed. I started to get worried.

I used my cell phone to call Coach Spears. His wife answered the phone.

"Jake. I forgot you were away. I guess you didn't hear."

This confused me. "Didn't hear what?"

She sighed. "My husband is still in the hospital. He's off the critical list but they want to keep him a while longer to make sure he's okay."

It took me a few seconds to digest what she'd said. "What happened? How long has he been in the hospital?"

She sniffed. "Eight days now."

I shook my head, unable to wrap my brain around what I'd just heard. *Why is he in the hospital? Did something happen? What about the rest of the team? I wondered why nobody showed up for practice.*

"I think I'd better let him tell you. He knows more about what happened."

I wanted to question her more but decided it would be useless. "Thanks for the info. I'll go see him. What room is he in?"

"He's in room 208. I think the nurses will let you see him even though you're not a family member."

I sighed. "Okay. I'll try to see him today."

"Give him my love."

"Will do."

***

When I got to the hospital, I gave the nurse my name and told her who I'd come to see.

"Yes. I think he's been expecting you. Room 208. Down the hall to the left."

I thanked her and headed to his room.

He appeared to be asleep so I said quietly. "Coach?"

He opened his eyes and smiled. "Jake. Good to see you. How are you?"

"I'm fine. What happened? I waited at the stadium for practice and nobody showed up."

He sighed. "We were attacked. The whole team." He closed his eyes. "Tim, Al, Jason and Mike are dead. Most of the rest of the team are suffering from major injuries. I've got a broken leg, a broken arm and some cracked ribs. They came just after we'd finished practice carrying bats and clubs. We were caught completely by surprise. The two security guards were found bound and gagged in another part of the building."

I sat there in shock, trying to process what he'd just said. Some of the guys dead, others injured? "Who attacked you, when and why?"

"From what the police told us it was a group from New York. They caught some of them, but not all. There's a warrant out for the arrest of their coach. The police think he might have instigated the attack."

I shook my head. "But why? Just because we beat them in the finals? That's ridiculous."

"Be that as it may, it looks like that was the reason. Actually, they were looking for you."

I stared at him open mouthed. "The team was attacked again because of me?"

"That's the way it seems. Some of them asked for you as they were beating us."

I sat there unable to believe some of my teammates had died because of me. I didn't know what to say, much less feel. With my hands hanging between my legs and my head down, I tried to process all I'd been told.

"Jake." His call interrupted my thoughts.

I looked at him, tears starting to form. "I'm responsible for the deaths of some of my team. How am I supposed to live with that?" I sobbed.

He reached for my hand. "You were the cause, but you're not responsible. You didn't harm or kill our guys. They did. Those that were caught will go on trial for murder and aggravated assault. I don't know what they'll do to Coach Ruggeri when they catch up with him."

"I hope they hang him by the balls." I chocked as tears streamed down my face.

"Jake. Let the authorities take care of this. It's too much for you. I know it'll prey on your mind, but don't let it eat you up. We can rebuild the team. It'll take some time but we can do it. Of course I'll need your help." He squeezed my hand to make sure I was paying attention. "Don't try to get revenge on your own. Promise."

"I don't know if I can do that, Coach. I don't know if I can promise." I took a tissue from the box on the stand next to the bed and dried my eyes.

"Jake, I can see you're angry. Let the police and courts take care of them. Don't get yourself in trouble."

I almost gave in to the pleading in his voice. Almost.

"I don't know, Coach. I'll have to think about it." I stood up and turned to leave.

"Jake, please!" he begged.

I shrugged and said, "We'll see. 'Bye coach."

***

On the way back to my apartment, I thought about not only what

I would do, but what I could do. I didn't know how many of them made it back to New York and how many were here in jail. *Could it have been the entire team? I had no way of finding out without going to New York. Even then I couldn't be sure. Of course, Townsend and Clay would be monitoring my moves.*

At home I made myself a lemon tea and sat on the couch, thinking.

Finally, I called my dad. "I guess you've heard about the attack on my team?"

"Yes, I did. We have several of the perpetrators in jail here in Las Vegas. They refused to give the names of the ones who got away. I think we were lucky to get the ones we did. The FBI is handling the New York end of the investigation since the crime was committed across state borders. I have full confidence in their abilities. With Director Grabowski in charge, they'll get the job done. You won't have to worry about taking any action. Coach Ruggeri won't be able to leave the country, even if he uses a fake passport."

"Thanks, Dad, that's very reassuring. I'd like to deal with him personally when they catch him."

"You'd put yourself in jeopardy. I don't think you'd want to do that."

I sighed. "I guess you're right."

"Work with Coach Spears on rebuilding the team. There's still the World Cup to think about too. You'll need to keep your head together for that team."

I smacked my forehead. "You're right again."

"Keep it in mind. Work with Spears and let the FBI do their jobs." He paused. "I have to get back to work. Take care. Love you."

"Love you too, Dad."

***

Sitting at home didn't help me think. I decided to go for a walk. After some time, I found myself in front of a Burger King. I went in and ordered a salad. When I got it, I sat at a table looking at it and thinking. Finally, I picked up the salad and took it home.

Back at the apartment, I made a lemon tea and drank it while eating my salad. *What can I do? How can I get revenge? I couldn't let the attack on my team be handled by someone else. The responsibility belonged to me.*

I had to make them pay. I had respect for the FBI, but the retribution had to meted out by me. The attackers had come for me and taken it out on my team instead. They weren't fair, I won't be either. My primary problem was the FBI. I had to find a way to get around them. I'd wait until I developed a plan. The winter holidays were coming up. I could wait.

***

I went to Milton for Thanksgiving. Mrs. Burns wasn't there. Dad introduced me to Mrs. Alexander. "Mrs. Burns had a family emergency and won't be back until next year. She asked Mrs. Alexander to look after us until she got back."

Mrs. Alexander looked to be in her mid-fifties. A widow with three children - a son twenty-five, a son twenty-three and a daughter twenty-one. Mrs. Alexander wore glasses and had a full head of fluffy, grey hair. I noticed she doted on my dad. He hardly had to ask for anything and he had it.

She was an excellent cook. Her meals rivaled those of Mrs. Burns. I was impressed. She invited us to her house for Thanksgiving dinner. "Might as well eat with us. We'll have plenty. Plus, it'll keep me from having to cook two meals."

Dad looked at me. I shrugged, "Why not?"

"It's settled then," she said. "My place at four. You'll get to meet the kids. I'm sure we'll all get along just fine."

I thought she'd winked but wasn't sure.

***

Her kids welcomed Dad and me as though we were old friends. We shared non-alcoholic punch while the men got acquainted. The women spent their time in the kitchen. We men were restricted to the living room. I didn't mind. Dad didn't either.

When we all sat down at the table, Mrs. Alexander said grace, then we all pitched in, passing plates and bowls around the table. A running conversation ran around the table along with the food. She outdid herself. The meal was super. A large turkey was accompanied by a three-bean casserole, mushroom-flavored stuffing, baked candied yams, and much more than all of us could possible eat.

After we all had eaten our fill, Mrs. Alexander and her daughter chased the guys out of the kitchen, again. When they finally joined us, I could see into the kitchen. It sparkled as if unused.

Mrs. Alexander told Dad, "I've put together some leftovers for you two. You won't have to cook for a few days."

Both Dad and I thanked her.

Just as we were thinking we couldn't eat another bite, she and her daughter brought out the pumpkin pie and whipped cream.

I didn't think I could eat any more, but I managed. I didn't really have to force myself. It was that good.

All during the meal, my thoughts drifted to Marla and her family. Would I would have been invited for the holiday meal?

***

Mrs. Alexander and her daughter helped us carry the bowls and plates of food back to our place. I kept noticing the way the older woman looked at my father. *Is she looking for a new husband? Not my problem. He's old enough to take care of himself.* I watched him as he spoke with the lady. *He's been alone for quite some time. I couldn't imagine a woman's companionship being something he wouldn't want.*

After the daughter left, Ms. Alexander spent quite a while talking with my dad. I made myself scarce.

When he finally closed the door after her, he looked at me and said, "Nice lady."

I nodded. "*Very* nice lady."

***

I spent the next few days trying to figure out how I was going to get to New York without the FBI finding out. I knew Coach Spears and my dad would prefer I let the authorities handle the situation. My conscience wouldn't allow me to let it go. I had to do something. The problem was, what could I do and when and how could I do it? I decided to wait until after the New Year to really think about it. I couldn't do anything until then, anyway.

The annual Christmas Party at my dad's work would be coming up soon. Since it occurred after the actual Christmas Day, I entertained the thought of taking Marla with me when I mentioned it to my father, he thought it was a great idea. "I'll finally get to meet

201

the woman who stole my son's heart."

We both laughed.

"Do you want to spend Christmas with her?"

"Actually, I thought it would be a great idea. I'm sure her parents would love to have me spend the day with them."

"Go for it. I'll see you at the party on the Friday after."

I hugged him. "Thanks, Dad. You're the greatest."

He winked. "I know."

We both laughed.

I spent the next week shopping before going to Franklin.

***

When I arrived at my place in Franklin, I called Marla.

She sounded glad to hear from me and wanted to know what my plans were for Christmas.

I told her I hoped I'd be invited to spend Christmas with her and her family. I thought she was going to come through the phone.

"My mom and dad were hoping you'd be able to be with us. What about your dad? How does he feel about you not being home with him?"

"He's okay with it. However, there's a problem."

I heard her breath catch.

"Not all that bad. We have to be in Las Vegas for the annual Christmas party at his office. It won't be until the Friday after Christmas. You'll have to wear a formal gown."

"That won't be a problem. When are you coming over?"

"As soon ss I get off the phone."

"Hang up so you can get started. I'm dying to see you."

"Bye." I said and disconnected.

***

I don't think I broke any laws getting to her place. At least I hoped I didn't. I had barely shut my car down when I saw her door open. *She must have been looking out the window, waiting for me.* She looked more beautiful than the last time I'd seen her. After locking the car, I ran to her, took her in my arms and kissed her long and deep.

She returned the kiss. "We should go inside," she suggested.

I was a little dismayed to find her parents at home. I made the best of it and greeted them with handshakes and hugs.

I told them I would be spending Christmas day in Franklin and hoped I could spend it with them.

Her mother clapped her hands and squealed. Her father stood up and grabbed my hand with both of his. I think he tried to shake it off my wrist.

The rest of the day was a blur. We talked about the holidays and the celebrations the town had started preparing. The decorations had been in full swing for over a week and the place looked like a fairy tale village.

I spent Christmas Eve at my place and arrived at Marla's in time for Christmas breakfast. We passed most of the day listening to choirs sing carols and joining them when we thought we knew the words.

Then it was time. I had them all sit on the couch. I stood before them and handed Mr. Santo-Dominguez an envelope.

He looked at it with a hint of suspicion. "Open it," his wife demanded.

He did. I watched as his face showed incredulity. He couldn't speak, only move his jaw up and down. His wife took the papers from him and he reaction was the same. Marla finally took the papers and her jaw dropped.

"Jake. Wow! Flight and hotel reservations for the World Cup next year in Russia!"

"Phew," I said. "I glad you can all read."

All three jumped off the couch and grabbed me, hugged and kissed me. Mr. Santo-Dominguez kept pounding me on my back and thanking me in Spanish and English.

His wife was crying buckets.

Marla said, "We've been thinking about going, but it's so far and so expensive. There would be no way we could afford it."

"A whole month. A whole month. We'll be able to see almost every game. We will watch and cheer for Spain and think of you. I won't insult you by asking how much it cost you and how you managed to get tickets and reservations."

"I appreciate that. Just think of it as my Christmas gift to you. I realize the holidays will be past but, hey, you'll have a holiday in Russia at the world's most prestigious event, outside of the

Olympics."

His wife held the papers and looked at them and cried and looked at them and cried some more. "How can we ever thank you?" he asked.

"Go there. Cheer for Spain and enjoy yourselves."

I didn't realize that during the whole time, Marla hadn't said a word. When her parents finally let go of me, she took me in her arms and kissed me. "Thank you, Jake Stettler. You've made us the happiest family in the world."

"It was more than a pleasure," I said. "Someone once said, 'The best gift you can give is the gift of pleasure'."

"I think you've outdone yourself." She kissed me again.

In the back of my mind, I tried to think of way I could use this trip to get to New York. I wouldn't be travelling with Marla and her family. I'd be traveling with the team. Would it be possible to sneak away for a little while to visit the Rebels? Something worth thinking about.

CHAPTER TWENTY-SIX

When we entered the courthouse building for the Christmas party, I noticed they had set up an area where we could check our coats. I checked mine then slid Marla's from her shoulders. I gasped when I saw her bare back. Her blue silk dress formed a large V from her shoulders to her waist. When she turned around, the dress formed a smaller V, showing cleavage. The rest of it clung to her like a second skin. I imagined myself wrapped in the soft warmth when she squeezed my shoulder.

"Give the lady my coat, Jake."

I blinked several times then handed the coat to the clerk. On the way to the elevator, I took Marla's left hand by the wrist. This made her switch her purse to her right. I moved my hand so I was holding hers when we entered the elevator. Just as the signal announced we had arrived at the third floor I held up her hand and slipped a ring on her finger. "You'll need to wear this," I said.

The doors opened before she had a chance to say anything. Judge Eichelmann happened to be passing by and saw us emerge.

"Jake Stettler! Welcome! Welcome! And you have your lady with you. Wonderful."

Marla's eyes switched between her hand and me.

"Oh! Excuse me." The judge shouted, "Hey everybody. Jake is here with his fiancé."

Before she could say anything, he put his across her shoulder arm and started lead her around the room, introducing her as he went.

She glanced over at me a few times as I followed them with my hands clasped behind my back and a big smile on my face.

The judge finally stopped when they reached my dad. "Stettler," he shouted. "Did you know your son got engaged?"

He smiled wide enough to swallow a barge. "No, I didn't. Jake, when did this happen?"

"Just before the elevator doors opened. I thought I'd surprise her." I didn't think I could smile any wider.

Dad wrapped his arms around Marla. "Welcome to the family." He held her at arm's length. "My son sure knows how to pick 'em." He grinned at me. "She's beautiful."

"I know, Dad. I know."

"When are you planning to tie the knot?"

"We hadn't gotten that far yet. We still have to let her parents know."

He was about to hug her again when she was surrounded by a bunch of well-wishing-women. During all this, she only managed to look at me and say my name once.

Before I knew it, she had disappeared into the crowd.

"Don't worry. You'll see her again before the night's over."

"It looks like it might be just before the festivities end."

He put his hand on my shoulder. "Hang in there, son. You'll probably get her back when they open the buffet line."

I nodded.

"What are you drinking?" he asked.

I think he only meant to distract me.

"I'll have a Roy Rogers."

He smiled. "Good choice."

"Marla drinks red wine."

He nodded and left to get our drinks.

By the time he got back, the ladies had returned Marla to me.

"That was sneaky, Jake Stettler," she pouted.

I smiled. "I'm glad you approve."

Trying to look cross and happy at the same time, she said, "You could have asked me."

"I didn't think I had to. You told me we had to get married so you could have my babies. Remember?"

She blushed. "Yes, I remember."

My dad stood next to us smiling as if he knew something we didn't. "Time to get in line for the eats. If we're fast enough, we might even get a table together."

We managed to get a score a table.

"When will you tell your parents?" Dad asked her.

"I've a good mind to call them right now." She gave me a look that attempted to show annoyance. It didn't make it.

"You might want to finish eating first. You'll be on the phone for a while."

She smiled and nodded.

While we ate, my dad asked her about life in Franklin and her parents.

She answered all his questions and seemed happy for to tell him all about her.

"Of course she'll be spending the night with us. Now that you're engaged, I think I might even let you sleep together." He had a wicked smile on his face.

"Gee, Dad, can we? I promise we'll be a quiet as possible."

He punched me gently on the shoulder. "Idiot."

Marla looked at us then laughed with us.

***

It was after midnight by the time we got back to the house.

"Don't forget to set the alarm. See you in the morning." Dad said as he turned to go to his room. "Mrs. Alexander will be surprised, but I don't think she'll mind. Good night."

I set the alarm and turned out the lights. Taking Marla by the hand I led her to my room. "This is where I grew up. You can explore my childhood tomorrow." We undressed and got into the bed.

"Tomorrow I'll stop taking the pill." she said before kissing me.

When we came up for air, I asked her, "Isn't that a little soon? We just got engaged tonight."

She rubbed her naked body against mine. "How long do you think we should wait?"

"I don't know. I don't want you in a wedding dress with a swelled belly."

"Then we should have the baby before we get married." She shut me up with her tongue in my mouth.

***

Mrs. Alexander wasn't very surprised when we walked into the dining room holding hands. Dad had already explained Marla to her and given her the news.

She hugged us both and congratulated us. "If you'll be patient, I'll fix you a breakfast fit for a king." She handed each of us a cup of coffee and sent us the living room to wait.

Mrs. Alexander outdid herself. We cooked steak, eggs, rolls, a plethora of diced fruit, orange juice and of course, more coffee.

Marla looked at all the food and, with a big smile said, "Are we supposed to eat all this at one sitting?"

Mrs. Alexander laughed. "I think you'll need to replenish the energy you spent last night."

We all laughed.

"I'm not so old I don't remember what it's like to be in love." She looked at Dad with a huge smile as she spoke.

Marla and I looked at each other and winked.

We managed to make a big dent in the food she had prepared.

While Mrs. Alexander cleaned up the kitchen after we had eaten all we could, the three of us went to the living room to relax and let the food settle.

Dad asked Marla, "Will you call your parents or wait until you see them to break the news?"

She looked at me. "When are we going back to Franklin?"

"I planned on leaving tomorrow."

"Then I'll wait until I see them. It'll be a nice surprise." She looked at my father. "Did Jake tell you about the Christmas present he gave us?"

He looked at me. "No, he didn't. Speak up, Jake. I like surprises too."

I blushed. "I got them airline tickets and hotel reservations for a month in Russia for the World Cup."

He sat quietly for a few moments. "Wow! That's some present.

I'm sure they'll be thanking you for the next four years."

I blushed some more and shrugged.

"Can you still get tickets and rooms?"

"I'm pretty sure I can. Do you want to go too?"

"You forget, I introduced you to the game. I've never been to a World Cup game and I would love to see Russia."

I nodded. "Consider it done. I should be able to arrange everything before the end of next week."

"That would be wonderful. I would love you for the rest of your life."

"You would anyway."

We all laughed.

***

While we watched the news and relaxed, thoughts of the New York Rebels and what they had done to my team kept creeping into my head. *How can I get to New York and avenge my team? The FBI will be watching my every move. Still, I have to find a way. I can't let them get away with what they'd done. It wasn't enough they beat up the guys, they didn't have to kill any of them. Somehow, I planned to make them pay. I almost didn't care if I got caught.* I wouldn't be careless, but I would be vengeful. I pushed the thoughts from my mind and tried to concentrate on the news on the TV.

The newscaster said, "The FBI is at a loss concerning the bodies that have been turning up around the country. They believe the same person or persons is responsible for all the deaths. Of particular concern is the four Mexicans who were killed in Florida, the five men killed in Bakersfield and the ten men killed in Vancouver. The only information the authorities have released is that all the victims were strangled. If anyone has information that can lead to the arrest and prosecution of the perpetrator or perpetrators, please call the Information Hot Line at the number at the bottom of the screen." The program turned to local news and we turned the TV off.

Marla said, "It seems like the killer is only after groups of people."

I nodded. "I noticed that too."

"I wonder if all the people that died are soccer players too?" Dad asked.

I said, "The reporter didn't mention if they were or weren't. It's something to think about, I guess."

Marla put her hand to her chin. "Why would a killer only target soccer players? It seems kind of strange."

I shrugged. "Maybe the killer doesn't like the game or the people that play it."

Dad shook his head. "If that were the case, more soccer players would be dead."

"You have a point there," I agreed.

"I guess we could find something a little less morbid to talk about," Marla suggested

Dad and I agreed.

I turned to Marla. "Care to go for a walk?"

"That sounds like a good idea. I think it'll help the food settle." As we headed outside she asked, "Does she cook like that all the time?"

"I don't really know. I spend most of my time in Franklin or on the road. I'd have to ask my father, but I don't think so. He'd be grossly overweight if she did. I'm assuming he doesn't stuff himself unnecessarily."

We both laughed and continued walking, holding hands and enjoying just being together.

***

The next day, after another huge breakfast, we headed for Franklin. We made small talk along the way, talking about how she thought her parents would react and when we should start planning the wedding.

"Do you really want to have a baby before we get married?" I asked.

"I was just joking. However, if it happens, it wouldn't make me unhappy. I think I'd be the happiest woman in the world." She reached over and stroked my leg.

"You'll have to wait until I stop the car."

She laughed so hard it brought tears to her eyes. "I'm glad you have a sense of humor. It's one of the reasons I love you."

"Just for the record," I asked. "When did you decide I was the one?"

"I'm not really sure. I'd seen you several times before. I think it was when we first spoke. Something in your eyes and manner touched me." She reached over and we held hands for a few seconds.

"And you?"

"I liked you when I first noticed you at the cash register, but I think I fell in love on our first date. You were so beautiful, so warm, so loving. I couldn't help myself if I'd tried."

We spent the rest of the trip in silence, just enjoying being with each other.

***

The first thing she did when we walked into her home was run to her mother to show her the ring.

I approached her father. "Sir, I hope you'll excuse my forwardness. I know I should have asked for your blessing first. It's just that the idea came to me short before we left for Las Vegas. I had already bought the ring but didn't have a chance to speak to you. Can you forgive me?"

He hugged me then held me at arm's length. "Of course I can. As happy as you make my daughter, I can forgive you almost anything. Keep her content and I will always be delighted with you."

Her mother broke away from Marla and wrapped me in a warm hug. She had tears in her eyes. She pulled a handkerchief from her pocket, wiped her eyes and put her arm around her husband with her head on his shoulder.

Later, as we sat down to dinner, he asked me, "How long do you think you'll continue to play soccer?"

"I'll play as long as they let me. I notice some players are still in the game at 35. I'll continue at least that long if I'm still healthy."

"What will you then?"

I grinned. "I'll send Marla out to work and I'll stay home and take care of the babies."

This got all four of us laughing.

After dinner, Marla's dad and I retired to the living room while the ladies cleaned up the kitchen. We talked soccer while he sipped a brandy and I had a glass of water.

When the ladies had the kitchen in order, the ladies joined us. We talked about the upcoming vacation and whether or not I'd be able to seem them during the trip.

"I don't see any problem. We won't be playing every day. I might even be able to join you when Spain plays."

"That would be wonderful," he said. "The three of us would be happy to have you with us."

Looking at my watch, I said, "I think it's time for me to head home. The Thunder don't have any games until the spring but I need to contact Coach Lindermann about practice." I gave all three of them hugs and headed for the door. Marla followed me and gave me an extra hug before I went to my car.

On the way home I got so involved in thinking about the New York Rebels, I almost passed my house. *I have to find a way. I can't let them get away with what they'd done. Even if they put them all in jail, I'll find a way to avenge my teammates.* Once inside my apartment I yelled at the walls. "New York Rebels, you will all pay for what you did." I would save Coach Ruggeri for last. I'd want to make him sweat, wondering when and how I'd be coming for him.

To calm myself down, I made a hot lemon tea and turned on the TV. I had no idea what I watched. I only know that it distracted me enough to calm down so I could sleep.

The next morning I awoke with a plan in mind. The more I thought about it, the happier it made me. There were a few wrinkles I needed to work out, the biggest being New York is a big place and it would take too much time to do them individually. I'd have to get as many as possible together. "YES!" I shouted to the walls. "New York Rebels, you are mine!"

I was bubbling with joy when I called Coach Lindermann to get the schedule for the coming weeks.

CHAPTER TWENTY-SEVEN

The season for the Franklin Thunder wouldn't start until March with practice beginning in February. The Men's National team had already qualified for the World Cup and had no regular games scheduled until then. I decided to spend my time in Orlando, Florida practicing with the Men's National Team. When I spoke with Coach Spears, he agreed with my decision since he was still in the process of rebuilding the Franklin team.

The Men's National Team started practice in March and Coach Lindermann had us on the pitch three days a week. I called Marla on the days we didn't practice. That way we could spend more time on the phone.

On the days when we weren't practicing, I looked up the names and addresses of the New York Rebels. Since I didn't need to hurry, I took my time, using the various search engines on the internet to get the information I needed. As it turned out, I'd spent quite some time getting what I anticipated. By the end of April I even had Coach Ruggeri's address and phone number.

***

The Men's National Team were scheduled to fly to Moscow,

Russia by way of Frankfurt, Germany. We would be leaving from New York three weeks before the tournament began.

Fate dealt me what I needed to accomplish my mission. When the Men's Team landed in New York, we were told we would be delayed for a week. Thankfully, this wouldn't present a problem getting to Russia before we were to play our first game. Coach Lindermann ranted and raved for what seemed like hours to no avail. We had to wait. The airline would only tell him there was a problem with the plane and flight schedules. The plane scheduled to take us had developed both mechanical and electrical problems. To make matters worse, the copilot didn't have the required visa to enter Russia. We had to wait for that to be corrected since the airline didn't have another person that could take his place.

I almost shouted with joy when I heard the news. This would give me the time I needed. The airline booked us into a hotel to wait, at their expense, of course.

While most of the guys used the time to explore the city, I spent my time getting prepared to take out a whole soccer team. I planned to save the coach for last.

After spending a day wondering where I could get them all together, it dawned on me that they had games scheduled and would be practicing. I found my way to their practice venue and spent an hour wandering around it, looking for ways in and out and places to hide.

After checking it out, I found it was perfect. They would all be in the locker room together getting ready for practice while Coach Ruggeri would be with them or in his office. A phone call to him from a burner phone would make sure of that. Now all I had to do was plan what day to strike.

***

We finally got word our plane had been repaired and the copilot had his required visa. All this had taken the better part of a week. This would cut our time getting ready in Russia a bit short, but Coach Lindermann's primary concern was that we get there more than one or two days before our scheduled first game.

Even though the repairs had been made to the aircraft, it still had to be loaded with food and drinks. Then, Coach had to round up the players and get all our gear loaded. I had less than twenty-four hours to accomplish my goal. This suited me just fine.

I took a bus to the stadium along with a few other people. On the way, I called Coach Ruggeri and told him my name was Art Samson and I would like a chance to play on his team. I told him I'd be at the stadium today and wanted to know if I could meet him in his office.

He said that wouldn't be a problem and he'd wait for me there.

I thanked him and hung up.

The spectators were checked at the entrance to the stadium by security guards for bottles, fireworks and other prohibited items. The guards advised us to stay in the stands. Only the players and team personnel were allowed in the locker areas. I followed the crowd most of the way. When I saw the stairs for the locker rooms I started a commotion by pushing the man in front of me. He turned to confront his pusher and I motioned to the man beside me. Pushing and shoving escalated to a small riot. I used the confusion to make my way to the locker rooms. I was in luck. The team were just finishing changing clothes and were getting ready to head to the field. Several of the players recognized me and asked what I was doing there.

"You come to get your ass kicked?" one of them asked.

Another said, "Yeah. He wasn't there when we visited his team."

I nodded. "So, you admit you attacked my team?"

Their goalie, a tall muscular man, came up to me and looked down on me. *He must be six-foot-four.*

"Yeah, it was us. Sorry we missed you. We can take care of that now. I guess I'll have the pleasure of sending your body parts back to Franklin." His ugly grin showed uneven and missing teeth.

"Back off. Your breath smells." I told him.

He laughed. "A wise ass, and stupid." He looked around. "You here by yourself?"

I nodded. "I am."

They all laughed and started to close in on me. I smiled and backed up to a locker. I closed my eyes and imagined them all encased in spider webbing. My smile grew wider as I listened to their cries of dismay and shouted curses.

"What the fuck is this shit?" "Hey, get this stuff off me." "What the hell. I can't get loose."

All of it was music to my ears. After a few minutes I opened my eyes and saw the whole group wrapped in six strands of white webbing. I didn't need to feed on them, Coach Ruggeri would satisfy that need.

The group yelled and screamed as the webbing got tighter and tighter. It would continue until they were all crushed. When the life had ebbed from them, it would disintegrate. I learned that from one of my earlier escapades. All that would be found would be a mass of crushed bodies. No fingerprints, no DNA. It made my heart jump for joy.

Now for Coach Ruggeri.

He had just left his office and was heading for the locker room when we met in the hall.

"What the hell are you doing here?" he shouted.

"I came to pay you and your team back for what you did to my team," I said quietly, not smiling.

He grinned. "You? All by yourself?" He started laughing. "You'll have to take us out one at a time." He chuckled. "I don't think that's gonna happen."

I smiled. "Already took care of your team. Your turn now."

His smile froze. He looked past me toward the locker room. "What the hell did you do?"

I shrugged. "I killed your team. As I said before, your turn now." I reached and grabbed his shirt with both hands. "Prepare to die."

When he gasped, I put my mouth on his and extended my tongue. It wasn't just feeding that made me feel good, it was knowing I had avenged my team.

After I'd finished with him, I dragged him back to his office and put him in his chair behind his desk. Assuming the guards didn't know exactly how many spectators they had let in, I left the stadium by the players' entrance and reentered through the spectator's entrance.

"Where the hell you been?" a guard asked me.

"Had to go to the bathroom."

He looked at me hard, then nodded and let me back into the main part of the stadium.

The crowd had gotten rowdy wondering where the players were.

After more than an hour of waiting, an announcer said practice for the day had been canceled. He asked that everyone please exit in an orderly manner.

I heard a lot of mumbling and grumbling as the crowd started to exit.

***

The scene outside the stadium looked like organized chaos. Police cars and ambulances with red and blue lights flashing, were strewn haphazardly throughout the area. Detectives in suits gave order to uniformed policemen. Yellow tape and sawhorses kept the cell phone-wielding crowd at bay.

Vans from all the local and national TV stations lined the perimeter just outside the police barrier. Reporters with microphones informed the public, via portable cameras, of what little they knew.

I eased my way through the crowd to get closer to the barricades. Without saying a word, just looked and listened.

" . . . almost the whole team has been wiped out. A security guard found them," I heard someone say.

"How many?" a woman shouted.

"Seventeen. I guess those who weren't there can thank their lucky stars."

"Any suspects?" another person yelled.

"One detective said something about spider webbing," an onlooker said.

"Spider webbing?" The questioner shuddered.

I nodded. Apparently some of the webbing hadn't completely disintegrated.

"Yeah. Spider webbing."

"That's silly. They're just little things. How can one grow big enough to kill a person, much less a whole group?"

A man shrugged. "Your guess is good as mine."

Another spectator joined the conversation. "Hey. Remember that woman who killed all those people some years ago?"

"Yeah. Her daughter killed a bunch of people too."

I listened, not commenting, not smiling. Just listening.

More were comments about what was found, what wasn't found and the state of the bodies swept through the crowd.

"I guess we'll have to wait until the cops brief the reporters."

I smiled, made my way out of the crowd and boarded a bus to return to my hotel.

***

Back at the hotel, I had barely enough time to gather my gear together to get it loaded on the team bus. In no time at all, we were headed for the airport.

As we were boarding the plane, the dull throbbing of being hunted hit me. I looked around for police but didn't see any. As I looked to the left side, lo and behold, there were Townsend and Clay. They just watched me as I followed the rest of the team to the aircraft. I didn't know whether to acknowledge them or not. It didn't matter, a few seconds later, they were out of sight. I kept expecting to be hauled off the plane and arrested. The further away I got from them, the less the pain. I breathed more than a sigh of relief when the plane took off and we were airborne. We were on our way to Germany. Soon after we were in the air, we were served a meal.

Everybody was excited about our trip. Except for Hans and Mohammed, none of us had never been out of the country.

Finally, we were on our way to Russia. I had accomplished my goal. My team had been vindicated. I was so wrapped up in my thoughts that I missed the first shout.

"Turn on the news!" someone yelled.

I turned on the video screen on the back of the seat in front of me. "What channel?" I yelled.

"Any news station," came the reply.

I found out later that ABC, CBS and NBC were all reporting on the same thing. The death of most of the NY Rebels soccer team. I turned the volume up.

". . . any indication of how this occurred or why?" a reporter asked the mayor.

"We're working on finding answers. Since it's an ongoing investigation, we can't disclose any information we have."

"Is it true the men were wrapped in spider webbing?" another asked.

"That has not been confirmed. We can only say that seventeen of the twenty-three team members died from being crushed."

218

All heads turned to the line of bodies in black bags being wheeled to waiting vehicles.

"Sir. The guy who called 911 said they were wrapped in sticky white rope. Can you confirm that?"

"No, I can't."

Another reporter asked, "Is this reminiscent of the killings by Myra James and her daughter, Blaire Winslow?"

"I can't confirm that," the mayor said. "They killed by another means. Also, they didn't commit mass murder." He raised his hand to forestall more questions. "That's all the time I have for questions at this time. We will keep the public updated on new developments." He turned and walked away ignoring the shouted questions.

I turned off the monitor, sat back, smiled and relaxed. "Sorry I missed you guys." *Apparently, three team members arrived late because of car troubles. They found the team and notified the authorities. Lucky for them they were late.*

***

We arrived in Russia the week before Marla and her family. I didn't get a chance to see them when they arrived. Practicing for the upcoming games was paramount.

We were in the group with England, Nigeria and Japan. Coach Lindermann told us that we had our work cut out for us. Boy, would he ever be right.

I managed to meet with Marla and her parents. We planned to get married two months after we were all back in Franklin. This would give the ladies time to make all the arrangements.

I stayed excited during the whole tournament. Oh, yeah. We won first place. Considering we didn't even qualify for the last World Cup, this turned out to be more than a step up. I won the MVP Award for the whole tournament. My dad was more than proud. Every time my picture appeared on a TV, he would say to all who would listen, "That's my son."

We had to pass the organizers as we received our medals. Afterward, they shot off the confetti canons as we held up our medals for the crowd to see.

Some concern arose about the man found dead one night during the tournament. The news only said that he had been strangled. The incident had only been mentioned once and we heard no other news reports about it for the rest of our stay.

***

A ticker tape parade awaited us in New York when we got back. Coach Lindermann rode in a convertible with the top down. The team was in an open-topped bus. We waved our medals and the crowds cheered. The mayor of the city and the governor invited us to a ceremony at the town hall. It was packed with reporters. There were more of them than there were of us. We didn't mind. We basked in the limelight.

However, all good things must come to an end. So it was with our celebration. Coach Lindermann gave us all a month off to go to our respective homes to celebrate with friends and relatives. Naturally, I went to Milton. I had an idea. Before I left New York, I'd found a shop where I could buy a wig and fake mustache and beard. Since the FBI would be tracking me for who knows how long, I figured a disguise could get me past them for the times I needed to feed. It wouldn't help me with Marla. That was another hurdle I'd have to face. *One thing at a time. One thing at a time.*

My dad had gotten home before I did and waited for me. Dad couldn't tell me often enough how proud he was of me.

I spent two days with him and then told him I had to go to Franklin.

He knew why.

When I arrived, I went straight to Marla's house. Marla and her parents greeted me like a long-lost son. It took almost an hour for me to get them to settle down so we could discuss the marriage. Between the four of us, we decided, as before, to hold the wedding in two months. After that was settled, I took Marla out for lunch. I wanted to spend some time alone with her.

"When are you going to make me dinner?" she asked.

"How about tonight?" I answered.

"Tonight would be fine. What are you going to cook?"

I thought for a few moments. "Let me go to the store to see what they have."

She nodded. "Whatever it'll be, I'll bring my bottle of wine."

"Sounds good to me. How does seven sound?"

"Seven sounds good. I'll have my dad drop me off."

I cocked my head to one side as I looked at her. "I guess you're planning to spend the night."

She smiled. "You are sharp, today."

We finished our lunch and I drove her back home.

***

After dropping her off, I thought about my feeding. *How would that work out? Would I be able to control my hunger so she wouldn't notice? What if my need to feed escalated? How could I hide it from her?* I almost forgot to shop due to my worries. I finally managed to get steaks and all the stuff that went with them. I spent the next few hours preparing and cooking.

Marla arrived with her bottle of wine just as I finished cooking. I opened the wine for her and we sat down to dinner. I toasted her with my lemon tea and she toasted me with her wine.

After we'd eaten, she helped me clear the dishes and put the leftover food in the fridge. We then settled down to just relax and enjoy each other's company. We watched TV for a while, then started kissing.

After a while, she said, "I'm ready for bed, Jake Stettler." She kissed me, then got up and headed for the bedroom.

I shut off the TV and turned off the lights, then followed her.

It turned out to be the most beautiful night of my life. We lay cuddled spoon fashion afterward. She had just fallen asleep when the tell-tale signs of my hunger showed itself. *Oh, no. Not now. I can't leave her. It'll have to wait.* I ignored the feeling long enough to be able to sleep.

The next day, while we were having breakfast, my hunger manifested itself again. *It's only been two months. I can't be hungry now.* Be that as it may, I needed to feed. The dilemma. How would I manage it? I couldn't do anything with her there. Also, it was daytime. I'd never fed this early in the day.

"Jake, you look worried. What's wrong?" she asked.

What should I tell her? How could I explain what I needed to do? "Before I left to join the Men's team, I found out that the Thunder had been attacked. I visited Coach Spears in the hospital. He told me four of the team had died as a result of the attack. He was in the process of rebuilding the team while we were in Russia. I need to find out how things have progressed since I've been gone."

"Oh, Jake. I'd heard about the attack but I didn't know some of the guys had died. I'm so sorry. Is there anything I can do?" She held both my hands in hers as she spoke.

I shook my head. "I need to see him to find out how things are progressing. If you don't mind, I'll take you home then go see him."

She looked me in the eyes for a moment, then nodded. "Okay. I need to change clothes, anyway. Call me after you've talked to him."

I nodded. "I will."

CHAPTER TWENTY-EIGHT

I went to see Coach Spears. He said the pain had not gotten worse and he expected to be up and around soon.

I asked, "How have you been managing rebuilding the team while you've been laid up?"

"I had a few of the guys who had recovered, looking for players. It helped keep their minds off their troubles. We had funerals for the dead while you were gone."

"Sorry I missed that."

He waved his hand in dismissal. "We knew you'd be gone and didn't want to keep you from your travel. We figured you'd be there in spirit anyway." He paused and took a deep breath. "We have a full team now. The guys have been taking turns running the practices. From what I hear, things have been working out very well. Do you plan to come back to the team?"

I smiled. "Of course I do. I owe the Franklin Thunder for my success. Franklin will always be my home team."

He smiled. "I'm really glad to hear that."

"Coach, I've got to go. I have something I have to take care of. I'll keep in touch and, of course, I'll be at practice soon."

"Good. The guys will be glad to see you again."

I stood and shook his hand., then left.

That visit didn't solve my problem on how I was going to feed. The hunger almost distracted me while talking with Coach Spears. *It's still daytime. How and where am I going to feed?* I drove around the city for what seemed like hours. Finally, I headed out of town. *Maybe I'll find another cyclist who can help me solve my problem.*

I'd been driving for about a half hour when I saw a cyclist. My heart leapt with joy. As I drove past him, I swerved and caused him to go off the road. Slamming on my brakes, I got out and ran back to him. "Are you okay?" I asked.

"Were you trying to kill me?" he yelled as he removed his helmet and surveyed the damage to his bike.

"I'm terribly sorry. I got distracted and didn't see you. Can I help you in any way?"

He looked at his bike with dismay. "You'll have to give me a ride back to town."

"No problem."

He looked at the bike and then turned to my beetle. "How are you going to get my bike in your car?"

"Let me worry about that," I told him.

He turned to me to ask another question and I hit him in the throat. As he gasped for air, I grabbed him and took advantage of his open mouth. When I'd finished, I leaned against the car for a few seconds, basking in the afterglow. *I have to get out of here before someone comes.* I dragged his bike out into the desert until it couldn't be seen easily from the road. I then did the same with his body and deposited it by his bike. Using my handkerchief, I wiped my fingerprints from the bike and even wiped his body where I'd held him. *Hope that's good enough.* "Thanks for the feed," I said out loud before I left.

How often would I be able to do this? I needed to feed every two months now. Am I losing control over this hunger? I hoped not. Time to get out of here. I went back to my car and drove home.

Back at the house, I made myself a lemon tea and sat on the couch in the living room to think about the direction my life was heading. I had to find a way to feed without letting Marla know. *Maybe I'll need to tell her the whole story so I won't have to hide. NO. NO. NO. She'd think I'm some kind of monster. I doubt she'd be able to live with me knowing what I was.*

***

It had been just over a month since my last feed. The way things were going I shouldn't have to feed again for about two or three weeks. In the meantime, I needed to work out a plan for using my disguise. I knew the Feds would be watching my house. They probably had it bugged, along with my car. *I hope they enjoyed listening to Marla and me making love, if the house was wired.*

To get my mind off Marla, I tried on the wig, beard and mustache. I didn't look too bad. I'm sure the FBI wouldn't recognize me. *You have to do more than change your appearance. People are recognized more often by the way they walk.* I nodded. *I guess I could develop a limp.* I'd just have to make sure I limped on the same leg every time. I smiled. Limp on the left leg going out, limp on the right leg coming in. That should make my watchers laugh. *Just kidding.*

To make my disguise more convincing, I went to a thrift shop and bought a pair of shoes, trousers and a shirt and jacket. I didn't care about the colors, just the fit. I made sure all the items were about a half-size too big. I decided to try out my disguises. Just before midnight, I left the house wearing the disguise. I limped slightly with my left leg. The stomach cramps let me know they were watching. I walked to the end of the block and turned the corner. No stomach cramps. I kept the limp up for another block, just in case. Still no stomach cramps. I discarded the limp and walked just for the sake of it. *Can't get back to the house too soon. Have to make it look like I had an errand to run.*

After walking for twenty minutes, I turned around and headed back to the apartment. I think I'd been gone long enough not to raise suspicion as to why I left the house.

Sure enough, when I turned the corner, the stomach cramps started. Although there were several cars parked on the street, it didn't matter which one they were in. I just needed to know they were there. I felt confident when I got back in my apartment. I didn't turn on the living room lights because they were in the front of the house. That would be a dead giveaway. I turned on the bedroom light. That was in the back of the apartment and wouldn't show in the front. I couldn't help myself. I had to peek through the blinds, even though I didn't know which car they were in. It just made me feel good knowing my plan had worked.

***

The next day as I headed to the stadium for practice, a thought hit me. *SHIT! I'm getting married in less than two months. I won't be able to use the disguise to get past the FBI. DAMN.* Without thinking I had banged on the steering wheel and stomped my foot. The blaring of horns, the squealing of tires and the shouts and curses brought me back to reality. I forgot that I had been driving. Using my three mirrors, I saw a jumble of cars and trucks behind me with drivers waving their fists and yelling and screaming. *Ooops.* I lowered my head into my shoulders and drove away as fast as I could.

At the stadium, I tried to keep my mind on the game. Even though it was practice, I still had to keep the ball out of the net. I stood next to a goal post thinking about my dilemma when someone shook my shoulder.

"Hey, Jake, are you okay?" Glen's brow furrowed.

I blinked. "Yeah. Why?"

"You let a ball get past you. You didn't even try to stop it. Is something wrong?"

I shook my head. "No. I'm all right. I had something on my mind that distracted me." Taking a deep breath, I said. "I'm in the game now. Let's play."

He and the other guys looked at me skeptically, but finally continued practice. I managed to keep the ball out of the net for the rest of the scrimmage.

After practice, when we had all showered, changed and left the stadium, I sat in my car and thought. *What am I gonna do? I'll have to feed. How can I work this out with Marla? Should I tell her? Could I tell her? Then that other question arose. What would she think of me? Would she leave me? I couldn't blame her if she did.*

Oh, well. *No sense sitting here stewing about it. I'll just have to wait and see how things go after we're married.* I tried to pay more attention to the road as I drove. *Don't need another incident like I had this morning.*

***

I had only been home a short time when the phone rang.

"You're invited for dinner. How soon can you be here?" Marla asked.

"About fifteen minutes."

"Good. See you then."

She hung up before I could respond.

I did a quick change of clothes and drove to her house. She must have seen me coming. The door opened before I could ring the bell.

We hugged on the porch and then went into the house where I greeted her parents. Her mother said a quick hello and then disappeared into the kitchen.

Her father said, "You might as well sit down. We men are not allowed in the kitchen. They'll call us when everything is ready."

I sat on the couch and waited for him to take his usual chair.

"Can I offer you a drink?" he asked, standing next to the couch.

"No, thank you. I'm sure they'll have drinks on the table when we eat," I responded.

He nodded, then sat down.

We spent the next few minutes talking about how Spain was doing in their league. It surprised me that we didn't talk about the World Cup. I wouldn't have minded. I had a lot to be proud of and would have been glad to relive my exploits.

We had just about run out of things to discuss when the ladies called us. The meal consisted of paella with a green salad and homemade bread. Glasses of iced tea stood at each person's place.

As we ate, we talked about the wedding. How many guests should we have? What day, precisely, would we have it? Where would we hold the reception?

Then, Mrs. Santo-Dominguez asked me the question I'd hoped nobody would.

"Are you Catholic?"

I inhaled and let it out slowly. "No, I'm not. Will that be a problem?"

Her mom brought her hand up to her mouth. Her dad said, "No. Not really. The church will marry you if you promise to bring you children up as Catholics."

I nodded. "I don't have a problem with that."

Her mother removed her hand from her mouth and smiled wide enough to swallow a truck. "You two will be so happy." She turned to her husband. "It will be wonderful being grandparents, won't it?"

He nodded and rolled his eyes. "Yes, my dear. It will."

After dinner, her dad and I relaxed in the living room while the women cleaned up the kitchen. It didn't take them long.

Marla took my hand and pulled me off the couch. "I'm staying at your place tonight."

I blinked several times. "As long as your parents don't mind, it's okay with me."

She hugged her parents and taking my hand, led me to the door.

On the way to the car, I asked, "Do your parents mind? I thought they were devout Catholics?"

"I guess you could call them the new breed. In the old country, us spending the night together before we were married would be unheard of. You would get castrated. I would be excommunicated."

As we drove off, I said, "Let's hear it for the new breed."

We both laughed.

At my place we had a beautiful night together if I hadn't kept thinking about my feeding problem. I managed to get some sleep though, but not much.

***

The next three weeks went by quick as a blink. We would be getting married in one week. I became as excited as Marla. Although we'd been acting as a married couple, being married would be different. She wouldn't have to go home to her parents. She would be mine and I would be hers. Parents would be people we would visit.

The wedding was a small one with family and a few friends. The two teams, with wives and dates, would show up for the reception.

At the reception, most of the members of both the Franklin Thunder and the Men's National team showed up. You couldn't have found a happier bunch of people.

Mr. Santo-Dominguez spent a lot of time talking with Coaches Spear and Lindermann. I assumed they talked soccer, knowing how big a fan he was.

Of course the Thunder members and the Men's team spent a lot of time trading stories. I joined them. As if I had a choice.

Marla always seemed to be in the middle of a bunch of women. I didn't mind. She'd be mine before the night ended.

The dancing and eating and drinking went on until almost midnight. With the help of her parents and my dad, we managed to escape while thing were still going strong.

We'd planned to spend our honeymoon in the Bahamas. We drove to my place, changed clothes and picked up our suitcases. I called Lyft while we were changing. It arrived shortly before we were ready. We held hands on the way to the airport.

***

When our honeymoon was over, we returned to Franklin and real life. I told Marla, although I enjoyed my apartment, it would get crowded when we started having children.

She laughed. "I'd thought about that too. Can we afford to buy a house?"

"Yes, we can. With the money I make from being on two teams and living alone, I've been able to set aside enough for a sizeable down payment. We can start looking for a place after we spend a day or two with your parents."

She nodded. "That sounds like a good plan. Have you thought about where we'd live?"

"Absolutely. I thought a three-bedroom, two-story house with a two-car garage would be perfect." She hit me in the arm. "Jake Stettler, you know what I mean. *Where* would you like the house
to be?"

I put my hand to my chin. "I think it should be on a sizeable lot with a backyard big enough for a pool and grass area for the kids to play in."

I ducked as she swung at me again. I grabbed her and held her while we both laughed. "I'll let you pick out the area. How's that?"

She smiled. "That sounds fair. I'll check for schools and other amenities and let you know where we'll live."

"Sounds like a plan." I looked at my watch and said, "Time to call your parents."

She nodded and picked up the phone.

***

A week later, we were preparing to go look at houses when the doorbell rang. When I opened the door, there stood Townsend and Clay.

I greeted them. "Hi, guys. Long time no see. How've you been?"

Neither one of them smiled. Townend said, "Jake Stettler, you are under arrest for suspicion of murder. Please put your hands behind your back." He brandished a pair of handcuffs.

"There must be some mistake. Are you sure you have the right person?"

"Quite sure. Turn around. Don't make this difficult."

Marla stood open-mouthed, unsure of what to make of the situation. Standing and watching while wringing her hands, "Jake. . . " was all she could say.

I reluctantly complied. No sense fighting. I first had to find out what they knew and what evidence they had. "Let your parents and my dad know."

Standing open-mouthed, she nodded.

She'd cry when the realization of what happened hits her. I hoped she'd be able to make the call to my dad. She'd probably do it at her parent's house.

CHAPTER TWENTY-NINE

After Townsend handcuffed me, they put me in their car and drove to Police Headquarters. There they fingerprinted me and took my picture.

After sending a night in jail, Townsend and clay escorted me to the to the courthouse. Townsend removed the handcuffs and said, "Run if you want to die."

I decided not to run.

We sat in the courtroom for several minutes when a man announced, "Case number 18-07-26-012, the people versus Jake Stettler on several count of murder in the first degree. All parties please step forward."

Townsend, Clay and I moved to the front of the court.

The judge asked, "How do you plead?"

I said, "Not guilty, your honor."

The DA said, "Your Honor, we request bail be denied because of the nature of the crimes. We also believe Mr. Stettler to be a flight risk."

The judge looked at me, then said, "Bail denied. Next case."

Townend smiled at me, then took my arm and led me out of the courtroom.

***

I didn't know the time of day since they took my watch, my belt and everything I had in my pockets, but I think it was late afternoon when a guard brought me a ham and cheese sandwich and a can of Coke. He didn't talk, just rapped on the bars and handed me the tray with the food.

He came back a little later and took the tray.

Before he left, I asked him if I could have a book or magazine to read. The way he acted, I felt like I'd been talking Greek.

He just looked at me for a few seconds, then walked away.

I spent the rest of the day sitting on the cot wondering what would happen next. Since I didn't know exactly what they'd found, I couldn't even begin to know how things were going to go.

It made me wonder. I didn't get interviewed or questioned or anything. They only fingerprinted me, took my picture and put me in a cell. I hadn't seen the two FBI agents since entering the police station. It got me wondering about what was really going on.

I found out later that I had been in a holding cell. After two hours, they took me out to a car and transported me to the county jail. In the vehicle, Townsend and Clay were my escorts, riding on either side of me in the back seat.

Once at the jail, two officers guided me to a bathroom.

"Strip to your underwear," one of the officers told me.

When done, he handed me a folded-up orange jump suit with DOC in large black letters on the back, a pair of white socks and a pair of slippers. I put them on and they took me to a cell. "There's no number on the suit. Am I anonymous or am I supposed to get lost in the system?"

I got no answer.

There were two cots in the cell. Only one had sheets, a blanket and a pillow. "I guess I don't get a roommate, do I?"

Again, silence.

"Can I get a book or magazine to read, please?" They made me feel like I hadn't spoken or they were deaf.

Somehow, during the night of pacing and sitting and pacing, I managed to fall asleep. The next morning, the guard woke me up by banging on the bars. "Breakfast," he called.

I took the tray and he walked away. What a wonderful way to

start the day. Two slices of buttered toast, a hardboiled egg and a cup of unsweetened tea. *What? No coffee?*

This went on for four days. I tried to get the guard to tell me what was going on. He must have had a gag order. He only delivered my food and looked at me with total disinterest. An orderly came in once a day to clean the cell. I had to wait outside in handcuffs while she worked.

Finally, on the fifth day a guard opened the cell and waited for me to exit.

When I did he pointed with his chin to the door at the end of the hall.

I went through it and stepped into the main part of the station. Townsend and Clay were waiting for me.

Townend said, "This way," and led me to an interrogation room.

When I entered, I saw a black man in a three-piece gray suit with a dark blue tie, white shirt and brown shoes, leaning against the wall with his arms and legs crossed. When he saw me, he unfolded and walked toward me. He held out his hand. "I'm Mahlon Washington, your lawyer."

I extended my hand. "Glad to meet you." My hand got lost in his huge fist. Looking straight ahead, I saw his neatly trimmed beard. It, along with his eyebrows, were mostly gray. He was bald on top of his head. I had to look up to see his eyes. They were brown and almost matched the color of his skin. They crinkled on the edges when he smiled.

He pulled out a chair from the table and motioned for me to sit. After I did, he took the chair next to me.

Townsend and Clay had taken the seats on the other side of the table.

"Do you know why you're here?" Townsend asked.

"You arrested my client on suspicion of murder. I should have you up on charges for several reasons. First, for not reading him his rights. Next for keeping him locked up for more than twenty-four hours without benefit of counsel. Should I continue?"

Townsend crossed his arms and said nothing.

Clay sat with his hands in his lap looking at a spot on the wall behind us.

Washington said, "Have you even thought about a bail hearing?"

Townsend leaned forward putting his hands flat on the table.

"Yes, we have. Unfortunately, all the judges are tied up for several weeks and we were not able to schedule one."

Washington snorted. "All the more reason to release him." He sat back. "You do realize the failure to read him his rights will get your arrest thrown out of court? I'm sure your superiors would be glad to hear about that."

Townsend leaned back and crossed his arms again. "I think we could make some kind of arrangement."

This time Washington leaned forward. "Did you even let the police know *why* you arrested him?"

"Yes, we did." He uncrossed his arms.

"I guess they didn't ask about reading him his rights, did they?"

"No. I take it they assumed we already did it when we arrested him."

Washington shook his head. "How long before you retire, Agent Townsend?"

He looked nervous as he said, "I've got three more years to do."

"I suppose you want to make it to that time, don't you?"

Taking a deep breath, Townsend answered, "Of course I do." He looked at Clay as if asking for help.

"Agent Clay," Washington said, fixing him with a hard stare. "Were you aware of the mistakes made concerning my client?"

Clay cleared his throat. "Yes, I was."

Washington glared at him. "Why didn't you say anything?"

Clay shrugged. "He's the lead agent. He makes the decisions. I do what I'm told."

Washington nodded. "I'm taking my client out of here. I don't think you'll want to stop me."

As he prepared to stand up, Washington looked at Townsend. "By the way. What murder is he accused of committing?"

Townsend took a deep breath. "He's accused of the murders of more than a few soccer players across the country."

Washington leaned forward on the table again. "And how did he commit those murders?"

Townsend looked down at the table, then at me. "By strangulation."

He nodded. "And what proof do you have?"

Townsend hesitated. "None, actually. However, he was unaccounted for during the times of the murders. That makes him the most viable suspect."

Washington sat back and laughed. "Since you can't account for *my* whereabouts during the times of the killings, does that make *me* a viable suspect?"

"Uh, no. Not really."

"And why is that?"

Townsend said quietly. "You don't have a motive."

"And what motive did my client have?" He pushed his face closer to Townsend, his eyebrows forming a large V.

Townsend cleared his throat and rubbed his hands together. "The killings occurred after several of his teammates had been attacked."

Washington leaned back and smiled. "So, you think they were revenge killings?"

"Yes. I and my superiors think so."

Still smiling, Washington said, "I find that interesting. I'll have to speak with your superiors about this."

Townsend merely nodded.

I felt sorry for Clay. Probably because of his lack of training or experience, he had been almost completely ignored during the whole exchange.

We all stood up and were about to leave the room when an officer entered. "There's been another one," he said.

"Another what?" Townsend demanded.

"Another one of those killings. They found the victim an hour ago. The ME said he'd been killed sometime between two and four this morning,"

Both Townsend and Clays mouths dropped open.

Townsend finally found his voice. "That's impossible. He's been in jail all night and with us."

Washington smiled. "This means you either have the wrong person or there's a copy-cat killer on the loose. Your thoughts?"

"This can't be. Only the police and the FBI know all the details of the murders." He looked frantically at the officer. "Is the ME absolutely sure the man died the same way?"

"It probably would be better if you went and spoke to him yourself," the officer said.

Townsend's eyes were open and glaring, wild with rage. He fidgeted, his hands forming, releasing and reforming into fists.

Clay stood next to him, his hands clasped behind his back, placidly waiting to see what would come next.

Finally, Townsend said, "The morgue." He tilted his head in Clay's direction. "Let's go."

When they were gone, Washington shrugged after they'd left. "I guess you're off the hook, at least for a little while. We'll see what happens after they talk to the ME. I'll get you out of here as soon as I can. Okay?"

"That would be a 'Yes.' By the way, how'd you know I'd been arrested?"

"Your father told me. It seems you didn't know that I'm your family lawyer. I do apologize for taking so long to get to you." As we walked out of the room he put his arm around my shoulder.

***

A guard gave me my clothes and led me to the bathroom where I changed as fast as I could out of the orange jumpsuit. It felt good to be back in my clothes again.

I went out and met Washington. We were about to leave the building when Townsend and Clay entered.

Townsend said, "Jake Stettler, you are under arrest on suspicion of murder." He read me my Miranda rights. "do you understand what I've just read to you?"

I stood there dumbfounded. I looked at Washington.

Veins in his head pulsed as his complexion turned darker as if a storm were brewing in his head.

"Do you understand your rights?" Townsend repeated, loudly.

I nodded. "Yes, I do."

"Please turn around and put your hands behind your back."

When I did, he handcuffed me. Looking at Washington, he said, "How did I do?" His grin spread almost the whole way across his face.

Washington raised a clenched fist and shook it at Townsend. "You'll pay for this, Townsend. That's a promise." He turned to me. "Say nothing," then stormed out of the building.

Townsend maintained his smile as he watched Washington leave.

Clay stood by, impassive as ever.

***

Back in my cell in the orange jumpsuit with no number, I again tried to get something to read. Still no luck.

The only change from my previous suit-up was I had a lawyer working for me. I hoped and prayed he could find a way to get me released.

After a week, I noticed my jumpsuit started to get a little looser. *Am I losing weight? It wouldn't surprise me considering my meager meals.* I wondered if they were trying to save money or starve me to death. That would save the state the cost of an execution. *Very funny.*

After another three days, the guard came and escorted me down the hall.

What's going on now?

In the interrogation room were Townsend and Clay. This time they had Washington along with them.

Washington was smiling.

"Okay guys tell me what's going on," I said.

"We have to let you go," Townsend grumbled.

My heart jumped as I tried to suppress my relief. "What happened? Did you find the real killer?" I asked.

"One of the things that had never been mentioned about the killings was that the killer somehow extracted the victim's brain. This latest victim had no brain when the ME completed the autopsy. This could not have been a copycat killing. We can only surmise that the perpetrator is still on the loose. As a result, since you've been incarcerated from before the killing, we have to assume that you are not the person we're looking for. You'll be released immediately."

Washington smiling, merely looked at Townsend. "I tried to tell you that you had the wrong person." He paused, looking down at the table. "I guess we can forget about your first screw-up."

Townsend smiled. "I would appreciate it. I must have been a little over-zealous. By the time you get changed, the paperwork for your release will be signed."

I sighed. "It will be good to get into my own clothes again."

The four of us stood and left the room. Washington waited while a guard handed me my clothes and I went to the bathroom to change.

When I was ready to leave, he escorted me to his car for the ride to my apartment and wife.

To say that she was glad to see me would be an understatement. I thought she tried to kiss me to death as she merged her body with mine.

CHAPTER THIRTY

Marla and I spent the next several hours getting reacquainted. After a short nap, we called her parents to let them know I had been released. They were excited to get the news.

"Do you need to call your dad?" Marla asked.

"I probably don't need to, but I will anyway, just to make sure he knows."

When I got my father on the phone, he informed me he already had heard from Mr. Washington.

He probably called him as soon as I had gotten out of his car. "By the way, did you hear about the man who got killed while I was in jail?" I asked him.

"Yes, I did. The police down here are wondering if there is another person that kills that way or if you were innocent to begin with."

"I don't suppose you have any thoughts on the subject?"

"I'm assistant to the DA, I'm not a cop. I stay out of things like this."

"Yeah. Okay." I didn't know what else to say. He knew about my need to feed , but since he didn't mention it, I didn't either.

"What are your plans for the immediate future?" he asked.

"Marla and I are going to look for a house. Since we plan on building a family, my apartment would get kind of crowded."

"Amen to that. When will you start looking? How big a place are you thinking of and where will it be?"

"Nothing like getting to the point all in one go. We thought we'd look this weekend since she still has her job. I thought a three-bedroom, two-story detached house with a backyard big enough for a pool and grassy play area. We'll be looking for something fairly close to her parents. That way, her mother can babysit if the need arises. Did I miss anything?"

"Like father like son. Why is she still working?"

"My health insurance only covers her minimally. If she got really sick, I'd have to bear the brunt of the costs. As it is, her job will cover most of her medical costs, including everything associated with a pregnancy."

"I see. Well, good hunting. Let me know where and when you find a place. I'll set up a house-warming."

"That would be nice. I'll keep you informed."

"Okay, son. Take care and keep in touch."

"I will. Bye."

***

By the weekend, I had four prospective houses for us to look at. I had made arrangements with the real estate agent to visit all four of them.

Saturday morning, Marla and I went house shopping. When we entered the third one, she said, "This is it." She turned to me and said. "We're home."

Dumbfounded, I looked at her and said, "You've only been in the first few feet. How do you know this is the right one?"

She looked at me with a huge smile. "A woman knows."

The agent, a women, smiled and greed with her.

All I could think of was, *Okay. Whatever.*

We went back to the apartment and called the estate agent. I told her which one *we* had decided on. She said it would be available immediately. Once the papers were signed, we could start moving in.

Marla was excited. I didn't know that she had been furnishing the house in her head on the way home.

Things went really fast. The house belonged to us by the

following Wednesday. I called my dad and gave him the good news and the address.

Of course he was happy for us and said he'd start making arrangements for the house-warming right way.

"Shouldn't we wait until we have furniture in the house?" I asked.

He laughed. "By the time I have everything arranged, you'll be ready to receive guests."

***

He was true to his word. We'd been in the house a week when he called and said the party would be that coming Saturday. I just shook my head in wonder and didn't ask any questions. It was a good thing we didn't have a game scheduled.

It was a blast. All of the Thunder and most of the Men's National team showed up with their wives and dates along with my dad and some of the people from his work. Marla and her mother made sure everybody had something to eat or drink. Her father spent most of his time talking with Coach Lindermann. I just wandered around getting involved in minor conversations.

The women all congratulated Marla on the way the house had been so nicely furnished. The decorations my dad had arranged made it seem really festive.

It was almost midnight when the last guest left. Marla's mom and dad had retired to one of the spare rooms. They would head home after breakfast.

All was going well but I still had to think about my feeding problem. Nights and weekends Marla would be with me all the time. During the week she would get home from work about a half-hour after I finished practice. With her around, I couldn't use my disguise. I thought about away games. Since she didn't work weekends, she would be with me there too. *What to do? What to do?*

I remembered she was a very light sleeper. The slightest move I made would wake her up. I nearly pulled my hair out trying to figure out a solution.

Then I saw the light at the end of the tunnel. She worked on Mondays' and I had that day off. Problem solved. I didn't have to get rid of my disguise. At least not yet. Then the thought hit me. I couldn't use it anyway. It would be okay if we were still in the apartment. With the FBI watching the house, it would be a dead giveaway if I left using the disguise. Problem *not* solved. *Damn*

While I was still working on my problem, a body turned up halfway between Franklin and Las Vegas. According to what my dad told me, the man had been strangled and his brain removed. *That sure sounds familiar. Who the hell was doing this? Is there someone else out there with my attributes?* I didn't know what was going on, but it got the FBI off my back.

That problem had been solved. I still needed to feed.

I put my disguise in a small backpack, dumped it on the back seat of my car and drove to the mall. After finding a parking space, I went to the biggest store and used their bathroom to change my appearance.

I left the store, wandered around until I found a suitable subject. I caught him between buildings. He appeared to be heading to one store after leaving another. "Excuse me," I said. "Could you spare a dollar or two so I can get something to eat?"

He looked me up and down before saying, "Are you sure you don't need a drink?"

"I'm sure, sir. I can't drink alcohol. It makes me sick."

He looked at me with his head cocked to one side. Then, looking around as if to see if anyone was watching, he dug out his wallet and handed me a five-dollar bill.

"Thank you, thank you. I'm so grateful." I put my arms around him and hugged him.

He tried to pull away but I held him even tighter. "What the hell?"

"Hush. Someone might think we're lovers." I held him tighter.

We were in a space between two buildings and would be hard to see.

When he opened his mouth to protest, I put my mouth on his and fed.

After finishing, I held him for a few moments. *What to do with the body?*

Then I heard voices and looked around. To my left a door opened and two men walked out carrying large garbage bags. I hadn't noticed the large green dumpsters near the end of the building. I pushed the man against the wall and pretended that we were kissing.

The two men looked at us. One shouted, "Get a room."

After they went back inside, I took the man and carried him to the nearest dumpster. I put him on the ground while I took several garbage bags out. I stuck him in the dumpster, then put the bags in on top of him. With luck, he'll be dropped at the dump along with the garbage. No telling how long it would be before they find him.

With a sigh of relief, I went back into the store and changed out of my disguise. I decided to wander through the stores just in case I had developed a tail. My body didn't indicate that I had, but better to be safe than sorry. I found my car and drove home. Satisfied in more ways than one.

***

We had been in the house just over a month, when one Sunday, Marla said, "We have to get started on our family. I've been off the pill for at least two months and I'm not pregnant. I want to have baby."

The look in her eyes told me I had to do something about it, right away. I took her hand and led her to the bedroom, even though it was still early afternoon.

She nodded and smiled.

An hour later, she asked, "Have you ever been raped?"

"No," I answered.

She smiled and kissed me.

I must have dozed off because I felt myself climbing out of the depths of sleep. Marla lay beside me, still sleeping, breathing gently. She had a satisfied look on her face.

My hips were sore. I didn't dare move for fear of waking her up so I closed my eyes and just relaxed.

A short time later, she did wake up. She stretched and smiled. After a quick kiss, she said, "For your sake, I hope I'm pregnant."

Considering what I'd just gone through, so did I.

We got out of bed and I relaxed in front of the TV while she made us lunch.

***

We spent the rest of the day walking around town, window shopping and enjoying each other's company. Neither of us

243

mentioned babies or her getting pregnant. *Thank goodness.*

I came to dread Sunday afternoons. She'd get that look in her eyes. Taking me in her arms, she would say, "Time to make a baby."

I love her with all my heart, but I wondered what it would take to get her pregnant.

I almost passed out with relief when one day she told me, "I'm late."

We made an appointment with her doctor who confirmed it. She was pregnant.

On the way home, she told me, "That doesn't relieve you of your husbandly duties."

"My God! Are you some kind of sex maniac?"

She smiled. "Only with you. It's your fault for being so good to me and with me."

***

Adam was born later that year.

When I took them home from the hospital several days later, Marla looked at me and said, "That's one."

"How many do we plan to have?" I asked with consternation.

"At least two or three. I'll decide when the next one will be due."

With a shudder, I asked, "How soon will that be?"

She shrugged. "I think we should wait at least a year."

I sighed with relief. "Sounds good to me."

Adam was beautiful. His grandparents doted over him. Mrs. Santo-Dominguez couldn't get enough of him. She wanted to feed him, hold him, rock him when he cried.

One day when they were visiting us, Mr. Santo-Dominguez told her, "You have to let his mother spend time with him. I think if she had her way, you'd move in with them and only let Marla have the boy when she needed to feed him."

The way Mrs. Santo-Dominguez blushed, we knew he'd hit the nail on the head. "I always wanted a boy too, one to be like his father. Is that so wrong?"

He put his arm around her shoulders. "No, my dear. It's not wrong. Providence only allowed us one child. I'm happy with her and I think you are too. Especially now that she has given you a grandson."

She smiled with tears in her eyes. "When will you go back to work?" she asked Marla.

"My company and insurance say I can wait two months.

"Will you take the whole two months?"

"Of course, mama. I want to spend as much time as possible with my son. You know I will welcome you every day."

Her mother beamed with delight. "Of course I'll come. Thank you."

***

Something was going on that I couldn't wrap my head around. I fed every other month. During the months I didn't feed, a body had been found with the brain missing. If it wasn't me, then who? The FBI knew it wasn't me because they had me under surveillance. I'm surprised Townend and Clay hadn't shown up at my house accusing me of hiring an accomplice. As if I could find one.

Obviously, one had found me. and had been doing my work for me. I guess I shouldn't call it work. For me, feeding was a necessity.

Should I worry about this other person? What if we crossed paths? How would I react? How would the other person react? I shook my head. No need to worry about it. The other person was out there, doing what I had been doing. I decided to let the authorities worry about him or her, whatever the case may be.

I continued my Monday feedings with the rest of my family ignorant of my doings. "Let sleeping dogs lie," as the saying goes.

CHAPTER THIRTY-ONE

Even though I controlled my hunger by feeding every other month, I suppressed the urge to feed more often. I managed to control myself.

This situation continued for the better part of a year. During that time I saw neither hide nor hair of Townsend and Clay. I did notice, occasionally, a car parked down the street from our house and experienced that tell-tale feeling alerting me to police presence.

I didn't mind. I kept my cool and didn't give them any reason to approach me.

One evening, Marla baked a tray of chocolate chip cookies. I got my hand slapped when I tried to take one.

"Who are they for? I don't recall a church bake sale or anything like that coming up."

"They're for the guys in the sedan down the street. This is just to let them know we know about them.

I looked at her and smiled. "So, you know about them too?"

She smiled back at me. "How could I not? It's the same car with the same guys in the same spot. The guys changed shift around six in the evening. They could at least bring in other people and move to a different spot. They could even change cars."

I went to hug her. She topped me and said, "Wait until I deliver these."

After she returned, we sat down and watched TV for a while. She asked, "What time is your practice tomorrow?"

"We start at ten. Why?"

"I guess I'll call my mom before I go to work so she'll be here before you leave. Can't leave Adam on his own. No telling what he might get into."

I looked at her confused. "She'll be here anyway. Besides, he's less than a year old. What can he get into?"

She smiled. "You never know. Kids grow up fast these days." Laughing, she kissed me then headed for the bedroom.

I shook my head, then followed her.

***

The next morning, I had my gear packed and slung my bag over my shoulder when the doorbell rang. Figuring it was my mother-in-law, I opened the door. Imagine my surprise when FBI Agent Clay stood before me. "Well, well. To what do I owe the pleasure?"

He stood just outside the door. "I just thought you'd like to know, Agent Townsend won't be bothering you anymore."

"Why is that? Does he finally believe I'm not responsible for the series of deaths?"

"Well, I don't know about that. The two times he arrested you didn't go unnoticed by our supervisors. He's been transferred to a single person station in Montana. I'm just here to let you know I won't make the same mistakes he did. This is not to say you're not still under suspicion. It's just that I intend to have more proof before I make a move." He nodded. I heard him mutter, "Have a nice day." He walked away.

As he drove off, my mother-in-law turned into our walk and headed for the house. I kept the door open for her.

"Good morning. I hope I'm not late."

"No, you're not. I had just spoken to the man who drove off in the car as you turned into the walk. I'm ready to go if that's okay with you?"

"Yes, of course. See you two when you get back. I'll have dinner ready so neither of you will have to cook." I started to protest, but she raised a hand. "No. I insist. It's no fun cooking for only two people. I love cooking and don't get to spoil anybody these days."

"But you cook for us almost every day of the week. What could you be missing?"

She sighed. "Being with my grandson and my children, every day and every night. I would love to sing him to sleep and be there when he wakes up during the night."

"Well, he sleeps through the night almost every night. Marla and I take turns when he wakes up. It doesn't take much to get him back to sleep. He's not much of a bother."

"Still, I miss having a baby to take care of all the time." She shrugged. "You better get going. Don't want you to be late for practice."

I kissed her on the cheek and headed out the door.

***

Things changed with Agent Clay in charge. The surveillance team only showed up two or three times a week. They used different guys and they changed the vehicle. Sometimes they used a gray sedan, sometimes a blue one. I could never anticipate what color car they would be using. In addition, they didn't always park in the same spot. They even changed which side of the street they parked on.

"Way to go, Agent Clay," I thought. "Keep me guessing."

Marla noticed the change too. "I had so looked forward to baking cookies every week," she pouted, half-smiling.

I put my arms around her. "I wouldn't mind home-baked cookies."

She pushed me away. "You don't need cookies. You might get fat. You need to keep in shape for your game."

I put on my best hang-dog expression. "If I promised not to eat them all at one time, could you bake me some?"

She pursed her lips. "I'll have to think about it."

***

Adam had just turned a year when Marla announced she was pregnant again.

I was, of course, ecstatic. "Your mom is gonna love you to death when she finds out."

We waited until Saturday to let her parents know. We surprised them by showing up around ten in the morning.

They were both anxious when we entered with Adam in tow.

"Is something wrong?" her father asked.

"Not really," Marla said. "We thought we'd come over for lunch."

"Oh," her mom said, her head cocked to one side. Worry creased her brow.

"Is that okay, Mom?"

"Of course it is, honey. You're always welcome." She still looked worried.

"Also, I just thought you'd like to know I'm pregnant again. The doctor said I'm eight weeks along."

I thought her mother would start dancing. She bounced up and down a few times. Mr. Santo-Dominguez watched her, shaking his head. "You'd think she just won a million bucks."

I took Adam from Marla thinking her mother would be hugging her. I got that right. As soon as I had Adam her mon rushed to her and wrapped her in a bear hug. "Oh, my darling child. How wonderful, how wonderful." She let her go and hugged her husband. "We will be grandparents again. How wonderful."

***

To keep Agent Clay and the rest of the FBI guessing, I'd sometimes travel to Las Vegas to feed. Just for a change, I'd travel to Milton. Just for a change. For more than a year, only one other person had killed the same way I did. This confused not only me, but also the FBI and the police as well. To make matters even more complicated, the most recent happened in Bakersfield, California, the same day I fed in Milton. *I'll have to ask my father if he has any ideas about this. Maybe together we could figure out who the other person was.*

I was happy with the way things were going and occasionally wondered what it would be like when I retired form the game. But I still had a few more playing years before that happened.

***

Adam was almost three and Thomas almost a year when my dad

came up to spend the weekend. Marla and her mom had gone shopping, leaving us men to take care of the babies.

When we were sure the boys were down for the count, I said, "I still wonder about those other killings. Especially with the timing and location of them."

He nodded, then looked me square in the eye. "Parents are supposed to protect their children."

It took a few seconds for this to register. When I did, I started to speak when he held u a hand and said, "I guess you're proud of your sons?"

"Yes, I am, Dad. . . ." Although still confused, my chest swelled.

"Let me give you something to think about," he dad said. "Myra James was bitten by a Black Widow spider. She had extraordinary abilities. Her daughter, Blaire Winslow, inherited those abilities. You were bitten twice. You have special abilities. You have two sons."

I thought about that for a moment. "Oh, my God!" I looked at my father with wide eyes. "Do you think . . . ?"

"I don't know. We'll have to wait and see."

I hid my face in my hands and moaned. "Lord, please, no. Not my babies, please."

***

In Las Vegas, Kirsten and Heidi were having a tea party in the yard when Heidi said, "Look what I can do!" She extended her arm full length with her palm facing up, then stuck her tongue out and picked up the candy in her palm with her tongue.

"Wow! I wish I could do that," Kirsten said. "Can you do it again?"

"Yep," Heidi said.

Curious, Greta looked at the two girls wondering what Heidi had done.

Heidi extended her arm again and once more picked up the candy from her outstretched hand.

Greta stared at her daughter with mouth and eyes open wide. She put her hands to her mouth and cried, "Oh my God, Oh my God!"

The End ???

ABOUT THE AUTHOR

Ernest lives in North Las Vegas, Nevada with his wife and son. He is the author of Novels *Myra James the Black Widow, The Black Widow's Daughter* and a collection of short stories entitled *Journeys in the Macabre*. He has also published four short stories, *Wolf, Her Mother's Daughter, Malcolm's House* and *Walking the Bristlecone Trail*

ernestwalwyn@gmail.com